THE

METAMORPHOSIS AND

OTHER STORIES

THE METAMORPHOSIS AND OTHER STORIES

FRANZ KAFKA

Translated by
Katja Pelzer

UNION
SQUARE
& CO.
NEW YORK

UNION SQUARE & CO.

NEW YORK

UNION SQUARE & CO. and the distinctive Union Square & Co. logo are trademarks of Sterling Publishing Co., Inc.

Union Square & Co., LLC, is a subsidiary of Sterling Publishing Co., Inc.

This 2021 edition published by Union Square & Co., LLC.

For information about custom editions, special sales, and premium purchases, please contact specialsales@unionsquareandco.com.

ISBN 978-1-4351-7230-2

Printed in Canada

4 6 8 10 9 7 5

unionsquareandco.com

Cover design: Igor Satanovsky and David Ter-Avanesyan
Cover images: Bridgeman Images: Private Collection; Shutterstock.com: Studio Barcelona (icon)

THE

METAMORPHOSIS AND

OTHER STORIES

CONTENTS

CONTENTS

CONTENTS

BEFORE THE LAW

BEFORE THE LAW STANDS A DOORKEEPER. A MAN FROM THE COUNTRY comes to this doorkeeper and asks for entry into the law. But the doorkeeper says that he cannot grant him entry now. The man considers and then asks whether this means that he may be allowed to enter later. "It is possible," says the doorkeeper, "but not now." Since the gate to the law stands open, as always, and the doorkeeper has stepped aside, the man bends forward to see inside through the gate. As the doorkeeper notices this, he laughs and says: "If it is so tempting, go ahead and try to enter although I have forbidden it. But remember: I am powerful. And I am only the lowest doorkeeper. From hall to hall stand doorkeepers, each more powerful than the other. The sight alone of the third is even more than I can bear." Such difficulties were something that the man from the country had not expected; after all, the law is supposed to be accessible to everyone all the time, he thinks, but as he now looks more closely at the doorkeeper in his fur coat, with his large, pointed nose, and long, thin, black Tartar's beard, he decides that it is better to wait until he has received permission to enter after all. The doorkeeper gives him a stool and allows him to sit down to one side of the door. There he sits for days and years. He makes many attempts to be let in and tires the doorkeeper with his requests. The doorkeeper often carries out little interrogations with him, asks him about his homeland and many other things, but they are apathetic questions such as those asked by great men, and at the end, he always tells the man that he cannot let him in yet. The man, who equipped himself with many things for his journey, uses everything, however valuable it may be, to bribe the doorkeeper, who accepts everything, but says: "I am only accepting this so you don't believe you have left anything out." During the many years, the man observes the doorkeeper almost continuously. He forgets the other doorkeepers; this first one seems to him to be the only hindrance to his entry into the law. He curses his bad fortune, recklessly and loudly in the first years, and later, as he becomes old, grumbling to himself. He becomes childish, and because he has been studying the doorkeeper for years and is familiar even with the fleas in the collar of his fur coat, he also asks the fleas to help him and change the doorkeeper's mind. In the end his eyesight becomes weak and he doesn't know whether it is truly growing darker, or whether his eyes are merely deceiving him. He does, however, discern a radiance among the darkness as it breaks forth inextinguishably from the door to the law. Now he has not much longer to live. Before his death, everything that he has experienced all this time collects in his head into one question that he had not yet asked the doorkeeper. He beckons him over, for he can no longer raise his stiffening body. The doorkeeper has to bend down low to him, as the difference in their height has changed very much to the man's disadvantage. "What more do you want to know now?" asked the doorkeeper. "You're insatiable." "Everyone strives for the law, do they not?" said the man. "How can it be that in all these many years no one other than myself has requested entry?" The doorkeeper recognizes that the man is already near his end and, in order to manage to reach his fading ear, he shouts at him: "No one else could have been granted entry, for this entrance was intended only for you. I shall now go and close it."

THE JUDGMENT

(For Fräulein Felice B.)

IT WAS ON A SUNDAY MORNING AT THE HEIGHT OF SPRING. GEORG Bendemann, a young businessman, was sitting in his private room on the first floor of one of the low, poorly built houses that extended along the river in a long row, discernable almost solely by their height and color. He had just finished a letter to a childhood friend now residing abroad; he lingered blithely as he sealed it, and then, his elbows resting on his desk, he gazed out the window at the river, the bridge, and the hills on the other bank with their fragile green.

He thought about how this friend, dissatisfied with his progress at home, had actually sought refuge in Russia many years ago. Now he ran a business in St. Petersburg, which had gotten off to a very good start, but seemed to have been stagnating for some time, as his friend complained during his increasingly seldom visits. So he was slaving away in his foreign country to no avail, his foreign beard poorly concealing the face that Georg had known since childhood, whose yellow complexion seemed to indicate an emerging illness. As he explained, he had no real ties to the colony of fellow countrymen there, and hardly any social interaction with local families either, and was therefore resigning himself to permanent bachelorhood.

What should you write to such a man, who had apparently taken the wrong track, whom you could pity, but whom you could not help? Should you maybe advise him to come back home, to shift his livelihood back here, to resume all his old friendly relations—for which there was certainly no hindrance—and to rely upon the support of his friends for everything else? This would mean nothing less than telling him simultaneously—the more gently, all the more insultingly—that his previous attempts had failed, that he should finally give them up, that he should return and be forced to let everyone stare with big eyes at one who has returned for good, that only his friends have a clue, and that he is an overgrown child who is to follow his successful friends who stayed home. And was it even certain that there was a reason for the burden that would be placed upon him? Perhaps you would not even succeed in bringing him home at all—he said himself, after all, that he no longer understood the state of affairs at home—and so, in spite of everything, he would stay in his foreign country, embittered by the suggestions, and all the more estranged from his friends. But were he to actually follow your advice and become—not intentionally, of course, but due to the circumstances—dejected, unable to reconcile himself with his friends or find his way without them, suffering from humiliation, truly having no home and no friends any longer, wouldn't it be much better for him to stay abroad as he was? Would it be possible under such circumstances to think that he would really make progress here?

For these reasons, you were not able, if you still wanted to even maintain your contact by letter, to really convey any information at all, such as you would convey to even the most distant acquaintance without hesitation. This friend had not been home for more than three years now and explained quite feebly that this was due to the uncertain state of political affairs in Russia, which would allegedly not permit a small businessman even the briefest period of absence, while hundreds of thousands of Russians were traveling the world as they pleased. During the course of these three years, however, many things had changed, especially for Georg. News of the death of Georg's mother, which had taken place about two years ago, and since which Georg and his old father had been sharing a common household, had apparently reached his friend, who expressed his condolences in a letter with a dryness that could only be the result of the fact that grief due to such an event becomes entirely unimaginable so far from home. Now since that time, however, Georg had tackled his business, as well as everything else, with greater determination. Perhaps his father had been a hindrance while his mother was still alive, only allowing his own opinion to be accepted and thus preventing his son from truly fulfilling his own function in their business; perhaps his father had become more reserved since the death of his mother, although he still worked in the business; perhaps fortunate coincidences—which was in fact very likely— played a far greater role, but in any case, their business had developed quite unexpectedly in these two years, they had had to double their staff, their revenue had increased fivefold, and further progress was doubtlessly imminent.

But his friend had no inkling of this change. Earlier, for the last time perhaps in that letter of condolence, he had wanted to persuade Georg to emigrate to Russia and had talked at length about the prospects in St. Petersburg for precisely Georg's line of business. The figures were vanishingly small in comparison to the scope that Georg's business had now taken on. But Georg had not felt like writing his friend about his business successes, and had he done it now, in retrospect, it would have certainly appeared strange.

So Georg confined himself to writing his friend only of meaningless events, which, when you are lost in thought on a quiet Sunday, pile up in your memory in no particular order. He wanted nothing other than for the image that his friend had no doubt made of his hometown during his long absence, and to which he had resigned himself, to remain intact. So it happened that Georg announced to his friend the engagement of one incidental person to an equally incidental girl three times in letters written at rather large intervals, until indeed, quite contrary to Georg's intention, his friend then began to become interested in this remarkable event.

Yet Georg would much rather write to him about such things than confess that he himself had become engaged to a Fräulein Frieda Brandenfeld, a girl from a wealthy family. He often spoke to his bride about this friend and the peculiar correspondence relationship he had with him. "So he won't come to our wedding at all then," she said, "although I have a right to meet all your friends." "I don't want to disturb him," answered Georg, "You see, he would probably come, at least I think so, but he would feel coerced and resentful, would maybe envy me and surely feel discontented; and, incapable of ever disposing of his discontentment, he would return home alone. Alone—do you know what that is?" "Yes, but couldn't he also hear of our marriage another way?" "That is indeed something I cannot prevent, but with his lifestyle it is unlikely." "If you have such friends, Georg, you shouldn't have gotten engaged at all." "Yes, we are both at fault; but I wouldn't have it any different now." And when she then, breathing quickly under his kisses, managed to say "It actually does upset me after all," he found it truly innocuous to tell his friend everything. "This is how I am, and this is how he must accept me," he told himself. "I cannot tailor myself into a person who may be more suited to his friendship than I."

And he did indeed report his engagement to his friend in the long letter that he wrote that Sunday morning with the following words: "The best news I have saved for last. I have become engaged to a Fräulein Frieda Brandenfeld, a girl from a wealthy family, who didn't settle here until long after your departure and who could therefore hardly be familiar to you. There will certainly be an opportunity for me to tell you more about my bride, but for today, be content to know that I am quite happy and that our mutual relationship has only changed to the extent that instead of having a very ordinary friend, you will now have in me a happy friend. Furthermore, you will acquire in my bride, who sends her warm greetings and who will be writing you herself soon, a sincere friend, which is not entirely without significance for a bachelor. I know there are many things holding you back from visiting us, but wouldn't my wedding be just the right occasion to throw all those obstacles aside for once? In any case, act without any sense of obligation and only as you see fit."

With this letter in his hand, Georg had sat for a long time at his desk, his face turned toward the window. As an acquaintance passed by and greeted him from the street, he had barely replied with an absent smile.

He finally put the letter in his pocket and walked from his room across a small hallway to his father's room, which he had not been in for months. It was not usually necessary to do so, for he was constantly in contact with his father in their business, they had their lunch in a restaurant at the same time, and although each had his evening meal as he pleased, they usually then sat for a while—unless Georg met with friends, as occurred most frequently, or nowadays visited his bride—each with his own newspaper, in their common living room.

Georg was amazed at how dark his father's room was, even on this sunny morning. So this was the shadow cast by the high wall that rose on the other side of the small courtyard. His father sat by the window in a corner decorated with various remembrances of his late mother and read the newspaper, which he held sideways before his eyes, in an attempt to compensate for some sort of visual impairment. On the table were the remains of his breakfast, of which not much seemed to have been eaten.

"Ah, Georg!" said his father and came at once to meet him. His heavy dressing gown opened as he walked, the skirts fluttering around him—"My father is still a giant," Georg said to himself.

"It's unbearably dark in here," he then said.

"Yes, it is dark indeed," answered his father.

"You've closed the window as well?"

"I prefer it that way."

"Well, it's very warm outside," said Georg, adding to his previous remark, and sat down.

His father cleared the breakfast dishes and placed them on a chest.

"Actually, I only wanted to tell you," continued Georg, who followed the old man's movements quite forlornly, "that I have announced my engagement in St. Petersburg after all." He pulled the letter out of his pocket a little and let it fall back again.

"In St. Petersburg?" asked his father.

"To my friend there," said Georg and sought his father's eyes.—"But at work he is completely different," he thought, "how he sits here broadly and folds his arms across his chest."

"Yes. To your friend," said his father with emphasis.

"But you know, Father, that I wanted to keep my engagement from him at first. Out of consideration, for no other reason. You know yourself that he is a difficult person. I told myself, he could possibly hear of my engagement from someone else, even though this is hardly likely given his solitary lifestyle—I can't prevent that—but he should not hear about it from me."

"And now you have had second thoughts?" asked his father, laying the large newspaper on the windowsill, and on the newspaper his glasses, which he covered with his hand.

"Yes, now I have had second thoughts. If he is my good friend, I told myself, then my happy engagement will also bring him happiness. And this is why I no longer hesitated in announcing it to him. But before I drop off the letter, I wanted to tell you."

"Georg," said his father, drawing his toothless mouth wide, "listen to me! You have come to me with this matter in order to consult with me. That honors you, no doubt. But it is nothing, worse than nothing, if you now fail to tell me the entire truth. I do not wish to stir up things that do not belong here. Since the death of our dear mother, certain unpleasant things have taken place. Perhaps the time will also come for them and perhaps it will come sooner than we think. Many things escape me at work, perhaps it is not being hidden from me—now I do not wish to assume that it is being hidden from me—I am no longer strong enough, my memory is deteriorating, I no longer have an eye for all the many things. First, that is the course of nature and second, the death of our dear little mother struck me far more than you.—But because we are talking about this issue in particular, about this letter, I beg you, Georg, do not deceive me. Do you really have this friend in St. Petersburg?"

Georg stood up, unsettled. "Let's forget my friend. A thousand friends cannot replace my father. Do you know what I think? You're not taking good enough care of yourself. But old age demands its dues. You are indispensable to me at work, this you know very well, but if work is threatening your health, I will close our business for good first thing tomorrow. That won't do. We will have to change your lifestyle. And fundamentally. You are sitting here in the dark and you would have such nice light in the living room. You nibble at your breakfast instead of strengthening yourself properly. You sit with closed windows and fresh air would do you so much good. No, my father! I'll fetch the doctor and we will follow his instructions. We will exchange rooms, you will move into the front room, I'll move in here. It will be no change for you, everything will be carried over with you. But there's time for all that later. Now lie down in bed for a while, you definitely need to rest. Come, I'll help you to get undressed, you'll see, I can do it. Or if you would like to move to the front room right away, you can lie down in my bed for the time being. That would be very sensible, by the way."

Georg stood right beside his father, who had let his head with its disheveled white hair sink to his chest.

"Georg," his father said quietly, without moving.

Georg knelt down immediately next to his father, he saw the pupils enlarged in the corner of his father's tired eyes directed at him.

"You have no friend in St. Petersburg. You've always been a clown and haven't even restrained yourself with me. How could you have a friend there, of all places! I can't believe that at all."

"Think back once again, Father," Georg said. He lifted his father from the armchair, and took off his dressing gown as he stood there rather feebly. "Now it was almost three years ago that my friend came to visit us. I still remember that you didn't like him particularly well. At least twice, I denied to you that he was my friend, even though he was sitting in my room. I could understand your aversion very well; after all, my friend has his peculiarities. But then again, you also conversed with him very well. I was so proud back then that you had listened to him, nodded, and asked questions. If you think about it, you must remember him. He told unbelievable stories about the Russian Revolution. For example, how on a business trip in Kiev he saw a priest on a balcony during a riot who cut a broad cross in blood into the palm of his hand, raised this hand and called to the crowd. You've told this story yourself every now and then."

Meanwhile, Georg had managed to sit his father back down and carefully take off the knitted pants that he wore over his linen underpants, as well as his socks. He reproached himself for having neglected his father at the sight of his not particularly clean underclothes. It had surely also been his duty to keep watch over his father's change of underclothes. He had not yet spoken explicitly with his bride about how they wanted to arrange his father's future, for they had quietly assumed that his father would remain in their old home alone. But now he decided quickly and with complete certainty to bring his father along into his future household. It almost seemed, on closer inspection, that the care that his father was to be provided with there could come too late.

He carried his father to bed in his arms. He had a terrible feeling when he realized during the few steps to his bed that his father at his breast was playing with his watch chain. He couldn't put him in bed right away, so tight was his grip on this watch chain.

But no sooner was he in bed than everything seemed fine. He covered himself up and even drew the bedcover up particularly high over his shoulders. His expression as he looked up to Georg was not unkind.

"You remember him after all, am I right?" Georg asked and nodded to him encouragingly.

"Am I covered up well now?" his father asked, as though he couldn't look to see if his feet were properly covered.

"So you like it in bed," Georg said and rearranged the blanket around him.

"Am I covered up well?" his father asked once again and seemed to pay particular attention to the answer.

"Just calm down, you are covered up well."

"No!" his father shouted, so that the answer thrust against the question, threw the blanket back with such strength that it unfolded completely during its moment of flight, and stood upright in bed. With only one hand he held lightly onto the ceiling. "You wanted to cover me up, this I know, my rascal, but I am not covered up yet. And even if this is the last of my strength, it's enough for you, too much for you. Of course I know your friend. He would have been a son after my own heart. That is why you have been deceiving him all these years. Why else? Do you think I haven't wept for him? That is why you lock yourself in your office, not to be disturbed, the boss is busy—just so you can write your deceitful little letters to Russia. But fortunately no one has to teach this father to see through his son. And now, just as you believed that you had gotten him down, so far down that you can sit on him with your backside without him stirring, my most distinguished son has decided to marry!"

Georg looked up to his father's terrible image. His friend in St. Petersburg, whom his father suddenly knew so well, moved him as never before. He imagined him lost in faraway Russia. He imagined him at the door of his empty, plundered store. He was just managing to stand between the ruins of the shelves, the shredded merchandise, the falling gas fixtures. Why did he have to go so far away!

"But look at me!" shouted his father, and Georg ran, almost absentmindedly, to his bed in order to grasp everything, but balked halfway in his tracks.

"Because she lifted her skirts," his father began to warble, "because she lifted her skirts like this, the disgusting cow," and to demonstrate this he lifted his shirt so high that you could see the scar on his thigh from his war years, "because she lifted her skirts like this and this and this, you had a go at her, and in order to satisfy your desires with her without interruption, you have violated our mother's memory, betrayed your friend, and put your father to bed, so he can't stir. But he can stir, can't he?"

And he stood entirely free and flung his legs. He radiated with insight.

Georg stood in a corner, as far as possible from his father. A long time ago he had firmly resolved to observe everything very precisely so that he could not be taken by surprise, indirectly somehow, coming from behind, down from above. Now he recalled his long-forgotten resolve and forgot it again, just as a short thread is pulled through the eye of a needle.

"But your friend has not been betrayed after all!" shouted his father, and his finger was wagged back and forth to reinforce it. "I was his representative here on site."

"Comedian!" Georg could not help calling out, recognizing the damage immediately and biting, only too late,—his eyes frozen— into his tongue, so that he buckled under the pain.

"Yes, I have indeed been performing a comedy! Comedy! A good word for it! What other consolation does the old widowed father have left? Tell me—and for the moment of your answer, remain my living son—what choice did I have, in my back room, persecuted by unfaithful staff, old to the bones? And my son went through the world in jubilation, closing deals that I had prepared, falling over himself with pleasure, and walked away from his father with the barred face of an honorable man! Do you believe I never loved you, I, from whom you stem?"

"Now he is going to lean forward," thought Georg, "what if he were to fall and shatter to pieces!" These words hissed through his head. His father leaned forward, but did not fall. Because Georg had not come closer as he had expected, he stood up again.

"Stay where you are, I don't need you! You think you still have the strength to come over here and only hold yourself back because you want to. You are mistaken! I am still the much stronger one. Alone I may have had to retreat, but as it is, your mother has given me her strength, I have bonded wonderfully with your friend, I have your customers here in my pocket!"

"He even has pockets in his nightshirt!" Georg said to himself and believed that he could embarrass him before the entire world with that remark. He thought this for just a moment, for he was constantly forgetting everything.

"Hook arms with your bride and come my way! I will sweep her from your side, you'll be amazed how!"

Georg grimaced in disbelief. His father merely nodded, asserting the truth of what he had said, into Georg's corner.

"How you amused me today when you came and asked whether you should write to your friend about your engagement. He knows all about it, silly boy, he knows all about it! I wrote him, of course, because you forgot to take my writing things away from me. That is why he hasn't been here for years, he knows everything a hundred times better than you yourself, your letters crumpled up and unread in his left hand, while he holds out my letters to read in his right!"

He swung his arm over his head in his enthusiasm. "He knows everything a thousand times better!" he cried.

"Ten thousand times!" said Georg, to ridicule his father but, still in his mouth, the words took on a deadly serious ring.

"For years now I've been waiting for you to come to me with this question! Do you think I worry about anything else? Do you think I read the news? Here!" and he threw Georg a newspaper that must have been carried along into his bed. An old newspaper with a name entirely unfamiliar to Georg.

"How long you have taken to grow up! Your mother had to die, she couldn't live to see the happy day; your friend is perishing in his Russia, three years ago he was already yellow enough to dispose of; and me, you see how things have become for me. You certainly have eyes for that!"

"So you've been lying in wait for me!" cried Georg.

His father said compassionately: "You probably wanted to say that earlier. Now it's out of place."

And louder: "So now you know what there was other than yourself; until now you only knew about yourself! After all, you were actually an innocent child, but more actually you were a devilish person!—And therefore be aware: I condemn you now to death by drowning!"

Georg felt chased out of the room, he still carried the blow, with which his father fell onto the bed behind him, in his ears. On the stairs, over whose steps he rushed as though they were a slanted surface, he startled his maid, who was on her way upstairs to clean up the room after the night. "Jesus!" she cried and covered her face with her apron, but he was already gone. He leapt through the gate, compelled to cross the road toward the water. He was already clinging to the railing, like a hungry man to his food. He flung himself over, like the excellent gymnast that, to his parents' pride, he had been in his youth. He still held on with increasingly weak hands, spotted an omnibus between the bars of the railing that would easily cover the sound of his fall, called softly, "Dear Parents, I always did love you," and let himself fall.

At this moment, a positively endless stream of traffic passed over the bridge.

THE METAMORPHOSIS

I

As Gregor Samsa awoke one morning from restless dreams, he found himself transformed in his bed into a monstrous insect. He lay on his hard, armor-like back and saw, when he lifted his head a little, his curved, brown abdomen, segmented by stiff arches, the height of which was barely covered by his blanket, which was ready to slip down entirely at any moment. His numerous and, in comparison to his girth, pathetically thin legs flickered helplessly before his eyes.

"What has happened to me?" he thought. It was not a dream. His room, a proper human being's room, only slightly too small, lay calmly between the four familiar walls. Above the table, on which an unpacked collection of textile samples was spread out— Samsa was a traveling salesman—hung the picture that he had recently cut from an illustrated magazine and placed in a pretty, gilded frame. It depicted a lady, who, dressed in a fur hat and fur boa, was sitting upright and raising toward the viewer a heavy fur muff, in which her entire forearm had disappeared.

Gregor's gaze then turned to the window, and the dreary weather—one could hear raindrops striking the tin windowsill— made him quite melancholy. "What if I were to sleep a little longer and forget all this foolishness," he thought, but that was entirely unfeasible because he was accustomed to sleeping on his right side, and in his current state he was unable to bring himself into this position. No matter how much force he used to throw himself onto his right side, he always rocked back to lie on his back. He must have tried it a hundred times, closed his eyes so he didn't have to see his wriggling legs, and only let off when he began to feel a slight, dull pain in his side that he had never felt before.

"Oh God," he thought, "what a strenuous profession I have chosen! Traveling around day in, day out. The business dealings are much more demanding than those in the actual business at home, and I am additionally burdened with the menace of traveling, worrying about train connections, the irregular and bad meals, a stream of people that is constantly changing, never lasting, never becoming more cordial. Let the devil take it all!" He felt a slight itching high on his abdomen; pushed himself slowly on his back closer to the bedpost in order to raise his head better; found the place that was itching, which was covered with small white spots that he was not able to assess; and wanted to feel the area with one of his legs but pulled it back immediately, for his touch sent a wave of cold shivers through him.

He slid back into his previous position. "Getting up so early," he thought, "makes one entirely stupid. People must have their sleep. Other traveling salesmen live like harem women. If I return to the guesthouse during the morning, for example, in order to transfer the acquired orders, these men are still sitting at the breakfast table. I should try that with my boss; I would be thrown out on the spot. Who knows, by the way, whether that wouldn't be quite good for me. If I weren't holding myself back on account of my parents, I would have quit long ago. I would have stood before the boss and spoken my mind from the bottom of my heart. He would have fallen from his desk! It is a peculiar habit, after all, to sit on the desk and talk down to one's employees, who are also forced to approach the desk quite closely because the boss is hard of hearing. Well, all hope is not yet lost; once I have the money together to pay off the debt that my parents owe him—it may take five to six more years—I'll carry it out for sure. Then I'll make a big cut. For the time being, however, I must get up, for my train leaves at five."

And he looked over at his alarm clock, which was ticking on the chest. "Heavenly Father!" he thought. It was half past six and the hands were progressing steadily; they had actually passed the half-hour mark already and had almost reached three-quarters. Had the alarm failed to ring? One could see from the bed that it was set correctly at four o'clock; it had certainly also rung. Yes, but was it possible to sleep peacefully through that furniture-rattling noise? Well, his sleep had not been peaceful, after all, but probably all the sounder for it. But what was he to do now? The next train left at seven o'clock; in order to catch it, he would have to hurry around ridiculously, and the collection was not yet packed, and he himself was definitely not feeling particularly fresh and agile. And even if he caught the train, a good scolding was not to be avoided, for the shop's attendant had waited at the five o'clock train and long since reported his failure to appear. He was the boss's creature, spineless and stupid. And what if he said that he was ill? That would be extremely embarrassing and suspicious, for Gregor had not been ill even once during his five years of service. The boss would certainly arrive with the health insurance doctor, would reproach his parents for having such a lazy son, and stifle all objections with a reference to the health insurance doctor, for whom there are only completely healthy people, after all, with an aversion to work. And would he be entirely wrong in this case? Aside from a drowsiness that was really unreasonable considering that he had slept so long, Gregor felt quite well, in fact, and was even feeling particularly hungry.

As he contemplated all of this in great haste, without being able to decide to leave his bed—the alarm clock had just struck a quarter to seven—there was a cautious knock at the door behind the head of his bed. "Gregor," someone called—it was his mother—"it's a quarter to seven. Weren't you going to leave town?" That gentle voice! Gregor was startled as he heard his voice responding, for although it was unmistakably his own voice, it had been mixed, as though from below, with an insuppressible, painful chirping sound that allowed his words their formal clarity at first, only to destroy them as they resonated so that one was not sure if they had been heard correctly. Gregor wanted to answer thoroughly and explain everything, but limited himself, given the circumstances, to saying: "Yes, yes, thank you, Mother, I'm getting up." Due to the wooden door, the change in Gregor's voice did not seem to be noticeable outside, for his mother was reassured by this explanation and shuffled away. But through this brief conversation, the other family members were now aware that Gregor, contrary to their expectations, was still at home, and soon his father knocked on one side door, weakly, but with his fist. "Gregor, Gregor," he called, "what's wrong?" And after a little while, he urged again with a deeper voice: "Gregor! Gregor!" But at the other side door, his sister pleaded softly: "Gregor? Are you not well? Do you need anything?" Toward both sides Gregor answered: "I'm already finished," and tried, with the most careful pronunciation and by inserting long pauses between the individual words, to remove all conspicuousness from his voice. And his father returned to his breakfast, but his sister whispered: "Gregor, open the door, I beg you." But Gregor wouldn't even think of opening the door, and instead commended himself for the precaution to which he had become accustomed from traveling of locking all doors at night, even at home.

First he wanted to get up calmly and, without disturbance, get dressed, and, most importantly, eat breakfast before thinking about the rest, because, as he was well aware, thinking would not come to any sensible conclusion in bed. He remembered having often felt some slight pain in bed, perhaps caused by lying in an awkward position, which then turned out to be purely imaginary when he got up, and he was curious to find out how today's illusions would gradually dissolve. He did not doubt in the least that the changes in his voice were nothing but the first signs of a bad cold, an occupational illness for traveling salesmen.

Throwing the blanket off was quite simple; he only needed to inflate himself a little and it fell on its own. But beyond that, things became difficult, especially because he was so incredibly wide. He would have needed arms and hands to prop himself upright; but instead of these he had only the many little legs, which were continually moving about in different directions and which he could not control to begin with. If he tried to bend one of them, it was the first one to stretch out; and by the time he finally succeeded in getting one leg to do what he wanted it to, all the other legs would be waving about as though set free at the greatest, most painful, level of excitement. "It's no good staying in bed unnecessarily," Gregor said to himself.

He wanted to get out of bed with the bottom part of his body first, but this bottom part, which he had, by the way, not yet seen, and which he could not really picture, proved to be too inflexible; it moved so slowly. When he had finally grown almost wild, gathered his strength, and thrust himself forward without restraint, he had chosen the wrong direction and slammed heavily against the bedpost. The burning pain that he felt instructed him that particularly the bottom part of his body was perhaps the most sensitive at the moment.

He therefore tried to get his upper body out of the bed first, and turned his head carefully toward the edge of the bed. This worked easily, and eventually, despite its width and weight, the bulk of his body slowly followed his turning head. But as he finally held his head freely in the air outside of his bed, he became afraid of moving forward in this fashion, for if he were to ultimately let himself fall in this way, it would take a downright miracle for his head not to be injured. And his consciousness could not be lost now at any cost; he would sooner remain in bed.

However, after repeating the effort only to lie there sighing just as he was before, and seeing his little legs fighting one another again, possibly worse than before, and finding no possibility of bringing peace and order into this arbitrariness, he told himself again that he could not possibly remain in bed, and that it would be the most sensible decision to sacrifice everything, even if there was only the slightest hope of freeing himself of his bed. But at the same time he didn't forget to remind himself from time to time that calm, the calmest deliberation, was much better than desperate decisions. At such moments he focused his eyes as sharply as possible on the window, but unfortunately the sight of the morning fog, which even enveloped the other side of the narrow street, offered little by way of assurance or cheer. "Already seven o'clock," he said to himself as the alarm clock struck anew. "Already seven o'clock and still such a fog." And for a while he lay calmly, breathing shallowly, as though he were expecting the utter stillness to return everything to its real and natural state.

But then he said to himself: "Before it strikes a quarter-past seven, I must absolutely have gotten myself completely out of bed. Besides, someone from the office will have come by then to ask after me, for the office is opened before seven o'clock." And then he began to rock the entire length of his body steadily out of bed. If he were to let himself fall out of bed in this way, his head, which he intended to lift sharply as he fell, would presumably remain uninjured. His back seemed to be hard; it was unlikely that anything would happen to it as he fell on the carpet. His greatest reservation was his deliberation about the loud crash that would certainly result, and the concern, if not fear, that it was certain to provoke behind all the doors. That would have to be risked however.

As Gregor was already jutting halfway out of bed—the new method was more of a game than a strain, all he needed to do was rock back and forth jerkily—it occurred to him how easy everything would be if someone were to come help him. Two strong people—he thought of his father and the maid—would suffice entirely; they would only have to slide their arms beneath his arched back, extract him in this way from his bed, bend down under his weight, and then simply wait carefully for him to complete his swing over onto the floor, where his legs would hopefully gain some purpose. Now, quite apart from the fact that the doors were locked, should he really call for help? Despite all distress, he could not suppress a smile at this thought.

He had already gotten to the point where he was rocking so strongly that he could barely maintain his balance, and he would have to make a final decision very soon because it was five minutes before a quarter-past seven—when the doorbell rang. "That's someone from the office," he said to himself and almost froze, while his little legs only danced all the more urgently. For a moment, everything remained quiet. "They're not going to open," Gregor told himself, caught in some sort of senseless hope. But then, of course, the maid walked in firm steps to the door and opened it, as always. Gregor only needed to hear the visitor's first word of greeting and already knew who it was— the chief clerk himself. Why did Gregor have to be the one condemned to serve in a company that immediately conceived the greatest suspicions at the slightest lapse? Were all the employees, the whole lot, scoundrels with not one faithful, obedient person among them who, if he failed to exploit even a few morning hours for the business, would go mad with remorse and be literally incapable of leaving his bed? Would it really not have sufficed to have an apprentice ask after him—if this asking was even necessary? Did the chief clerk have to come himself, and, in doing so, show his entire, innocent family that the investigation of this suspicious matter could only be entrusted to the chief clerk's judgment? And more as the result of the agitated state that Gregor had reached through this deliberation than as the result of a proper decision, he swung himself with all his might out of bed. There was a loud thud, but not an actual crash. The fall was alleviated slightly by the carpet, and his back was also more elastic than Gregor thought, producing a not-so-conspicuous dull sound. But he had not managed to hold his head carefully enough and had hit it; he turned it and rubbed it on the carpet in anger and pain.

"Something has fallen in there," said the chief clerk in the room to the left. Gregor sought to imagine whether something similar to what had happened to him today could also happen to the chief clerk; this possibility really must be acknowledged, after all. But as if in blunt response to this question, the chief clerk then took a few decisive steps in the next room and let his patent leather boots creak. From the room to the right, his sister whispered to inform Gregor: "Gregor, the chief clerk is here." "I know," said Gregor under his breath; but he didn't dare to raise his voice loudly enough for his sister to have been able to hear.

"Gregor," said his father then from the room to the left, "the chief clerk has come and is inquiring about why you didn't depart with the early train. We don't know what we should tell him. For that matter, he would like to speak with you in person. So please open the door. He will be good enough to excuse the disorder in your room." "Good morning, Herr Samsa," the chief clerk interjected amiably. "He's not feeling well," said his mother to the chief clerk while his father was still speaking at the door, "he's not feeling well, believe me, sir. How else would Gregor miss his train! The boy has nothing in mind other than business, after all. It almost irritates me that he never goes out in the evenings; now he has been in town for eight days, but has spent every evening at home. He sits there with us at the table and reads the newspaper or studies train schedules. It's distraction enough for him to busy himself with fretwork. He cut a little frame, for example, over the course of two, three evenings; you'll be amazed how pretty it is; it is hanging in his room; you'll see it in just a moment, when Gregor opens the door. I am grateful, by the way, that you are here, sir; we alone would not have been able to convince Gregor to open the door; he's so stubborn; and most certainly not feeling well, although he denied it this morning." "I'll be right there," said Gregor slowly and deliberately and didn't stir so as not to miss one word of the conversations. "Nor can I, dear lady, think of any other explanation," said the chief clerk. "Hopefully it is nothing serious. While I must say, on the other hand, that we businessmen—unfortunately or fortunately, as you will—must very often simply overcome slight illnesses for the sake of business concerns." "So can the chief clerk come into your room?" asked his impatient father and knocked again on the door. "No," said Gregor. An awkward silence entered the room to the left; in the room to the right his sister began to sob.

Why did his sister not join the others? She must have just gotten out of bed and had not even begun to get dressed. And why was she crying? Because he hadn't gotten up and wouldn't let the chief clerk in, because he was in danger of losing his position, and because then his boss would pursue their parents with the old demands again? But these were surely unnecessary worries for the time being. Gregor was still here and hadn't the slightest intention of leaving his family. At the moment, he seemed to be lying on the carpet, and no one who knew of his condition would have seriously demanded of him that he let the chief clerk in. But Gregor could not really be immediately dismissed on account of this little discourtesy, for which a suitable excuse could easily be found later. And it seemed to Gregor that it would be far more sensible for them to leave him in peace now, instead of bothering him with crying and pleading. It was the uncertainty, however, that distressed the others and excused their behavior.

"Herr Samsa," called the chief clerk now with a raised voice, "what is the matter? You're barricading yourself in your room, answering only with yes and no, giving your parents grave, unnecessary cause for concern, and neglecting—this mentioned only incidentally—your business obligations in a manner that is actually outrageous. I am speaking here in the name of your parents and your boss and ask you quite seriously for an immediate, clear explanation. I'm astonished, astonished. I thought I knew you to be a quiet, sensible person, and now you seem to want to suddenly start showing off your strange whims. Although the director implied a possible explanation for your absence this morning—it concerned the task of cash collection, with which you have been entrusted as of recently—I almost pledged my word of honor that this explanation could not apply. But now I see your incomprehensible stubbornness here and am losing all desire to advocate for you in the slightest. And your position is certainly not the most stable. I originally had the intention of telling you this in confidence, but as you are letting me waste my time here uselessly, I don't know why your parents should not hear it as well. So your recent performance has been very unsatisfactory; admittedly, it is not the season for doing particularly good business, this we recognize; but a season for doing no business at all doesn't exist, Herr Samsa, cannot exist."

"But sir," cried Gregor frantically, forgetting everything else in his excitement, "I'll open the door immediately, this very moment. A slight illness, a bout of dizziness, prevented me from getting up. I am still lying in bed. But now I am feeling quite fresh again. I am now getting out of bed. Just a moment's patience! It's not yet going so well as I thought. But I am already feeling quite well again. Incredible, how a person can be overwhelmed by such a thing! Only yesterday evening I was feeling quite fine. My parents know for sure. Or rather, yesterday evening I already had a little premonition. They must have noticed it. Why didn't I notify the office! But one always thinks that one can overcome the illness without staying home. Sir! Spare my parents! There is no reason for all the accusations that you are now making; no one has mentioned a single word about it to me. Perhaps you haven't read the last orders that I sent. I'll be traveling with the eight o'clock train, by the way, the few hours rest have given me strength. Don't let me keep you, sir; I will be in the office myself soon, and please be good enough to tell them that, and give my regards to our esteemed director!"

And as Gregor emitted all this hastily, hardly knowing what he was saying, he had easily drawn himself closer to the chest, probably due to the practice he had already had in bed, and was now attempting to straighten himself up against it. He truly did want to open the door, truly did want to let himself be seen and to speak to the chief clerk; he was eager to hear what the others, who were demanding him so eagerly, would say at the sight of him. If they were frightened, then Gregor would no longer bear responsibility and could be calm. If they accepted everything calmly, however, then he would also have no reason to fret and could, if he hurried, actually be at the train station at eight o'clock. At first he slid off the smooth chest several times, but finally gave himself one last swing and stood there upright; he no longer paid any attention to the pain in his lower abdomen, however much it burned. Now he let himself fall against the backrest of a nearby chair, the edges of which he held onto with his little legs. In doing so, he had also gained control of himself and fell silent, for now he was able to hear the chief clerk.

"Did you understand a single word?" the chief clerk asked his parents. "He's not making fools of us, is he?" "For God's sake," cried his mother, already in tears, "maybe he is seriously ill, and we are agonizing him. Grete! Grete!" she then screamed. "Mother?" called his sister from the other side. They were communicating through Gregor's room. "You must go to the doctor this instant. Gregor is ill. Rush for the doctor. Did you hear Gregor speaking just now?" "That was an animal's voice," said the chief clerk, in a noticeably quiet voice, compared to his mother's screaming. "Anna! Anna!" called his father through the hallway into the kitchen, clapping his hands, "Fetch a locksmith at once!" And the two girls were already running with rustling skirts through the hallway—how had his sister gotten dressed so quickly?—and tearing open the apartment door. One didn't even hear the door slamming shut; they must have left it open, as is customary in apartments in which a great misfortune has taken place.

Gregor had become much calmer, however. So his words were no longer understandable, although they had seemed to be clear enough, clearer than before, maybe as a result of the adaptation of his ears. But after all they now believed that something was not quite right with him and were prepared to help him. The assurance and certainty with which the first arrangements had been made had done him good. He felt included again in the human sphere and hoped for great and surprising achievements from both men, the doctor and the locksmith, without entirely distinguishing among them. In order for his voice to become as clear as possible for the imminent crucial consultations, he cleared his throat a little, making an effort, however, to mute the sound, for it was possible that this sound was also already different from the sound of a human cough, which he no longer trusted himself to decide. In the next room, meanwhile, it had become entirely silent. Perhaps his parents were sitting with the chief clerk at the table and whispering, perhaps they were all leaning against the door and listening.

Gregor pushed himself slowly toward the door with the armchair, let go of it there, threw himself toward the door, held himself upright against it—the pads on his little legs were a bit sticky—and rested there for a moment to recover from the strain. But then he set about turning the key in the lock with his mouth. Unfortunately, it seemed that he lacked proper teeth,—what was he to grasp the key with?—but his jaws, on the other hand, were certainly very strong; and with their help, he actually got the key moving and paid no attention to the fact that he was undoubtedly causing himself some kind of damage, for a brown fluid came out of his mouth, ran over the key, and dripped onto the floor. "Listen," said the chief clerk in the next room, "he is turning the key." That was a great encouragement for Gregor; but they all should have called out to him, including his father and mother: "Go on, Gregor!" they should have called, "Keep at it, keep at the lock!" And, imagining that everyone was following his efforts with excitement, he bit senselessly into the key with all the strength he could muster. In accordance with the progress of the turning of the key, he was dancing around the lock; he was now only holding himself upright by his mouth and hanging himself on the key, or pushing it down with the entire weight of his body, as necessary. The louder sound of the lock as it finally clicked back positively awoke Gregor. With a sigh of relief, he told himself: "So I didn't need the locksmith after all," and lay his head on the handle to open the door completely.

Because he had to open the door in this way, it was actually already open quite widely while he himself could not be seen. He first had to maneuver himself slowly around the one wing of the door, and to do so very carefully, if he didn't want to fall clumsily onto his back just before his entrance into the room. He was still busy with this difficult movement and hadn't had time to pay attention to anything else, when he already heard the chief clerk emitting a loud "Oh!" It sounded like the wind whistling, and now he could see him as well, how he, who was the one closest to the door, pressed his hand against his open mouth and retreated slowly, as though he were being expelled by some invisible, evenly lingering force. His mother—she was standing there, despite the chief clerk's presence, with her hair still disheveled from the night and standing high on end—looked first with folded hands at his father, then took two steps toward Gregor and fell to her knees in the midst of the skirts that spread out around her, her face sunk to her breast, nowhere to be seen. His father clenched his fists with a hostile expression, as though he wanted to repel Gregor back into his room, but then looked around the living room uncertainly, shaded his eyes with his hands and cried, so that his mighty breast shook.

Gregor did not enter the room at all now, but leaned against the locked wing of the door so that only half of his body was visible, as well as his head tilted sideways above it, with which he was peering over at the others. It had become much brighter in the meantime; clear was the view of a section of the endless, gray-black house on the other side of the street—it was a hospital—with its regular windows starkly interrupting its façade; the rain was still falling, but only in large drops that were individually visible, and literally also being individually thrown down to the ground. An excessive number of breakfast dishes were still on the table, for his father regarded breakfast as the most important meal of the day, drawing it out for hours as he read various newspapers. On the wall directly opposite, there hung a photograph of Gregor during his time in the military, depicting him as a lieutenant, demanding, hand on his sword with a carefree smile, respect for his stance and uniform. The door to the hallway was open, and, because the front door was also open, one could see out to the forecourt and to the top of the downward-leading stairs.

"Well now," said Gregor and was well aware that he was the only one who had maintained his calm, "I'll get dressed right away, pack the collection together, and leave. Would you, would you like to let me leave? Well, chief clerk, you see that I am not obstinate and enjoy my work; the traveling is burdensome, but I couldn't live without traveling. Where are you going, sir? To the office? Yes? Will you report everything faithfully? A person can be unable to work at the moment, but that is precisely the right time to recall his previous accomplishments and to consider that later, after the hindrance has been eliminated, he will certainly work more with more diligence and concentration. I am so indebted to the director, after all; this you know quite well. On the other hand, I am responsible for my parents and my sister. I'm in a quandary, but I'll work my way out of it. But don't make it harder for me than it already is. Put in a good word for me at the office! No love is lost on traveling salesmen, I know. One thinks, they earn a fortune and lead a great life. One simply has no particular reason to better think through this preconception. But you, sir, you have a better overview of the circumstances than the rest of the personnel, yes, between you and me, even a better overview than the director himself, who, in his capacity as employer, lets himself be misled to the slight disadvantage of his employees. You also know quite well that the traveler, who is outside the office for almost the entire year, easily becomes the victim of gossip, coincidence, and unfounded complaints, against which he cannot possibly defend himself, because he usually doesn't even hear about them, and then, when he returns home exhausted from a journey, he comes to feel the terrible consequences of these causes that he can no longer decipher. Sir, please don't leave without having said one word to me that shows me that you agree with me at least a little bit!"

But the chief clerk had already turned away at Gregor's first words and only over his twitching shoulder did he look back at Gregor with his lips flung apart. And during Gregor's speech, he hadn't stood still for a moment, but moved away without taking his eyes off Gregor, against the door, but very gradually, as though it were secretly forbidden to leave the room. He was already in the hallway and, after the sudden movement, with which he had finally pulled his foot out of the living room, one could have believed he had just burned his sole. But in the hallway, he stretched his right hand far in front of him toward the stairs, as though nothing less than heavenly salvation were awaiting him there.

Gregor realized that there was no way he could let the chief clerk leave in this state of mind without putting his position in the company in grave danger. His parents didn't understand all of this very well; they had developed the conviction over the long years that Gregor would be provided for by this company for his entire life, and besides, they were now so busy with their current concerns that all foresight had been lost. But Gregor possessed this foresight. The chief clerk must be held back, calmed, convinced, and finally won over; Gregor and his family's future depended on it! If only his sister were here! She was clever; she had already wept when Gregor was still lying calmly on his back. And surely the chief clerk, that lady's man, would have let her guide him; she would have closed the front door and talked him out of his shock in the hallway. But his sister was simply not there; Gregor himself had to act. And without thinking that he was not even familiar with his current abilities to move yet, also without thinking that his speech could possibly, indeed probably, not be understood again, he left the wing of the door; pushed himself through the opening; intended to approach the chief clerk, who was already clinging ridiculously to the railing in the forecourt with both hands; but fell down immediately, searching for support, with a little cry onto his many little legs. No sooner had this happened than, for the first time this morning, he felt physical comfort; his little legs had solid ground beneath them; they obeyed perfectly, as he observed with pleasure; they even strove to carry him away, wherever he wished; and already he believed that the final improvement of all suffering was imminent. But at that same moment, as he was lying there not far away from his mother, rocking with restrained movement, just across from her on the floor, she who had seemed so entirely sunken within herself sprang up suddenly with arms stretched out widely and fingers spread, and screamed: "Help, for God's sake, help!" tilting her head as though she wanted to see Gregor better, but ran, contradictory to this, back senselessly; she had forgotten that the table, which was still laid, was behind her; when she reached it, she sat down upon it hastily, as though in absence of mind; and seemed not to notice at all that a great stream of coffee was spilling from the large coffee pot that had been thrown over beside her onto the carpet.

"Mother, Mother," said Gregor softly, and looked up at her. He had entirely forgotten the chief clerk for a moment; but at the sight of the flowing coffee, he could not resist snapping his jaws in the air several times. At that his mother screamed out again, fled from the table and fell into his father's arms as he rushed toward her. But Gregor had no time for his parents now; the chief clerk was already on the stairs; with his chin on the railing, he was looking back for the last time. Gregor made a running start to be sure and catch up to him. The chief clerk must have sensed something, for he took a leap down several stairs and disappeared. "Aah!" he was still crying; it sounded throughout the entire stairwell. Unfortunately, the chief clerk's escape appeared to have also entirely confused his father, who until now had been relatively calm, for instead of running after the chief clerk himself, or at least refraining from hindering Gregor in his pursuit, he grabbed with his right hand the chief clerk's cane, which he had left behind on an armchair along with his hat and overcoat, took with his left hand a large newspaper from the table, and set about stamping his feet as he swung the cane and the newspaper in an attempt to drive Gregor back into his room. None of Gregor's pleas helped; no pleas were understood, however submissively he turned his head; his father simply stamped all the more strongly with his feet. Despite the cool weather, his mother had flung open the window on the other side of the room, and as she leaned out, she pressed her face, far outside the window, into her hands. A strong draft had arisen between street and stairwell, the draperies flew open, the newspapers rustled on the table, and individual sheets blew across the floor. His father drove him back relentlessly, making hissing noises like a wildman. As Gregor hadn't had any practice at all yet in walking backwards, it really went quite slowly. If only Gregor had been allowed to turn around he would have been in his room right away, but he was afraid of making his father impatient with the time-consuming rotation, and, after all, the cane in his father's hand was threatening at any moment a deadly blow to his back or his head. But ultimately, Gregor had no choice, for he noticed with horror that when he went backwards, he didn't even know how to keep going in the right direction; and so he began, with incessant fearful sideways glances toward his father, to turn himself around as quickly as possible, which was, in fact, only quite slowly. Perhaps his father noticed his good intent, for he didn't disturb him in his efforts, and even directed his turning movements from a distance with the tip of his cane. If only his father would have stopped his unbearable hissing! It made Gregor lose his head entirely. He had almost turned around completely when he, constantly hearing this hissing, even made a mistake and turned himself back a ways. But when he had finally happily reached the doorway with his head, it became apparent that his body was too wide to simply pass through. Of course, it didn't even remotely occur to his father in his current state to open the other wing of the door, for instance, to create a suitable passage for Gregor. His fixed idea was simply that Gregor must get into his room as quickly as possible. He never would have allowed the inconvenient preparations that Gregor needed to pull himself upright and perhaps pass through the door this way. On the contrary, he drove Gregor forwards, as though there were no obstacle, now with exceptional noise. Behind Gregor, it didn't at all sound like merely the voice of his one father; now it was really no longer a joke, and Gregor thrust himself—come what may—into the doorway. The one side of his body rose. He lay aslant in the doorframe, his side was scraped raw, the white door covered with ugly stains. Soon he was stuck and would no longer have been able to move on his own. His little legs on the one side hung quivering up in the air while the others were being painfully pushed to the ground. Then his father gave him a powerful push from behind, which was truly liberating this time, and he flew, bleeding heavily, far into his room. The door was slammed shut with the cane, and then it was finally still.

II

It was not until dusk that Gregor awoke from his heavy, coma-like sleep. He would certainly also have awoken a little later without being disturbed, for he had recovered sufficiently and felt well-rested, but it seemed to him that fleeting footsteps and a cautious closing of the door to the hallway had awoken him. Here and there the glow from the electric streetlight lay pallidly on the ceiling and the upper parts of the furniture, but down by Gregor it was dark. He slowly pushed himself toward the door, still searching around awkwardly with his feelers, which he was only now learning to appreciate, to see what had happened there. His left side seemed to be a single long, unpleasantly tense scar, and he actually had to limp on his two rows of legs. One little leg had also been badly injured during the course of the morning's events—it was almost a miracle that only one had been injured—and dragged behind lifelessly.

Only at the door did he realize what had actually lured him there. It had been the smell of something edible, for there stood a bowl filled with sweet milk, in which small pieces of white bread were swimming. He could have laughed with joy, for he was even hungrier than he had been in the morning and he quickly plunged his head into the milk, almost covering his eyes. But he soon pulled it back in disappointment; not only was eating causing difficulties due to his sensitive left side—and he could only eat when his entire body collaborated, puffing and panting—but the milk, which was usually his favorite drink, and which his sister had certainly brought him for that reason, didn't taste good, so he turned away from the bowl, almost with reluctance, and crept back to the center of the room.

In the living room, the gas was lit, as Gregor saw through the crack in the door, but although his father usually read the afternoon paper at this time of day in a raised voice to his mother and sometimes also to his sister, not a sound was now to be heard. Well, perhaps this habit of reading aloud, which his sister had always told and written him about, wasn't even practiced anymore of late. But it was also so quiet all around, despite the apartment certainly not being empty. "What a quiet life his family lived after all," said Gregor to himself and felt, as he stared before him into the darkness, great pride that he had been able to provide such a life in such a fine apartment for his parents and sister. But what if all the peace, all the affluence, all the contentment were now to come to a dreadful end? To keep from losing himself in such thoughts, Gregor instead set himself in motion and began crawling up and down the room.

Once during the long evening, one of the side doors was opened, and once the other door was opened a small crack and quickly closed again; someone must have felt the need to come in, but had too many reservations after all. So Gregor began stopping directly in front of the living room door, determined to bring the hesitant visitor in somehow, or at least to find out who he was; but now the door was not opened again, and Gregor waited in vain. Early that morning, when all the doors had been locked, everyone had wanted to come in, but now that he had unlocked the one door and the others had been apparently unlocked during the day, no one came, and the keys were now on the other side of the locks.

It was not until late at night that the light in the living room was put out, so it was easy to conclude that his parents and his sister had stayed awake for so long, for as one could hear exactly, all three of them were now leaving on tiptoe. Certainly no one would enter Gregor's room again until morning, so he had a long time to contemplate how to rearrange his life without being disturbed. But the high, spacious room, in which he was forced to lie flat on the ground, frightened him, although he was unable to determine the reason, for it was, after all, the room that he had inhabited for the past five years—and with a partially instinctive turn, and not without a little shame, he hurried under the sofa, where, despite his back being slightly squashed and despite no longer being able to raise his head, he immediately felt very comfortable and only regretted that his body was too wide to be entirely accommodated under the sofa.

He remained there the entire night, which he spent partially in a half-sleep, from which hunger had repeatedly awoken him, and partially in a state of worry and vague hope, which all led to the conclusion that he must behave calmly for the time being and, through patience and the greatest consideration, make the inconvenience, which he was forced to cause in his present state, as bearable as possible for his family.

Early in the morning, it was almost still night, Gregor already had the opportunity to test the strength of the resolution he had just made, for his sister opened the door from the hallway, almost completely dressed, and looked inside with suspense. She didn't find him right away, but when she noticed him under the sofa—good heavens, he had to be somewhere, after all, he couldn't have flown away—she was so startled that she, unable to restrain herself, slammed the door again from outside. But then, as though regretting her behavior, she immediately opened the door again and, as though she were visiting one who was critically ill or even a stranger, entered the room on the tips of her toes. Gregor had pushed his head forward just to the edge of the sofa and was observing her. Would she notice that he had left the milk untouched, and that it was due in no way to a lack of hunger, and would she bring him a different dish that suited him better? If she didn't do it on her own, he would rather starve than call her attention to it, although he actually felt an immense urge to shoot out from beneath the sofa, throw himself at his sister's feet and beg her for something good to eat. But his sister noticed at once with astonishment that the bowl was still full, with just a little milk spilled around it. She picked it up right away, not with her bare hands, of course, but with a washrag, and carried it out. Gregor was incredibly curious to see what she would bring instead and made all kinds of speculations about it. But he never could have guessed what his sister, in all her kindness, really had done. She brought him, in order to try out his taste, an entire assortment, everything spread out on an old newspaper. There were old, half-rotten vegetables; bones from supper that were covered in hardened white sauce; a few raisins and almonds; a cheese that Gregor had declared inedible two days before; one piece of dry bread, one piece of buttered bread, and one piece of bread that had been buttered and salted. In addition, she also put down the bowl, which was probably now reserved for Gregor once and for all, and which she had filled with water. And out of sensitivity, for she knew

Gregor would not eat in front of her, she departed as quickly as possible and even turned the key in the door so Gregor could understand that he could make himself as comfortable as he wanted. Gregor's little legs whizzed as he now went to eat. His wounds, for that matter, must have already healed completely, for he no longer felt any hindrance. He was amazed at this and thought of how he had slightly cut his finger with a knife more than a month ago, and how this wound had still been painful enough the day before yesterday. "Might I be less sensitive now?" he thought, already sucking greedily at the cheese, to which he had felt immediately and particularly attracted before all the other food. One after another and with eyes tearing with satisfaction, he consumed the cheese, the vegetables, and the sauce. The fresh foods, on the other hand, didn't taste good to him at all; he couldn't tolerate their smell at all and even dragged the things that he wanted to eat a little farther away. He was long since finished with everything and was lying lazily in the same place when his sister slowly turned the key to signal that he should withdraw. This startled him immediately, although he was already almost dozing, and he hurried back under the sofa. But it cost him a great amount of willpower to stay under the sofa, even if only for the short time during which his sister was in the room, for his body was slightly rounded from the ample meal and he could hardly breathe in the tight space. Between brief bouts of suffocation, he watched with somewhat protruding eyes as his unsuspecting sister swept together not only the leftovers, but also the food that Gregor had not touched, as though it too were no longer of any use, and how she hastily poured everything into a bucket that she closed with a wooden lid and carried everything out. Hardly had she turned around, when Gregor had already pulled himself out from under the sofa and stretched and puffed himself up.

Gregor now received his meals in this manner every day, once in the morning, while his parents and the maid were still sleeping, the second time after the common lunch, for then his parents would also sleep for a little while and his sister would send the maid away on some errand. Surely they didn't want Gregor to starve either, but perhaps they could not have endured learning more about his food than through hearsay. Perhaps his sister wanted to spare them even a possibly small amount of grief, for they were truly suffering enough at the moment. With which excuses they had managed to get the doctor and the locksmith out of the apartment on that first morning, Gregor could not find out, because due to the fact that he could not be understood, no one, including his sister, thought that he could understand the others, and so he had to be satisfied with listening to his sister's occasional sighs and appeals to the saints when she was in his room. It wasn't until later, when she had grown somewhat accustomed to every-thing—it was, of course, impossible to speak of becoming entirely accustomed—Gregor sometimes caught a comment that was meant kindly or could be interpreted as such. "He certainly liked his food today," she said when Gregor had cleaned his plate dili-gently, while in the opposite case, which had gradually become increasingly frequent, she was accustomed to almost sadly saying: "Now it's all been left again."

Although Gregor could not learn any news directly, he heard many things from the adjoining rooms, and, as soon as he heard even just one voice, he would run directly to the relevant door and push himself with his entire body against it. Especially in the early days there was no conversation that didn't somehow, even if only secretly, concern him. For two days, consultations were to be heard at all meals about how they should now react; but they also spoke of the same topic between the meals, for at least two family mem-bers were always at home, as no one apparently wanted to stay home alone and there was no way that they could all leave the apartment together. Already on the first day, the maid had begged his mother on her knees to be immediately dismissed—it wasn't quite clear what and how much she knew about what had occurred—and when she took her leave fifteen minutes later, she thanked them in tears for her dismissal, as though for the greatest of good deeds that had been bestowed upon her here, and, although no one had demanded it of her, gave a dreadful oath to never betray even the smallest detail to anyone.

Now his sister, together with his mother, also had to do the cooking; that wasn't much trouble, however, because they ate hardly anything. Again and again, Gregor could hear one of them encouraging another in vain to eat, receiving no other answer than "Thank you, I've had enough" or something similar. Perhaps they didn't drink anything either. His sister often asked his father if he would like a beer, and affectionately offered to get it herself, and when he remained silent, she then said, to remove any reservations, that she could send the caretaker to fetch it. But then his father finally uttered a big "No," and it was not spoken of again.

Already during the course of the first day, his father had presented their entire financial situation and prospects to his mother as well as his sister. From time to time he rose from the table and removed some document or notebook from his little home safe, which he had salvaged from the collapse of his business five years ago. One could hear how he opened the complicated lock and, following the removal of what he had been looking for, locked it again. These explanations by his father were in part the most pleasant news that Gregor had heard since his captivity. He had believed that his father's business had left him with nothing at all, at least his father had told him nothing to the contrary, and Gregor had admittedly never asked him about it. Then, Gregor's only concern had been to do his utmost to enable his family to quickly forget the financial misfortune that had driven everyone to a state of complete hopelessness. He had therefore begun to work with particular zeal and almost overnight, the little clerk had turned into a traveling salesman, who had entirely different possibilities to earn money, of course, and whose business successes could be transformed immediately as commissions into cash that could be laid on the table at home before his amazed and delighted family. Those had been good times, and never had they recurred thereafter, at least not in this glory, although Gregor had later earned so much money that he was able to carry the expenditures of his entire family, and also did so. They had simply become accustomed to it, the family as well as Gregor. They took the money gratefully, he was glad to provide it, but no particular warmth emerged anymore. Only his sister had still remained close to Gregor, and it was his secret plan to send her, who, unlike Gregor, loved music deeply and could play the violin movingly, to the conservatory next year, regardless of the great expense that it would entail, which he would have to earn in some other way. During his brief stays in the city, the conservatory was often mentioned in conversations with his sister, but always only as a beautiful dream, whose realization was unthinkable. Their parents didn't even like to hear these innocent references, but Gregor had thought about it quite distinctly and intended to announce it ceremoniously on Christmas Eve.

Such thoughts, entirely useless in his present state, went through his head while he was stuck there upright against the door, eavesdropping. Sometimes he couldn't even listen any further due to general tiredness and he carelessly let his head bump against the door, but immediately held it firmly again for even the slight noise that he had made was heard next door and made everyone fall silent. "What's he up to now, I wonder," said his father after a while, apparently facing the door, and only then did they gradually continue their interrupted conversation.

Gregor was well enough informed now—for his father was in the habit of repeating his explanations often, partly because he had not dealt with these matter himself for a long time now, and partly because his mother had not understood everything the first time—that despite all misfortune, some assets still existed from the old days, which had grown slightly in the meantime due to the untouched interest. And furthermore, the money that Gregor had brought home every month—he had only kept a small amount for himself—had not been used up entirely and had accumulated into a small amount of capital. Gregor, behind his door, nodded eagerly, delighted at this unexpected foresight and thrift. Of course, he actually could have used these excess funds to further pay off his father's debt to his boss, and that day when he would have been rid of his position would have been much closer, but now it was undoubtedly better the way his father had arranged things.

This money, however, was by no means enough for his family to be able to live on its interest; it was maybe enough to support his family for one or two years at the most, but not more than that. So it was merely an amount that was actually not to be touched and that had to be saved for emergencies; but the money to live on had to be earned. Now although his father was a healthy man, he was also an old man who hadn't worked at all for five years and, in any event, would not consider himself to be capable of very much; he had gained a lot of weight in these last five years, which had been the first holiday of his arduous yet unsuccessful life, and had therefore become quite sluggish. And was his old mother now to earn money, she who suffered from asthma, for whom a walk through the apartment was strenuous, and who spent every second day with breathing difficulties on the sofa by the open window? And was his sister to earn money, she who was still a child at seventeen years of age and was so happily granted a lifestyle that, up until now, had consisted of dressing herself nicely, sleeping late, helping out in the household, joining in a few humble pleasures, and, above all, playing the violin? When the conversation arrived at the necessity to earn money, Gregor always let go of the door first and flung himself on the cool leather sofa next to it, for he was quite hot with humiliation and grief.

Often he lay there the whole long night through, not sleeping a wink and only scrabbling for hours on the leather. Or he did not shy away from the great effort of moving an armchair to the window, crawling up to the window sill, and, propped up in the armchair, leaning himself against the window, apparently only as some sort of remembrance of the liberating sensation he used to feel when gazing out the window. For in fact, he was beginning to see even things that were only a small distance away less clearly by the day. He could no longer catch sight of the hospital on the opposite side of the street, the all-too-frequent sight of which he had previously cursed, and had he not known for sure that he lived in the quiet, but entirely urban Charlottenstrasse, he could have thought he was gazing out of his window at a desolate landscape, in which the gray sky and the gray earth merged indistinguishably.

Only twice had his attentive sister needed to see that the armchair was by the window before she began pushing the armchair right back over to the window each time she had cleaned up his room, and from now on she even left the inner window sash open.

If only Gregor had been able to speak to his sister and thank her for everything she had to do for him, he could have endured her services more easily; but as it was, he suffered because of it. His sister certainly tried her best to erase the awkwardness of the whole thing, and the more time passed, the more she succeeded at it of course, but Gregor also came to see through everything much more clearly with time. Already her entrance was terrible for him. Hardly had she entered than she ran straight to the window, without taking time to close the doors, however careful she usually was to spare everyone the sight of Gregor's room, and tore it open with hasty hands as though she were almost suffocating, and stayed at the window for a little while, even on the coldest of days, breathing deeply. She alarmed Gregor twice daily with her running and clamoring; he trembled all the while under the sofa, knowing quite well that she would certainly have spared him all this commotion if it had been at all possible for her to be in the same room as Gregor with the window shut.

Once—a month must have already passed since Gregor's transformation and his sister no longer had particular reason to be astonished at Gregor's appearance—she came a little earlier than usual and found Gregor, motionless and propped upright quite frighteningly, still gazing out the window. It would not have been unexpected for Gregor if she had not entered, for in his position he prevented her from opening the window straight away, but not only did she not enter, she even shrank back and closed the door; a stranger could almost have thought that Gregor had been lying in wait for her and had wanted to bite her. Of course Gregor hid himself immediately under the sofa, but he had to wait until midday before his sister returned, and she seemed much more anxious than usual. He concluded from this that the sight of him was still unbearable to her and was certain to remain unbearable, and that it must require great strength for her to keep from running away at the sight of even the small part of his body that protruded from beneath the sofa. One day, in order to spare her this sight as well, he carried the linen cloth from the sofa on his back—he needed four hours for this task—and arranged it in such a way that he was now completely covered and his sister could not see him, even if she bent down. If she had considered this linen cloth to be unnecessary, she could have removed it, after all, for it was clear enough that Gregor did not find amusement in entirely closing himself off in this way. But she left the linen cloth where it was, and Gregor even believed to have caught a grateful glance once as he carefully lifted the cloth a little to see how his sister found the new arrangement.

During the first two weeks, his parents could not bring themselves to come into his room, and he often heard how they gave his sister complete recognition for the work she was doing, whereas before they had often been irritated by her for she seemed to them to be a somewhat useless girl. Now, however, both his father and mother waited in front of Gregor's room while his sister cleaned it up, and, hardly had she come out when she had to tell them exactly how the room looked, what Gregor had eaten, how he had behaved this time, and if perhaps a slight improvement could be observed. His mother, incidentally, had wanted to visit Gregor relatively soon, but his father and sister had initially held her back with rational arguments, which Gregor listened to quite attentively and approved of fully. But later on, she had to be held back by force, and when she then cried: "Let me see Gregor, after all he is my poor son! Can't you understand that I must see him?" then Gregor thought that it might be good after all if his mother came inside, not every day, of course, but perhaps once a week; she understood everything much better than his sister, who, despite all her efforts, was still a child, after all, and perhaps for this reason had taken on such a difficult task out of childish carelessness.

Gregor's wish to see his mother was soon fulfilled. During the day, Gregor didn't want to show himself at the window, solely out of consideration for his parents; nor could he crawl much on the few square meters of floor; lying calmly was already difficult for him to bear at night, and eating soon brought him not the least amount of pleasure: so for diversion, he developed the habit of crawling to and fro across the walls and ceiling. He was particularly fond of hanging from the ceiling; it was much different than lying on the floor; one could breathe more freely; a slight swaying passed through one's body; and in the state of almost happy diversion in which Gregor found himself up there, it could happen that, to his own surprise, he would let go and crash to the ground. But now, of course, he had more control over his body than before and didn't hurt himself even during such a big fall. His sister noticed at once the new form of amusement that Gregor had found for himself—after all, he also left his sticky traces here and there as he crawled—and she set her mind to allowing Gregor the largest amount of crawling space possible by removing the furniture that was hindering him, primarily the chest and the desk. But she was not able to do this on her own; she didn't dare to ask her father for help; the housemaid would certainly not have helped her, for although this girl of about sixteen had been holding out bravely since their previous cook's resignation, she had requested the privilege of being allowed to keep the kitchen door constantly locked and only having to open it when specifically asked to do so; so his sister had no other choice than to fetch his mother, once during his father's absence. And with cries of excited joy, his mother did approach, only to fall silent at the door to Gregor's room. First, his sister looked to see if everything was in order in the room; only then did she let her mother enter. With the greatest haste, Gregor had pulled the linen cloth even further down with more folds, the whole thing really looked as though a cloth had been casually thrown over the sofa. Gregor refrained from spying from under the linen cloth this time as well; he refrained from seeing his mother this time and was happy that she had come after all. "Come on, you can't see him," said his sister, apparently leading his mother by the hand. Gregor then heard how the two weak women moved the old but heavy chest from its place, and how his sister consistently took most of the work upon herself without listening to the warnings of her mother, who was afraid she was going to overexert herself. It took a long time. Already after a quarter hour's work, his mother said they should just leave the chest there; first of all, it was too heavy, they wouldn't be finished by the time his father returned, and with the chest in the middle of the room, Gregor's every movement would be blocked, and second, it was not at all certain that they would be doing Gregor a favor by removing the furniture. It seemed to her that the opposite was true; the sight of the empty wall truly weighed upon her heart; and why shouldn't Gregor feel the same, since he had been accustomed to the furniture for so long and would therefore feel abandoned in an empty room. "And is it not the case," concluded his mother very quietly, almost in a whisper, as if she wished to prevent Gregor, whose exact whereabouts she didn't know, from hearing even the sound of her voice, for she was convinced that he didn't understand her words, "and is it not the case that by removing the furniture, we are showing him that we have lost any hope of his recovery and have ruthlessly abandoned him? I think it would be best to try and keep the room in the exact condition that it was before, so that Gregor, when he returns to us, will find everything unchanged and be all the more able to easily forget what happened in the meantime."

As he heard his mother's words, Gregor realized that the complete lack of direct human contact during these past two months, combined with his monotonous life in the midst of his family, must have confused his mind, for there was no other way to explain how he could have seriously wanted his room to be emptied. Had he really wanted to have his warm room, comfortably equipped with inherited furniture, transformed into a cave, in which he would surely be able to crawl around unimpeded in all directions, but at the same time quickly and completely forget his human past? Indeed, had he already been close to forgetting just now, before his mother's voice, which he hadn't heard for a long time, jarred him awake? Nothing was to be removed; everything had to stay; he could not manage without the positive influence of the furniture on his condition; and if the furniture was a hindrance for his senseless crawling about, it not only did him no harm but was also a great advantage.

But unfortunately his sister was of a different opinion; when discussing matters related to Gregor with her parents, she had become accustomed to acting as the special expert, which was admittedly not entirely unjustified. So now his mother's advice was also reason enough not only to insist on the removal of the chest and desk, which his sister had initially thought of on her own, but the removal of all furniture, with the exception of the indispensable sofa. Of course, it was not only childish defiance and the self-confidence that she had so unexpectedly and arduously acquired of late that led her to determine this course; she had actually observed, after all, that Gregor required a lot of room to crawl, whereas it appeared that he did not use the furniture at all. Perhaps a role was also played by the emotional sensibility of girls her age, which seeks gratification at every opportunity, and by which Grete was now letting herself be tempted to make Gregor's situation even more terrifying in order to then be able to help him even more than before. For no one other than Grete would dare to enter a room in which Gregor alone was solely in control of the empty walls.

And so she refused to be dissuaded from her decision by her mother, who also seemed to be unsure in this room out of sheer anxiousness and soon fell silent and made every effort to help his sister get the chest out. Now, if need be, Gregor could do without the chest, but the desk had to stay. And hardly had the women left the room with the chest, on which they pressed themselves groaning, than Gregor stuck his head out from under the sofa to see how he could intervene as carefully and considerately as possible. But unfortunately it had to be his mother who returned first, while Grete held her arms around the chest in the next room and swung it back and forth on her own, without, of course, managing to move it at all. His mother, however, was not accustomed to the sight of Gregor; it could make her ill, and so he anxiously hurried backwards to the other end of the sofa, but was no longer able to avoid making the front of the linen cloth move slightly. That sufficed in getting his mother's attention. She paused, stood still for a moment, and then went back to Grete.

Although Gregor told himself repeatedly that nothing unusual was happening, after all, that only a few pieces of furniture were being rearranged, he soon had to admit that the women's walking back and forth, their little shouts, the scratching of the furniture on the floor, all affected him like a great tumult fed from all sides, and he inevitably had to admit to himself that, no matter how tightly he pulled his head and legs in and pressed his body down to the floor, he would not be able to stand it for much longer. They were clearing out his room, taking everything that was dear to him; they had already carried out the chest, in which his fretsaw and other tools were stored; they were now loosening the desk, which had already dug itself firmly into the floor, and at which he had completed his assignments as a business school student, as a secondary school student, and yes, even as a primary schoolboy. He really had no more time to assess the good intentions of the two women, whose existence he had incidentally almost forgotten, for in their exhaustion they were now working in silence, and all that could be heard were the heavy steps of their feet.

And so he burst out—the women were leaning against the desk in the next room to catch their breath a little—changing his direction four times as he ran. He really didn't know what to save first, when he saw the picture of the lady clad entirely in furs hanging conspicuously on the otherwise empty wall. He crawled hurriedly up to it and pressed himself against the glass, which held him tight and felt good on his hot abdomen. At least this picture, which Gregor was now covering completely, would certainly not be taken from him. He turned his head toward the door to the living room in order to see the women when they returned.

They hadn't given themselves much rest and were already returning; Grete had laid her arm around their mother and was almost carrying her. "So, what shall we take now?" said Grete, looking around. Her eyes met Gregor's on the wall. It was probably due to her mother's presence that she kept her composure. She leaned her face to her mother's to keep her from looking around and trembled as she said thoughtlessly: "Come, shouldn't we go back to the living room for a moment?" Grete's intention was clear to Gregor; she wanted to bring her mother to safety and then chase him down from the wall. Well, she could go ahead and try! He was sitting on his picture and was not going to give it up. He would rather jump out at Grete's face.

But Grete's words had only unsettled her mother, who stepped aside, beheld the enormous brown spot on the floral wallpaper, and before actually becoming aware that it was Gregor she was looking at, exclaimed in a rough, screaming voice: "Oh God, oh God!" and fell with outstretched arms, as though she had given up entirely, onto the sofa and did not move. "Gregor!" shouted his sister with a raised fist and stern expression. These were the first words she had spoken directly to him since his transformation. She ran into the next room to fetch some sort of essence with which she could awaken her mother from her unconsciousness. Gregor also wanted to help. There was still time to rescue his picture, but he was stuck fast to the glass and had to tear himself away with force. Then he too ran into the living room, as though he could give his sister some kind of advice, as he used to in the past. But instead he had to stand idly behind her while she rummaged around in various little bottles, managing to startle her as she turned around; a bottle fell on the floor and shattered; a splinter injured Gregor in his face and some sort of corrosive medicine flowed around him. Without further delay, Grete then took as many little bottles as she could hold and ran with them to her mother, slamming the door shut with her foot. Gregor was now cut off from his mother, who was perhaps near death because of him. He was not allowed to open the door, for fear of chasing away his sister, who had to stay with his mother. He could now do nothing but wait, and, beset with self-reproach and concern, he began to crawl. He crawled over everything, walls, furniture, and the ceiling, and finally, in his desperation, as the whole room had already begun to spin, he fell onto the middle of the big table.

A little while passed as Gregor lay there listlessly. All around him it was quiet; perhaps that was a good sign. Then the doorbell rang. The maid was locked in the kitchen, of course, so Grete would have to answer it. His father had arrived. "What has happened?" were his first words; Grete's appearance must have revealed everything to him. Grete answered with a muffled voice, as she was apparently pressing her face on her father's breast: "Mother was unconscious, but she is already feeling much better. Gregor has escaped." "I expected he would," said his father "I always told you he would, after all, but you women didn't want to listen." It was clear to Gregor that his father had interpreted Grete's all-too-brief report falsely and assumed that Gregor was guilty of committing some act of violence. Gregor therefore had to try and appease his father, for he had neither the time nor the ability to explain things to him. And so he fled to the door of his room and pressed himself against it, so that his father could see right when he entered the hallway that Gregor had the best intention of returning to his room at once, and that there was no need to force him back, for one simply needed to open the door, and he would disappear right away.

But his father was not in the mood to notice such subtleties. "Aha!" he shouted the moment he entered in a voice that sounded as though he was simultaneously angry and pleased. Gregor withdrew his head from the door and lifted it toward his father. He had truly never imagined his father as he was standing there now. Recently, due to his new habit of crawling around, Gregor had neglected to follow the activities in the rest of the apartment as he had done before; otherwise, he should have actually been prepared to encounter some changed circumstances. Nevertheless, nevertheless, was this still his father? The same man who tiredly lay buried in bed as Gregor marched off on a business trip, who had greeted him on the evening of his return in his dressing gown from his armchair, who had not been entirely capable of standing up, but instead had only raised his arms as a sign of his joy, and who, during their seldom strolls together on a few Sundays a year and on high holidays, between Gregor and his mother, who were already walking rather slowly, had walked even a little more slowly, wrapped up in his old overcoat, working his way forward with his carefully positioned walking stick, and almost always standing still and gathering his companions around him whenever he wanted to say something? But now he was standing upright quite well, dressed in a close-fitting blue uniform with gold buttons like those worn by the attendants at the banking institutions, his strong double chin unfolded above the high, stiff collar of his coat; his black eyes gazing out boldly and attentively from beneath his bushy eyebrows; his white hair, usually disheveled, combed down into a meticulous, shining side part. He tossed his cap with its gold monogram, probably that of a bank, in an arc across the entire room onto the sofa and walked, with the tails of his long uniform coat thrown behind him and his hands in his pockets, toward Gregor with a sullen expression on his face. Perhaps he didn't know himself what he intended to do; after all, he lifted his feet unusually high. Gregor was amazed at the enormous size of his boot soles, but he did not linger in doing so, for he had known from the first day of his new life that his father believed only the utmost severity to be appropriate in his treatment of Gregor. And so he ran away from his father, paused when his father stopped, and hurried forward again the moment his father stirred. They circled the room several times in this manner, without anything decisive occurring, indeed without the entire thing even having the appearance of a pursuit, it was so slow. Gregor therefore remained on the floor for the time being, especially because he feared that his father could regard his escape onto the walls or ceiling as particularly mischievous. In any case, Gregor had to tell himself that he would not be able to keep up this running for long, for each of his father's steps required him to carry out a whole host of movements. He had already begun to notice a shortness of breath, just as he had not possessed entirely reliable lungs in earlier times. So he staggered along in order to save all his strength for the chase, hardly keeping his eyes open, not even thinking, in his stupor, of any way to escape other than running. He had already almost forgotten that he was free to use the walls, although here they were obstructed by carefully carved furniture full of prongs and spikes—when something, flung lightly, flew down just beside him and rolled around in front of him. It was an apple. A second one quickly followed. Gregor stood still in terror; running further was useless, for his father had decided to bombard him. He had filled his pockets from the fruit bowl on the sideboard and was now throwing apple after apple without taking careful aim. These small red apples rolled around on the floor and bumped into one another as though electrified. A lightly thrown apple grazed Gregor's back, but slid off harmlessly. The one that flew immediately after it, on the other hand, actually penetrated Gregor's back. Gregor wanted to drag himself further, as though the surprisingly unbelievable pain could disappear with a change of location, but he felt as though he were nailed down and stretched himself out in thorough confusion of all his senses. It was only with his last glance that he still managed to see the door to his room being flung open, and in front of his screaming sister, how his mother was hurrying forward in her shift, for his sister had undressed her to allow her to breathe freely in her unconsciousness, and running toward his father, and how along the way her untied skirts slid to the ground one after another, and how she threw herself at him tripping over her skirts, and embraced him, in complete union with him—now Gregor's sight was already failing—with her hands on the back of his father's head, begging him to spare Gregor's life.

III

Gregor's serious injury, from which he suffered for more than a month—the apple, which no one dared to remove, remained stuck in his flesh as a visible reminder—seemed to have caused even his father to remember that Gregor, despite his present sad and repulsive form, was a member of their family, and that they should not be treating him as an enemy. Rather, in accordance with family duty, they should swallow their reluctance and bear it.

And although Gregor had probably lost some of his mobility forever and presently required many long minutes to cross his room like an old invalid—crawling up on the walls was unthinkable—he believed that he was fully compensated for this worsening of his condition when every evening the living room door, which he was in the habit of observing sharply one or two hours beforehand, was opened so that he, who was lying in the darkness of his room and not visible from the living room, was able to see the entire family at the well-lit table and listen to their conversation, with their general permission as it were, entirely different than before.

Admittedly, they were no longer the lively conversations of earlier times, which Gregor had invariably thought of in his little hotel room with some longing as he threw himself tiredly into the damp bedding. Now things were usually quite calm. His father fell asleep soon after supper in his armchair; his mother and sister warned one another to be quiet; his mother, bent far forward beneath the light, sewed fine garments for a fashion store; his sister, who had taken a job as a salesclerk, studied stenography and French in the evenings in order to perhaps one day attain a better position. Sometimes his father woke up, and, as though he didn't know that he had been asleep, said to his mother: "How long you've been sewing again today!" and fell asleep again immediately, as his mother and sister smiled wearily at one another.

With a kind of obstinacy, his father refused even at home to take off his messenger's uniform; and while his dressing gown hung uselessly on the coat hook, his father dozed fully dressed in his seat, as if he were always ready for duty and waiting even here for his supervisor's voice. Hence the uniform, which was not new to begin with, lost its cleanliness right from the start, despite all diligence on the part of his mother and sister, and Gregor often spent entire evenings looking at this jacket, with its many stains, shining with its unfailingly polished golden buttons, in which the old man slept quite uncomfortably yet peacefully.

As soon as the clock struck ten, his mother tried gently to encourage his father to wake up and go to bed, for he was not getting proper sleep here, which his father, who had to appear for duty at six o'clock, desperately needed. But with the obstinacy that had grasped him since becoming a messenger, he always insisted on staying at the table even longer, although he regularly fell asleep and could only then be persuaded to exchange his arm-chair for his bed with the greatest difficulty. However much his mother and sister tried to pressure him with little warnings, he shook his head slowly for a quarter of an hour with his eyes closed and did not get up. His mother tugged at his sleeve, spoke cajoling words in his ear; his sister left her work to help her mother, but his father would not become roused. He simply sank deeper in his armchair. Only when the women seized him under his arms did he open his eyes, look back and forth between his sister and mother, and say: "What a life. So this is the peacefulness of my old age." And supported by both women, he rose, laboriously, as though he were the greatest burden to himself, let himself be led by the women to the door, where he waved them away and went on by himself, while his mother hastily threw down her sewing, and his sister her pen, and ran after his father to assist him further.

Who in this overworked and exhausted family had time to care for Gregor any more than was absolutely necessary? The house-hold had been reduced even further. The maid had been dis-missed after all. A huge, bony cleaning woman with white hair flying about her head came in the morning and evening to do the hardest chores. Everything else was managed by his mother in addition to her large amount of sewing work. It even happened that various pieces of family jewelry that his mother and sister had worn with great delight to social events and celebrations had been sold, as Gregor learned in the evening from the general discus-sion of the prices they had fetched. The greatest complaint, how-ever, was always that they could not leave their apartment, which was far too large for their present circumstances, because they could not even begin to contemplate how to relocate Gregor. But Gregor nevertheless realized that it was not only consideration for him that prevented them from relocating, for he could be trans-ported easily in a suitable box with a few air holes, after all. The primary reason preventing them from changing apartments was far more their utter hopelessness and the thought that they had been struck by misfortune the likes of which no one in their entire circle of friends and relations had seen. What the world demands of the poor they fulfilled to the utmost; his father brought the little bank clerk his breakfast, his mother sacrificed herself for the garments of strangers, his sister ran back and forth behind the counter at the customer's command, but the family's strength could be stretched no further. And the wound in Gregor's back began to pain him anew when his mother and sister returned from bringing his father to bed, left their work unfinished, and moved close together, already sitting cheek to cheek. When his mother then said, pointing to Gregor's room: "Close that door, Grete," and when Gregor was then in the dark again, in the next room the women mingled their tears or even stared at the table tearlessly.

Gregor spent his nights and days almost entirely without sleep. Sometimes he imagined that the next time the door was opened, he would take his family's affairs in hand again just as he did before. After such a long time, his thoughts returned to the director and chief clerk, the salesmen and the apprentices, the simpleminded porter, two or three friends from other stores, a chambermaid from a country hotel, a dear, fleeting memory, a cashier girl from a millinery whom he had courted seriously but too slowly—they all appeared intermixed with strangers or those already forgotten, but instead of helping him and his family, they were all inaccessible and he was glad when they disappeared. But then he was not at all in the mood to worry about his family, but filled only with rage at their poor treatment of him, and although he could not imagine anything that he might wish to eat, he still made plans for getting into the pantry in order to take what was still due to him, even though he didn't happen to be hungry. Without thinking anymore about what Gregor might particularly favor, his sister hurriedly shoved any old food into his room with her foot before rushing to the store in the morning and afternoon, and then sweeping it out with a pivot of the broom in the evening, regardless of whether the food had been only tasted or, as was the case most often, left entirely untouched. Cleaning his room, which she always did in the evenings now, couldn't be done quickly enough. Streaks of dirt ran along the walls; here and there lay balls of dust and refuse. Initially, Gregor would position himself in particularly dirty corners upon his sister's arrival in order to reproach her, to a certain extent. But he could have remained there for weeks, it seemed, before his sister had made any progress at all; she saw the dirt just as well as he did, after all, but she had simply decided to leave it there. And yet, with a touchiness that was entirely new to her, and which had indeed grasped the entire family, she made sure that the task of cleaning Gregor's room remained reserved for her. Once his mother had subjected Gregor's room to a thorough cleaning, which she had only managed with the use of several buckets of water—all the dampness also displeased Gregor, however, and he lay outstretched, resentful, and immobile on the sofa—but his mother did not escape punishment. For hardly had his sister noticed the change in Gregor's room that evening than she ran into the living room, highly offended, and despite her mother's imploringly raised hands, broke out in a fit of tears which her parents—her father, of course, had been startled out of his armchair—observed first in amazement and helplessness. Then they too began to stir. His father admonished his mother to his right for not leaving the cleaning of Gregor's room to his sister; while to his left, he screamed at his sister that she would never again be allowed to clean Gregor's room. Meanwhile his mother was trying to drag his father, who was beside himself with agitation, into the bedroom; his sister, shaken by sobs, was hammering on the table with her little fists; and Gregor was hissing loudly in his anger that no one had thought to close his door and spare him this spectacle and commotion.

But even if his sister, exhausted from her work, had become tired of caring for Gregor as before, it was by no means necessary for his mother to step in for her and there was no reason that Gregor had to be neglected, for now the cleaning woman was there. This old widow, who must have endured the most terrible things in her long life with the help of her powerful frame, was not actually disgusted by Gregor. Without being curious in any way, she happened to open the door to his room once, and, at the sight of Gregor, who, taken by complete surprise, began to run to and fro although no one was chasing him, she stood still in astonishment, her hands folded before her. Since then, she never failed to briefly open the door a little in the mornings and evenings and look in on Gregor. In the beginning she also called for him with words that she probably thought to be friendly, like "Come on over, you old dung beetle!" or "Just look at that old dung beetle!" Gregor did not respond to such appeals but remained motionless where he was, as though the door had not been opened. If only this cleaning woman had been ordered to clean his room daily, rather than being allowed to bother him uselessly whenever she felt like it! Early one morning—a heavy rain, perhaps already a sign of the coming spring, was beating against the window panes— the cleaning woman began calling to him again and Gregor was so resentful that he turned against her, albeit slowly and feebly, as if to attack. But the cleaning woman, instead of being afraid, simply lifted a chair that stood near the door up high above her, and as she stood there with her mouth opened wide, it was clear that she only intended to close her mouth when the armchair in her hand had struck down on Gregor's back. "Can't go any further, can you?" she asked, as Gregor turned around again, and put the armchair calmly back in the corner.

Gregor was now eating almost nothing. Only when he happened to pass by the food that had been prepared for him did he take a bite for the fun of it in his mouth, hold it there for hours, and usually spit it out again. At first he thought that his sadness about the state of his room was keeping him from eating, but it was precisely these changes to his room that he reconciled himself to very quickly. The family had become accustomed to putting things in his room that they could not store elsewhere, and these things were many, for they had let one room in the apartment to three boarders. These serious gentlemen—all three had full beards, as Gregor ascertained once through a crack in the door—were meticulously intent on orderliness, not only in their room, but, as they had taken lodgings here, in the entire household, particularly in the kitchen. They did not tolerate things that were unnecessary, let alone dirty. And furthermore, they had for the most part brought their own furnishings with them. For this reason, many things that could not be sold, but that they also didn't want to throw away, had become superfluous. All these things made their way into Gregor's room and the ash can and rubbish bin from the kitchen as well. The cleaning lady, who was always in a hurry, simply hurled anything that happened to be useless at the moment into Gregor's room; fortunately, Gregor usually saw only the object in question and the hand that was holding it. The cleaning woman may have intended to fetch these things again, given time and opportunity, or to throw them out all at once, but in fact they remained where they had been initially thrown, unless Gregor shifted them as he wriggled through all the clutter, first out of necessity, for no other place was free for him to crawl, but later with growing pleasure, although he lay motionless again for hours after such excursions, deadly tired and sad.

Because the boarders sometimes took their evening meal in the common living room, the living room door remained closed some evenings, but Gregor could do quite easily without the door being opened. After all, he had not taken advantage of it on some evenings when the door had been open, but had lain in the darkest corner of his room without his family noticing. On one occasion the cleaning woman had left the door to the living room open slightly, and it remained open, even when the boarders entered in the evening and the lamps were lit. They seated themselves at the head of the table, where his father, mother, and Gregor used to sit, unfolded their napkins and took their knives and forks in hand. His mother appeared immediately in the door with a dish of meat, and close behind her followed his sister with a dish piled high with potatoes. From the food rose a dense cloud of steam. The boarders leaned over the dishes that had been placed before them, as though they intended to assess them before eating, and indeed the one sitting in the middle, who was apparently regarded as the authority by the other two, cut a piece of the meat while it was still on the dish, apparently to determine whether it was tender enough and whether it may need to be sent back to the kitchen. He was satisfied, and mother and daughter, who had watched with suspense, began to smile as they breathed a sigh of relief.

The family itself ate in the kitchen. Nevertheless, the father came into this room before he went into the kitchen and took a single bow as he walked around the table with his cap in hand. All three boarders rose and mumbled something into their beards. Then, when they were alone, they ate in almost perfect silence. It seemed strange to Gregor that one could always discern the sound of chewing teeth from all the multiple eating sounds, as if to show him that one needed teeth in order to eat, and that even with the finest of toothless jaws one could accomplish nothing. "I do have an appetite," Gregor told himself worriedly, "but not for these things. How these boarders feed themselves, while I perish!"

On this same evening—Gregor could not remember having heard the violin all this time—its sound could be heard from the kitchen. The boarders had already finished their supper; the middle one had pulled out a newspaper, given the other two one page each, and they now leaned back as they read and smoked. As the violin began to play, they became attentive, rose, and walked on tiptoe to the doorway to the hall, in which they stopped and stood huddled together. They must have been heard from the kitchen, for his father called: "Are the gentlemen disturbed by the violin playing? It can be stopped right away." "On the contrary," said the gentleman in the middle, "wouldn't the young lady like to come in here and play in the living room, where it is far more pleasant and comfortable?" "Oh, certainly," called the father, as though he were the violinist. The gentlemen went back into the room and waited. His father soon came with the music stand, his mother with the music, and his sister with the violin. His sister calmly prepared everything for playing. His parents, who had never let a room before and were therefore excessively polite to the boarders, did not dare to sit in their own armchairs. His father leaned against the door, his right hand stuck between two buttons of his fastened uniform jacket. His mother, however, was offered a chair by one of the gentlemen and sat off to the side in a corner, where he had happened to set it down.

His sister began to play; his father and mother, each from their side, followed the movements of her hands attentively. Gregor, attracted by her playing, had dared to venture a little farther and his head was already in the living room. He hardly found it surprising that he had shown so little consideration for the others lately; previously such consideration had been a great source of pride. And he now had all the more reason to hide, for due to the dust that lay all over his room and flew around at the smallest movement, he too was entirely covered with dust. He dragged threads, hair, and scraps of food around with him on his back and sides. His indifference toward everything was far too great for him to lie down on his back as he used to do several times a day and scrub himself against the carpet. And despite his condition, he was not ashamed to advance a little farther onto the flawless living room floor.

And indeed, no one paid any attention to him. His family was entirely absorbed in the violin playing. The boarders, on the other hand, who had initially positioned themselves with their hands in their pockets so close behind the sister's music stand that they could all have read the music, which certainly must have disturbed her, soon withdrew to the window where they stayed, conversing in low voices with bowed heads, and being observed by the father with concern. It now appeared to be more than obvious that their expectation of hearing a pleasant and entertaining violin concert had been disappointed, that they were tired of the entire performance, and were only allowing their peace and quiet to be disturbed out of politeness. Particularly the manner in which they all blew their cigar smoke toward the ceiling through their noses and mouths implied great nervousness. And yet his sister was playing so beautifully. Her face was tilted to the side and she followed the staves considerately and sadly with her eyes. Gregor crept forward a little farther and kept his head close to the floor so that he could possibly catch her glance. Could he be a beast if music could seize him like this? He felt as though he were being shown the way to the unknown nourishment he longed for. He was determined to go up to his sister, to tug at her skirts to indicate that she should come into his room with her violin, for no one here was worth playing for as much as he would be. He would not let her out of his room again, at least not as long as he lived. For the first time his repulsive shape would be useful to him; he wanted to be at all doors in his room simultaneously and hiss at the attackers. His sister should not be forced, but stay with him voluntarily. She should sit next to him on the sofa, her ear leaned down toward him, and he would then confide to her that he firmly intended to send her to the conservatory, and that, if misfortune had not interfered, he would have told everyone last Christmas—surely Christmas had passed already?—ignoring any objections. After this declaration his sister would be moved to tears, and Gregor would raise himself up to her shoulder and kiss her neck, which she kept bare since she began going to work without ribbon or collar.

"Herr Samsa!" called the gentleman in the middle to the father, and without wasting another word pointed his finger at Gregor, who was slowly moving forward. The violin fell silent, the middle boarder first smiled at his friends, shaking his head, and then looked back at Gregor. Rather than chasing Gregor away, his father seemed to find it more necessary to first calm the boarders down, although they were not excited at all and seemed to be more entertained by Gregor than the violin playing. He hurried over to them and with outstretched arms tried to urge them into their room and simultaneously block their view of Gregor with his body. Now they really did become a little angry. It wasn't clear anymore whether this was due to the father's behavior or because it was now dawning on them that they had been living with Gregor as their neighbor without their knowledge. They demanded explanations from the father, raised their arms as well, pulled anxiously at their beards, and only slowly retreated toward their room. In the meantime, Gregor's sister had recovered from the bewilderment she had fallen into after her playing had been abruptly interrupted. After holding violin and bow for a while in her loosely hanging hands and continuing to look at the music as though she were still playing, she suddenly pulled herself together, lay the instrument on her mother's lap—she was still sitting on her chair and having difficulty breathing with her heaving lungs—and ran into the next room, which the boarders, urged by her father, were now quickly approaching. One could see how the blankets and pillows on the beds flew upwards and arranged themselves in his sister's skillful hands. Before the gentlemen had even reached the room she had finished making the beds and slipped out. His father seemed to be so caught up in his obstinacy again that he forgot all the respect that he still owed his tenants. He just kept urging them, all the way to the door of their room, where the gentleman in the middle stamped his foot thunderously, bringing the father to a halt. "I hereby declare," he said, raising his hand and looking around for the mother and sister, "that in consideration of the revolting conditions that prevail in this apartment and family"—here he spit spontaneously on the floor—"I am giving my notice immediately. I will, of course, not pay a cent for the days that I have already spent here; on the contrary, I will consider whether I shouldn't proceed against you with claims that—believe me—will be quite easy to substantiate." He fell silent and looked straight in front of him, as though he were expecting something. And indeed his two friends chimed in right away with the words: "We also give notice immediately." At that he grasped the door handle and closed the door shut with a bang.

Gregor's father staggered, groping his way to his armchair, and let himself fall; it looked as though he were stretching out for his usual evening nap, but the intense nodding of his seemingly unsupported head revealed that he was by no means sleeping. All this time Gregor had been lying quietly in the same place where the boarders had caught sight of him. His disappointment at the failure of his plan and perhaps also the weakness caused by being hungry for so long made it impossible for him to move. He feared with some certainty that at any moment a catastrophe would erupt above him and he waited. Not even the violin startled him as it slipped from beneath his mother's shaking fingers and gave off a clanging sound as it fell from her lap.

"Dear Parents," said his sister, striking the table with her hand in introduction, "things cannot go on this way. Maybe you don't realize it, but I do. I do not wish to speak the name of my brother in front of this monster, and so I will only say: we must try to get rid of it. We have tried everything humanly possible to care for it and tolerate it. I don't think anyone could reproach us in the slightest."

"She's absolutely right," Gregor's father said to himself. His mother, who was still struggling for air, began to cough hollowly into the hand she held over her mouth with an insane expression in her eyes.

His sister ran over to her mother and held her forehead. Her words seemed to have given her father more decisive thoughts, for he was now sitting up straight, playing with his messenger's cap between the plates that were still lying on the table from the boarders' supper, and glancing over at the motionless Gregor from time to time.

"We must try to get rid of it," said the sister only to her father this time, for her mother heard nothing over her coughing. "It will kill both of you, I see it coming. If we all have to work so hard, we can't also bear this endless torment at home as well. I can't bear it either anymore." And she broke into such heavy sobs that her tears fell onto her mother's face, which she wiped with a mechanical movement of her hand.

"My child," said her father compassionately and with remarkable understanding, "but what should we do?"

Gregor's sister only shrugged her shoulders as a sign of the helplessness that had taken hold of her while she was crying, in contrast with her earlier self-assurance.

"If only he could understand us," said her father half questioningly, but she shook her hand vehemently in the midst of her tears as a sign that it was entirely unthinkable.

"If only he could understand us," repeated her father and closed his eyes to acknowledge her conviction that this was impossible, "then it may be possible to reach an agreement with him. But as it is—"

"It has to go," the sister cried. "That is the only way, Father. You must simply try to get rid of the thought that it is Gregor. Our real misfortune is that we've believed it for so long. But how can it be Gregor? If it were Gregor, he would have realized long ago that people cannot possibly live together with such an animal and he would have left on his own accord. We would then have no brother, but could carry on with our lives and honor his memory. But instead this creature plagues us, chases our boarders away, apparently wants to take over the entire apartment, and have us sleep in the street. Just look, Father," she screamed suddenly, "he's at it again!" And in a state of panic that was completely incomprehensible to Gregor, his sister even left her mother, literally sprang from her armchair as though she would rather sacrifice her mother than remain in Gregor's vicinity, and hurried behind her father, who, agitated solely because of her behavior, also stood up and raised his arms halfway as if to protect her.

But Gregor had no intention of frightening anyone, least of all his sister. He had simply begun to turn himself around in order to wander back to his room, although this admittedly looked rather conspicuous because in order to achieve the difficult turns, his afflicted condition forced him to rely on the use of his head, which he lifted and struck against the floor several times. He paused and looked around. His good intention seemed to have been recognized; it had only been a brief scare. Now everyone was looking at him sadly in silence. His mother lay in her armchair, legs stretched out and pressed together, her eyes almost falling shut from fatigue; his father and his sister were sitting next to one another, and his sister had laid her hand around her father's neck.

"Now maybe they'll let me turn around," Gregor thought and began to work again. He couldn't keep from panting from the strain, and now and then he also had to rest. In any case, no one was forcing him; it was all left to him. When he had completed the turn, he immediately began to crawl straight back. He was amazed at the great distance separating him from his room and didn't understand at all how he, in his weak state, had traveled the same path a short time ago, almost without noticing it. Concerned only with crawling swiftly, he hardly noticed that there were no words, no outcries from his family to disturb him. It was not until he was already in the doorway that he turned his head, not completely, for he felt his neck stiffening, but he still saw that nothing had changed behind him, only that his sister had risen. His last glance fell upon his mother, who had now fallen fast asleep.

He was hardly inside his room when the door was shut hastily, bolted, and locked. Gregor was so startled by the sudden racket behind him that his little legs buckled beneath him. It was his sister who had been in such a hurry. She had already been standing there and waiting when she leapt forward nimbly—Gregor had not heard her coming—and called out "Finally!" to her parents while she turned the key in the lock.

"And now?" Gregor asked himself and looked around in the dark. He soon discovered that he could no longer move at all. This did not surprise him, for it struck him as unnatural that he had until now actually been able to move at all on these skinny little legs. Otherwise he felt relatively comfortable. Although he felt pains in every part of his body, they seemed to be gradually growing weaker and weaker and would eventually cease altogether. The rotten apple in his back and the inflamed area around it, which were covered entirely in soft dust, were already hardly noticeable. He thought back on his family with affection and love. His conviction that he must disappear was possibly even more resolute than that of his sister. He remained in this state of empty and peaceful contemplation until the clock tower struck three in the morning. He lived to see the sky begin to grow lighter outside his window. Then his head sank involuntarily to the floor and his final breath streamed feebly from his nostrils.

When the cleaning woman came early in the morning—out of sheer strength and haste, she slammed all the doors so loudly, no matter how often she was asked to avoid doing so, that it was impossible to sleep peacefully anywhere in the apartment from her arrival onwards—at first she found nothing to be out of the ordinary during her usual brief visit to Gregor. She thought he was deliberately lying there motionless and pretending to sulk; she presumed he possessed all kinds of intelligence. Because she happened to be holding the long broom in her hand, she tried to tickle Gregor from the doorway. When this also proved unsuccessful, she became annoyed and poked into Gregor a little, and only when she had pushed him from his spot without meeting any resistance, did she become more attentive. When she soon recognized the situation at hand, she opened her eyes wide, whistled to herself, and did not linger for long, but tore open the door to the bedroom and called with a loud voice into the darkness: "Come and have a look; it's dead; its lying over there, dead as a doornail!"

The Samsas sat upright in their double bed and struggled to overcome the shock of being woken by the cleaning woman before they got around to grasping her announcement. But then Herr and Frau Samsa got out of bed, each on their side, as quickly as they could. Herr Samsa threw the blanket over his shoulders, Frau Samsa appeared only in her nightgown; in this state they entered Gregor's room. In the meantime, the door to the living room, in which Grete had slept since the boarders had moved in, had also opened; she was completely dressed, as though she had not slept at all, as her pale face also seemed to confirm. "Dead?" said Frau Samsa and looked up inquiringly at the cleaning woman, although she could, after all, investigate everything herself and recognize it even without investigation. "I should think so," said the cleaning woman and pushed Gregor's corpse well to the side with her broom as proof. Frau Samsa moved as though she wanted to hold the broom back, but did not do so. "Well," said Herr Samsa, "now we can thank God." He crossed himself and the three women followed his example. Grete, who had not taken her eyes off the corpse, said: "Look how thin he was. He had not eaten anything for such a long time, after all. The food was taken out just as it had been brought in." Gregor's body truly was completely flat and dry, as one could actually only recognize now, for he was no longer elevated by his little legs and there was nothing else to distract the eye.

"Come into our room for a while, Grete," said Frau Samsa with a melancholy smile, and Grete followed her parents, not without looking back at the corpse, into the bedroom. The cleaning woman closed the door and opened the window wide. Despite the early morning hour, a mildness had been mixed into the fresh air. It was, after all, already the end of March.

The three boarders emerged from their room and looked around in astonishment for their breakfast; they had been forgotten. "Where is our breakfast?" the gentleman in the middle sullenly asked the cleaning woman. She, however, placed a finger before her lips and then gestured hastily and silently to the gentlemen that they should enter Gregor's room. They did enter and, with their hands in the pockets of their somewhat shabby coats, they stood around Gregor's corpse in the room, which was now full of daylight.

Then the door to the bedroom opened and Herr Samsa appeared in his uniform with his wife on one arm and his daughter on the other. They were a bit teary eyed; Grete pressed her face onto her father's arm from time to time.

"Leave my home at once!" said Herr Samsa and pointed at the door without letting the women go. "What do you mean?" said the gentleman in the middle, somewhat aghast with a mawkish smile. The other two held their hands behind their backs, rubbing them together incessantly, as though in pleasant anticipation of a big fight that would have to turn out well for them. "I mean exactly what I said," answered Herr Samsa and walked straight up to the boarder with his two companions. At first the boarder stood there calmly and looked at the floor, as though the things in his head were being rearranged into a new order. "Then we will be going," he said and looked up at Herr Samsa, as though he had been overcome by a sudden wave of humility and was requesting further permission even for this decision. Herr Samsa merely nodded to him briefly several times with his eyes opened widely. At that, the gentleman immediately walked into the hallway with long steps; his two friends had already been listening attentively for some time with calm hands and now they almost hopped after him, as though they were afraid that Herr Samsa could enter the hallway before them and disturb their connection to their leader. In the hallway, all three removed their hats from the coat rack, pulled their canes from the umbrella stand, bowed in silence, and left the apartment. In his mistrust, which proved to be entirely unfounded, Herr Samsa walked with his two women out onto the forecourt; leaning on the railing, they watched the three gentlemen slowly but steadily descending the long staircase, disappearing at each level in a particular bend in the stairway and reappearing a few moments later; the further they descended, the more the Samsa family lost interest in them, and, when a butcher with proud posture and a tray on his head had climbed the stairs toward them and then high above them, Herr Samsa and the women left the railing and, as if relieved, returned to their apartment.

They decided to use the day to rest and take a walk; they had not only earned this respite from their work, they desperately needed it. And so they sat at the table and wrote three letters of excuse, Herr Samsa to his director, Frau Samsa to her client, and Grete to her boss. While they were writing, the cleaning woman came in to tell them that she was leaving, for her morning chores had been completed. The three writers merely nodded at first without looking up; only when the cleaning woman still had not left the room did they look up in annoyance. "Well?" asked Herr Samsa. The cleaning woman stood in the doorway smiling as though she had great news to announce to the family but would only do so after being thoroughly questioned. The almost vertical little ostrich plume on her hat, which had bothered Herr Samsa the entire time she had worked for them, swayed slightly in all directions. "So, what is it then?" asked Frau Samsa, for whom the cleaning woman still had the most respect. "Yes," answered the cleaning woman, whose friendly laughter prevented her from continuing right away, "well, you needn't worry about how to dispose of the things from next door. It has been taken care of." Frau Samsa and Grete bent over their letters, as though they wished to continue writing. Herr Samsa, who noticed that the cleaning woman was about to begin describing everything in detail, dismissed this firmly with his outstretched hand. Since she was prevented from telling her story, she remembered that she was in a great hurry, and, obviously insulted, she called: "Farewell everyone," turned around wildly and slammed the doors terribly as she left the apartment.

"She'll be dismissed this evening," said Herr Samsa, but he received no answer from his wife or his daughter, for it seemed that the cleaning woman had disturbed the peacefulness again just as it had been restored. They rose, went to the window, and remained there embracing one another. Herr Samsa turned around in his armchair and observed them in silence for a little while. Then he called: "Come on over here. Let the old things go. And have a little consideration for me, too." The women obeyed him, rushed to him, caressed him, and hastily concluded their letters.

Then all three of them left the apartment together, which they had not done in months, and took a trolley to the countryside outside the city. The car in which they sat alone was entirely filled with warm sunshine. Reclining comfortably in their seats, they discussed their prospects for the future, which, on closer inspection, turned out to be not bad at all, for all three had positions that were quite good and especially promising for the future. Of course, the greatest improvement to their situation at the moment would easily come about with a change of apartments; they now wanted to take an apartment that was smaller and cheaper, but better situated and generally more practical than their current one which had been chosen by Gregor. As they were conversing, it occurred to Herr and Frau Samsa almost simultaneously at the sight of their increasingly lively daughter that, despite all the worry that had made her cheeks pale, she had blossomed into a pretty and voluptuous young woman. Growing quieter and communicating almost unconsciously through their glances, they thought that it was almost time to find a decent husband for her. And it seemed to them to be a confirmation of their new dreams and good intentions when, at their journey's end, the daughter rose first and stretched her young body.

THE STOKER

(A Fragment)

AS SIXTEEN-YEAR-OLD KARL ROSSMANN, WHO HAD BEEN SENT TO
America by his poor parents because a servant girl had seduced
him and had his child, sailed into the New York harbor on the
slowly moving ship, he beheld the Statue of Liberty, which he had
been observing for some time as though it were illuminated by a
sudden flash of sunlight. The arm holding the sword rose as
though recently thrust upwards, and around her figure the free
breezes were blowing.

"So high!" he said to himself and, as he hadn't even thought of
departing, he was gradually pushed by the continuously swelling
crowd of porters passing by until he reached the ship's railing.

A young man, with whom he had become fleetingly acquainted
during the journey, said in passing: "Well, don't you feel like getting off yet?" "Oh, I'm ready," said Karl with a laugh and in his
enthusiasm, and because he was a strong young man, he hoisted
his trunk onto his shoulder. But as he looked past his acquaintance, who swung his stick a little as he moved along with the
others, he realized with dismay that he had forgotten his own
umbrella down in the ship. He quickly asked his acquaintance,
who didn't seem very pleased, if he would be kind enough to wait
by his trunk for a moment and, surveying his surroundings in
order to find his way back, he hurried off. To his regret, he found
that a passageway down below that would have considerably

shortened his route was barred for the first time, which probably had to do with the disembarkment of all the passengers, and he was forced to arduously find his way through a myriad of small rooms, down short staircases that followed one another endlessly, through perpetually bending corridors, through an empty room with an abandoned desk until he actually managed—due to his having only gone this route once or twice and always in a larger group—to become absolutely lost. In his helplessness, and because he encountered no one and heard only the continuous shuffling of a thousand human feet above him and noticed from afar, like a breath of air, the final strokes of the already shut-down engines, he began to pound without deliberation on an arbitrary little door that he had halted in front of as he strayed about.

"It's open," called a voice from inside, and Karl opened the door with a genuine sigh of relief. "Why are you pounding on the door so madly?" asked a huge man, hardly even glancing at Karl. Turbid light, which had long since been used up in the decks above, fell through some overhead hatch into the miserable cabin, in which a bed, a closet, an armchair, and the man stood side by side, closely as though they had been put into storage. "I've lost my way," said Karl. "I didn't really notice it during the journey, but this is a terribly large ship." "Yes, you're right about that," said the man with a degree of pride, fiddling with the lock of a small trunk, which he kept pushing closed with both hands in order to hear the bar snapping into the catch. "But come inside!" the man continued. "You don't want to stand outside!" "I'm not bothering you?" asked Karl. "How should you be bothering me!" "Are you German?" Karl sought to assure himself, for he had heard many things about the dangers, especially from the Irishmen, that threatened newcomers in America. "That I am, that I am," said the man. Karl still hesitated. Suddenly the man grabbed the handle of the door, sweeping Karl into his cabin as he hastily closed it. "I can't stand it when people look in on me from the corridor," said the man, who was working on his trunk again. "Everyone walks by and looks in; it's unbearable!" "But the corridor is completely empty," said Karl, who stood there pressed awkwardly against the bedpost. "Now, yes," said the man. "But we are talking about now," thought Karl. "This man is difficult to talk to." "Why don't you lie on the bed; you'll have more room there," said the man. Karl crawled in as best he could and, as he did so, laughed out loud at his first failed attempt to swing himself over. But no sooner was he in bed than he cried: "Good God, I've completely forgotten about my trunk!" "Where is it?" "Above deck. An acquaintance is looking after it. What was his name again?" And he pulled a visiting card from a secret pocket that his mother had inserted into his coat lining for the journey. "Butterbaum, Franz Butterbaum." "Do you really need the trunk?" "Of course." "Well why did you give it to a stranger then?" "I had forgotten my umbrella below and ran to get it but didn't want to drag my trunk along. Then I got lost as well." "You are alone? Without a companion?" "Yes, alone." "Perhaps I should stick with this man," Karl thought. "Where am I to find a better friend?" "And now you have lost your trunk as well. Not to mention your umbrella." And the man sat in the armchair, as though Karl's concern had now gained considerable interest for him. "But I think my trunk is not yet lost." "Blessed are the faithful," said the man and vigorously scratched his dark, short, thick hair. "On a ship, the morals change along with the ports. In Hamburg, Butterbaum may have looked after your trunk, but here there is most likely no trace of either anymore." "Then I must go up and look right away," said Karl and looked around for a way out. "Why don't you stay," said the man and thrust him quite roughly with a hand against his chest back onto the bed. "Why should I?" asked Karl angrily. "Because there's no point," said the man. "In a little while, I will go as well, and we can then go together. Either the trunk is stolen, then it is no use, or the man has left it there, and it'll be all the more easy to find when the ship is entirely empty. And your umbrella as well." "Do you know your way around the ship?" Karl asked mistrustfully, and it seemed to him that there must be a catch hidden in the otherwise convincing notion that his things were best found on an empty ship. "I'm a stoker, after all," said the man. "You're a stoker!" Karl cried with joy, as though all his expectations had been exceeded, and propped himself up on his elbows to look at the man more closely. "Just in front of the cabin where I slept with the Slovak there was a porthole through which one could see into the engine room." "Yes, that's where I was working," said the stoker. "I have always been so interested in technology," said Karl, who followed a certain line of thought, "and later I would have certainly become an engineer if I had not had to leave for America." "Why did you have to leave?" "Oh, that!" said Karl and discarded the entire story away with his hand. As he did so, he looked at the stoker with a smile, as though he were asking for leniency regarding something he had not even admitted. "There was surely a reason," said the stoker in such a way that one couldn't be sure if he intended to encourage him or prevent him from disclosing this reason. "Now I could also be a stoker," said Karl. "My parents are now entirely indifferent about what I am to become." "My position will be free," said the stoker, and in full awareness of this fact he put his hands in his trouser pockets and threw his legs, which were clad in wrinkled, leathery, iron-gray trousers, onto the bed to stretch them out. Karl had to move farther toward the wall. "You're leaving the ship?" "That's right, we're departing today." "But why? Don't you like it?" "Well, this is the way it is, things are not always decided by whether one likes them or not. You are right, by the way; I also don't like it. You're probably not thinking seriously about becoming a stoker, but this is exactly when it is easiest to become one. So I definitely advise you against it. If you wanted to study in Europe, why don't you want to do so here? After all, the American universities are incomparably better than those in Europe." "It is possible, I suppose," said Karl, "but I have almost no money for studying. I did read about someone who worked in a store during the day and studied at night until he got his doctor's degree and became mayor as well, I think, but that requires a great amount of perseverance, right? That is something I lack, I'm afraid. Besides, I was not a particularly good student; it was not really difficult for me to bid my school farewell. And perhaps the schools here are much stricter. I can hardly speak any English.

People here are generally quite biased against foreigners, I think."
"Have you also experienced that already? Well that's good then.
Then you're my man. You see, we are on a German ship. It
belongs to the Hamburg-America line. Why are we not all Germans here? Why is the chief engineer a Romanian? His name
is Schubal. It's unbelievable. And this mean bastard grinds us
Germans on a German ship. Don't think"—he ran out of breath,
he waved his hand—"that I'm complaining just to complain. I
know that you have no influence and are yourself a poor lad. But
it is too horrible!" And he pounded on the table several times
with his fist and didn't take his eye off it as he pounded. "But I
have served on so many ships"—and he stated twenty names in
succession as though they were one word, Karl became quite
confused—"and have excelled and been praised; I was a worker
to the liking of my captains; I was even on the same merchant
ship for several years."—He rose, as though this was the culmina-
tion of his life—"And here in this tub, where everything is done
by the book, where no wit is required, here I am worthless, here
I am always standing in Schubal's way, I am a sluggard, I deserve
to be thrown out, and receive my pay only out of mercy. Can you
understand that? I can't." "You can't put up with it," said Karl
excitedly. He had almost lost the feeling that he was on the
unstable floor of a ship, on the coast of an unfamiliar continent,
so at home he felt here on the stoker's bed. "Have you already
been to see the captain? Have you already sought justice with
him?" "Oh, go away, just go away. I don't want you here. You
don't listen to what I say and then you give me advice. How am I
supposed to go to the captain?" And the stoker tiredly sat down
again and laid his face in both hands.

"I can't give him any better advice," said Karl to himself. And
besides, Karl thought he should have gone to get his trunk rather
than staying here and giving advice that was only considered stupid. As his father had handed over the trunk for good, he asked
him jokingly: "How long will you keep it?" and now this valuable
trunk might truly be lost. The only consolation left was that his
father could hardly learn of his current situation, even if he

should inquire. Only that he had come along to New York, that's all the shipping company could say. But Karl was sorry that he had hardly used the things in the trunk, even though he ought to have changed his shirt a long time ago, for example. So he had been economical in the wrong place; now, at the beginning of his career, when it was especially necessary to present oneself cleanly dressed, he would have to appear in a dirty shirt. Otherwise the loss of the trunk would not have been so terrible, for the suit that he was wearing was actually better than the one in the trunk, which was only an emergency suit that his mother had had to mend just before his departure. Now he also recalled that there was still a piece of Veronese salami in his trunk that his mother had wrapped up for him as an extra gift, from which he had only been able to eat the smallest bit because he had had no appetite during the journey, and the soup that came to be served in the steerage had sufficed him amply. Now, however, he would have liked to have that sausage at hand so that he could offer it to the stoker. Such people are easy to win over, after all, if you slip them some kind of trifle. This Karl knew from his father, who won over all the lower employees with whom he did business by distributing cigars. Now all Karl had left to give away was his money, which he didn't want to touch for the time being, considering that he had maybe already lost his trunk. Again his thoughts returned to the trunk, and now he failed to understand why he had watched it so attentively during the journey that it had almost cost him his sleep, just to allow the same trunk to be taken away from him so easily. He remembered the five nights during which he continuously suspected a little Slovak, who lay two bunks to the left of him, of being after his trunk. This Slovak was just lurking in wait for Karl, overcome by tiredness, to doze off for a moment, so that he could pull the trunk over to him with the long pole that he was always playing or practicing with during the day. During the day, this Slovak looked innocent enough, but no sooner had night fallen than he began to rise from time to time from his bed and look sadly over at Karl's trunk. Karl could see this very clearly, for now and then someone with the restlessness of an emigrant always lit a little light, although this was forbidden according to the ship's regulations, and attempted to decipher the incomprehensible brochures of the emigration agencies. If such a light was nearby, Karl could drift off a little, but if it was far away, or if it was dark, then he had to keep his eyes open. The strain had thoroughly exhausted him, and now it may have been in vain. That Butterbaum, if he should ever meet him somewhere!

At that moment, small short taps like those from children's feet sounded from the distance into the perfect silence; they came closer with intensified strength and became the calm sound of men marching. Apparently they were walking single file, as was natural in the small corridor, and one could hear a clinking sound as though from weapons. Karl, who was almost prepared to stretch himself out for a sleep that was free from all worries of trunk and Slovaks, startled and gave the stoker a push to finally alert him, for the head of the troop appeared to have just reached the door. "That's the ship's band," said the stoker, "they played on deck and are now going to pack up. Now everything's finished and we can go. Come along!" He took Karl by the hand, snatched at the last moment a framed picture of the Madonna from the wall above the bed, stuffed it in his breast pocket, grabbed his suitcase, and together with Karl he hurriedly left the cabin.

"Now I am going to the office to give the gentlemen a piece of my mind. There are no more passengers around; one doesn't need to be considerate." The stoker repeated this in various different ways, and as he walked, he tried to trample down a rat that was crossing their path with sideward jabs of his foot, but only drove it faster into its hole, which it managed to reach just in time. He was generally slow in his movements, for although he had long legs, they were too heavy after all.

They passed through a part of the kitchen where several girls in dirty aprons—they were dousing themselves on purpose—were cleaning dishes in large tubs. The stoker called over a girl by the name of Line, laid an arm around her waist, and carried her along a bit as she coquettishly pushed against his arm. "It's time to get paid; do you want to come along?" he asked. "Why should

I bother, why don't you bring me the money instead?" she answered, slipped out under his arm and ran away. "Where did you pick up that handsome fellow, anyway?" she called afterwards, but didn't wait for an answer. One could hear the laughter of all the girls who had interrupted their work.

They kept going, however, and reached a door that had a small pediment above it carried by small, gilded caryatides. This looked rather extravagant for the fittings of a ship. Karl noticed that he had never been in this area, which had probably been reserved for the first- and second-class passengers during the journey, but now the separating doors had been removed for the big ship cleaning. They had, in fact, already met several men carrying brooms on their shoulders who had greeted the stoker. Karl was amazed at all the bustle; on his steerage deck, he had hardly caught wind of any of it. Electrical wiring also ran along the corridor and one could constantly hear a small bell.

The stoker knocked respectfully on the door, and as someone called "Come in" he prompted Karl with a movement of his hand to enter without fear. He did enter but stopped and stood by the door. Before the room's three windows he saw the waves of the ocean, and as he observed their cheerful movement, his heart beat as though he had not been looking at the ocean incessantly for five long days. Large ships crossed one another's paths and gave way to the waves' pounding only so far as their weight permitted. With squinted eyes, these ships appeared to be staggering under their enormous weight. On their masts, they carried flags that were narrow but long and, despite being tautened by the speed of the ship, they fluttered to and fro. Cannon salutes sounded, most likely from war ships; the barrels of such a ship passing not very far away were radiant with the reflection of its steel coat, appearing to be nestled in the safe, smooth, though not horizontal movement. The small ships and boats could only be seen in the distance, at least from the door, as they sailed in numerously between the large ships. But behind all of this, New York stood and looked at Karl through the hundred thousand windows of its skyscrapers. Yes, in this room one knew where one was.

At a round table three men were seated; one, a ship's officer in the blue ship's uniform, the other two officials of the harbor authority in black American uniforms. On the table lay a high stack of various documents, which the officer first skimmed over with a pen in his hand, before handing them to the other two, who quickly read, quickly excerpted, quickly placed them in their portfolios, except when one, who was almost constantly making a little noise with his teeth, dictated something to his colleagues for the protocol.

At the window, with his back to the door, a short gentleman was sitting at a desk, busy with large ledgers that he had arranged on a strong bookshelf at the height of his head. Next to him was an open and, at first glance, empty cash box.

The second window was unoccupied and had the best view. Near the third, however, stood two gentlemen conversing in low voices. One leaned next to the window, also wore the ship's uniform, and played with the hilt of his sword. He with whom he was speaking faced the window, revealing now and again through a movement part of the row of medals on the other man's chest. He wore civilian clothes and had a thin bamboo cane, which, as both hands were holding on to his hips, protruded like a sword.

Karl didn't have much time to survey everything, for an attendant approached them and asked the stoker what he wanted with a look that indicated that he did not belong here. The stoker answered, as quietly as he had been asked, that he wanted to speak to the chief purser. The attendant, for his part, declined this request with a movement of his hand, but nevertheless walked on the tips of his toes, avoiding the round table by a wide margin, to the gentleman with the ledgers. This gentleman—as could clearly be seen—all but stiffened at the attendant's words, but eventually turned around toward the man who wished to speak to him and waved his arms about, stringently repelling the stoker and, for good measure, the attendant as well. The attendant then returned to the stoker and said, in a confiding tone of voice: "Get out of this room at once!"

At this reply, the stoker looked down at Karl, as though he was his heart, to which he silently lamented his sorrows. Without further deliberation, Karl took off, walked straight through the room, even managing to slightly brush the officer's armchair; the attendant ran after him, stooped forward with arms ready to enfold him as though he were hunting some large insect, but Karl was the first to reach the chief purser's desk, which he held onto tightly, in case the attendant attempted to drag him away.

Of course the whole room became lively. The ship's officer at the table sprang to his feet; the gentlemen from the harbor authority watched calmly but attentively; the two men at the window stepped next to one another; the attendant, who believed he no longer had any business being at a place of interest for the superior gentlemen, took a step back. The stoker by the door waited tensely for the moment at which his help would be needed. The chief purser finally made a big rightabout turn with his armchair.

Karl rummaged in his secret pocket, which he had no reservations about showing these people, and pulled out his passport, which he laid on the table in lieu of further introduction. The chief purser appeared to consider this passport irrelevant, for he flicked it aside with two fingers, whereupon Karl pocketed his passport again, as though this formality had been satisfactorily taken care of.

"I take the liberty of saying," he then began, "that in my opinion the stoker has been treated unjustly. There is a certain Schubal here who has it in for him. The stoker himself has served on many ships before, all of which he can name for you, to the utmost satisfaction. He is diligent, takes his work seriously, and it is really incomprehensible why he should not be suitable for work on this of all ships, where his duties are not overly difficult, such as on merchant ships. It can therefore only be slander that is hindering him in his advancement and cheating him of the recognition that he would otherwise certainly not be lacking. I have only spoken of this matter in general terms, he will submit his specific complaints to you himself." Karl had addressed his speech to all the gentlemen, because all of them had actually been listening, and because it seemed much more likely to find the righteous man among them all than that the chief purser should turn out to be the righteous one. Out of cleverness, Karl had also withheld the fact that he had only known the stoker for such a short time. Apart from that, he would have spoken even better had he not been unsettled by the red face of the gentleman with the bamboo cane, which he now saw from his current location for the first time.

"It's all correct, word for word," said the stoker, before anyone had asked, before anyone had even looked at him. This hastiness on the part of the stoker would have been a great mistake if the gentleman with the medals, who, as it now dawned on Karl, was surely the Captain, had not obviously made up his mind to hear the stoker out. He stretched out his hand and called to the stoker: "Come here!" with a voice solid enough to be hit with a hammer. Now everything depended upon the stoker's behavior, for as far as the righteousness of his cause was concerned, Karl had no doubts.

Fortunately, this occasion showed that the stoker had gotten about in the world. With exemplary composure, he removed from his little suitcase a small bundle of papers with his first grasp, as well as a notebook, and took them, as though it were self-evident, completely neglecting the chief purser, to the Captain and spread his pieces of evidence out on the windowsill. The chief purser had no choice but to go over there himself. "The man is a well-known troublemaker," he said in explanation. "He spends more time at the cash box than in the engine room. He has brought Schubal, that calm person, to the point of despair. Now listen!" he turned to face the stoker, "you've really taken your meddling too far. How often have you already been thrown out of the pay rooms, just as you and your completely, utterly, and invariably unjustified demands deserved! How often have you run straight from there to the purser's office! How often have you been politely told that Schubal is your immediate superior, and that you alone must come to terms with him as his subordinate! And now you even come here when the Captain is present, aren't ashamed to harass even him, and have the audacity to bring this boy along, whom I am now seeing on this ship for the first time, as a trained mouth-piece for your tasteless accusations."

Karl physically held himself back from jumping forward. But the Captain was also there already and said: "Why don't we listen to the man? That Schubal has become far too independent for my taste anyway, not that I wish to imply anything in your favor." The last words were directed at the stoker; it was only natural that he could not stand up for him right away, but everything appeared to be going in the right direction. The stoker began his explana-tions and managed right from the start to get himself to address Schubal with the title of "Herr." How pleased Karl was next to the chief purser's abandoned desk, where he kept pressing down a letter scale for the sheer enjoyment of it.—Herr Schubal is unjust! Herr Schubal favors the foreigners! Herr Schubal expelled the stoker from the engine room and had him clean lavatories, which was certainly not the business of a stoker!—Once, the compe-tence of Herr Schubal was even challenged as being more appar-ent than actual. At this point, Karl stared with all his might at the Captain, confidingly, as though he were his colleague, just to prevent him from being influenced to the stoker's disadvantage by his awkward way of expressing himself. After all, one could not really learn anything substantial from all his talking, and even if the Captain was still looking ahead of himself, with determination in his eyes to hear the stoker out this time, the other gentlemen had grown impatient, and soon the stoker's voice no longer domi-nated the room unchallenged, which was cause for concern. First, the gentlemen in civilian clothing set his bamboo cane in motion and tapped, albeit softly, on the parquet floor. Of course, the other gentlemen looked over now and then; the gentlemen from the harbor authority, who were evidently pressed for time, picked up their files again and began, if somewhat distractedly, to look through them; the ship's officer moved a bit closer to his table again; and the chief purser, who believed he had won the game, breathed a deep ironic sigh. The only one who seemed untouched by the general dissolution of interest was the attendant, who sym-pathized in part with the suffering of this poor man set among great men and nodded earnestly to Karl as though he wanted to explain something.

Meanwhile, harbor life went on outside the windows; a flat barge with a mountain of barrels, which must have been wonderfully stowed to keep them from rolling, passed by and almost generated darkness in the room; small motor boots, which Karl could now have gotten a close look at had he had the time, rushed by in straight lines in accordance with the jerks of the hands of a man standing upright at the wheel; peculiar floating objects emerged here and there on their own from the restless water, were promptly drowned again, and sank before one's astonished eyes; boats from the ocean liners were being rowed feverishly forward by sailors and were full of passengers who were sitting still and expectantly just as they had been squeezed in, even if some could not help from turning their heads toward the changing scenery. A movement without end, a restlessness, conveyed from the restless element to the helpless people and their creations!

But everything urged for haste, for clarity, for precise depiction, and what was the stoker doing? He, however, was talking himself into a sweat; his shaking hands were long past being able to hold the papers on the windowsill. Complaints about Schubal streamed to him from all directions, and in his opinion, each would have sufficed to bury that Schubal for good, but all that he was able to present to the Captain was a sad, confused flurry of everything whirled together. The gentleman with the bamboo cane had long since been whistling quietly up to the ceiling; the gentlemen from the harbor authority were detaining the officer at their table and showed no intention of ever letting him go; the chief purser was clearly being prevented from intervening only by the Captain's calmness; the attendant was standing at attention expecting at any moment his Captain's orders concerning the stoker.

Karl could no longer remain idle. So he walked slowly over to the group, and as he walked, he thought all the faster about the most clever way of tackling the issue. It really was high time; only a little while longer and they could both very likely be thrown out of the office. The Captain might indeed be a good man, and furthermore, it seemed to Karl, he may currently have a particular reason for showing himself to be a just superior, but he was no instrument, after all, to be played into the ground—and that was just how the stoker was treating him right now, albeit from within his infinitely indignant core.

So Karl said to the stoker: "You have to explain it more simply, more clearly; the Captain can't appreciate it the way you are telling it. Does he even know all the engineers and cabin boys by name, let along their first names, so that he is able to know immediately whom you are referring to when you speak only such a name? Why don't you order your complaints, beginning with the most important one and then the others in descending order? Perhaps it will then not even be necessary to mention most of them anymore. You always presented it so clearly to me!" If you can steal trunks in America, you can also tell a lie here and there, he thought as an excuse.

If only it had helped! Might it already have been too late? The stoker had interrupted himself immediately when he heard the familiar voice, but with his eyes, which were entirely concealed by the tears of his offended male honor, the terrible memories, the extreme distress of the moment, he could not even recognize Karl very well anymore. How could he—Karl realized silently as he stood before the now silent stoker—how could he suddenly change his manner of speaking now, when he felt that he had already said everything there was to say without the slightest acknowledgment, and on the other hand, that he had said nothing at all, and could hardly expect these gentlemen to listen to everything over again. And at such a moment, Karl, his sole supporter, comes along and tries to give him good advice, but shows him instead that everything, everything is lost.

"If only I had come sooner instead of looking out the window," said Karl to himself, lowering his eyes before the stoker and dropping his hands to his trouser seams, as a sign that all hope had expired.

But the stoker misunderstood this, probably sensing in Karl some sort of secret accusations, and with the good intention of convincing him otherwise, he now crowned all of his achievements by beginning to argue with Karl.

Now, when the gentlemen at the round table had long since become appalled by the useless noise that was disrupting their important work, when the chief purser had gradually found the Captain's patience incomprehensible and was leaning toward an immediate outburst, when the attendant, now fully present again within the sphere of his superiors, measured the stoker with wild glances, and when finally the man with the bamboo cane, at whom even the Captain glanced amicably now and then, who had already become entirely callous toward the stoker, yes even disgusted by him, pulled out a small notebook and, apparently busy with other matters altogether, let his eyes wander between the notebook and Karl.

"Yes, I know, I know," said Karl, who had difficulty repelling the stoker's barrage that was now directed at him, but still had a friendly smile for him through all the quarreling, "You're right, quite right, I never doubted it." He would have liked to have held his flailing hands for fear of being hit; or better still, to have forced him into a corner and whispered a few soft, calming words that no one else need hear. But the stoker was beside himself. Karl already even began to take a kind of comfort in the thought that the stoker could overpower all seven men in the room, if necessary, with the strength of his desperation. On the desk, however, as informed by a glance in that direction, was a panel with far too many buttons on it for the electric line, and a hand, pressed simply upon it, could make the entire ship rebellious, with all its corridors filled with hostile men.

The rather uninterested gentleman with the bamboo cane stepped over to Karl and asked, not too loudly, but clearly above all the stoker's shouting: "So what is your name?" At this moment, as though someone outside had been awaiting this gentleman's remark, there was a knock at the door. The attendant looked over to the Captain, who nodded. The attendant then went to the door and opened it. Outside stood a man in an old military coat of medium build, who, judging by his appearance, was not really suited to working with the engines but was nevertheless— Schubal. If Karl had not recognized this from the look in everyone's eyes, which expressed a certain gratification from which not even the Captain was free, then he would have to have observed it with horror by watching the stoker, who clenched his fists on his tightened arms as though this clenching was the most important part of him, for which he was prepared to sacrifice everything he had in life. All his strength was in his fists, even that which was managing to hold him upright.

So here was the enemy, free and fresh in his festive suit, a ledger under his arm—most likely the stoker's pay sheets and work passes—and looked, with the bold acknowledgment of wanting to ascertain each individual's mood, into everyone's eyes, one at a time. All seven men were already friends of his, for although the Captain had previously had, or feigned to have, certain objections to him, he appeared to probably not find the slightest fault with Schubal anymore after the grief that the stoker had caused him. One could not be strict enough with a man like the stoker, and if Schubal were to be accused of anything at all, it would be the fact that he had failed to crush the stoker's rebelliousness in time to prevent him from daring to appear before the Captain today.

Now one could still assume that the confrontation between the stoker and Schubal would not fail to have the same impact on these men as it would on a higher court, for even though Schubal was a good dissimulator, he wasn't necessarily capable of keeping it up to the end. A brief flash of his wickedness should suffice to make it visible to these gentlemen; Karl wanted to make sure of that. He already had a rough idea about each gentleman's astuteness, weaknesses, whims, after all, and from that standpoint, the time spent here had not been lost. If only the stoker had been better on the playing field, but he appeared entirely unable to fight. If someone had held Schubal before him, he would have probably been able to pound on his hated skull with his fists. But even taking the few steps over to him was more than the stoker could manage. Why had Karl not foreseen that which was so easily foreseeable? Schubal was bound to come in the end, if not of his own accord then summoned by the Captain. Why had he not discussed a precise war plan with the stoker on the way here instead of doing what they had actually done, simply walking in, hopelessly unprepared, when they had found the door? Was the stoker even capable of speaking anymore, of saying yes and no, which would be necessary for the cross examination, which would only take place in the most favorable case? He stood there, his legs spread apart, his knees bent a little, his head slightly lifted, and air traveled through his open mouth as though he had no lungs within him to process it.

Karl, on the other hand, felt more strong and lucid than he had perhaps ever been at home. If only his parents could see him, championing the good cause in a foreign country before distinguished personalities, and although he had not yet achieved victory, he was entirely prepared for the final conquest! Would they revise their opinion of him? Sit him down between them and praise him? Look for once, just once, into the eyes so devoted to them? Uncertain questions and the most unsuitable moment to ask them!

"I have come because I believe that the stoker is accusing me of some sort of dishonesty. A girl from the kitchen told me she had seen him on his way over here. Captain, sir, and all of you gentlemen, I am prepared to refute all accusations by means of my documents, and with statements of unbiased and uninfluenced witnesses who are standing outside the door, if need be." So spoke Schubal. This was admittedly the clear speech of a man, and from the changed expressions on the listeners' faces, one could have thought these were the first human sounds they had heard in a long time. Of course, they failed to notice that even this nice speech had holes. Why was the first relevant word that occurred to him "dishonesty"? Was this perhaps the accusation that should have been made, instead of his nationalist prejudice? A girl from the kitchen had seen him on his way to the office and Schubal had understood immediately? Was it not his guilty conscience that sharpened his wit? And he had brought witnesses along straightaway and also called them unbiased and uninfluenced? Deceit, nothing but deceit! And the gentlemen tolerated it and even acknowledged it as proper conduct? Why had he clearly let so much time pass between the kitchen girl's announcement and his arrival here? For no other purpose than to allow the stoker to tire the gentleman out until they had gradually lost their capacity for clear judgment, which Schubal had most to fear? Had he, who had surely been standing behind the door for a long time, not waited to knock until the moment when, due to that gentleman's incidental question, he had reason to hope that the stoker was done for?

Everything was clear and also involuntarily presented as such by Schubal, but the gentlemen had to be shown differently, even more perceptibly. They needed to be shaken up. So Karl, quickly, at least made the most of the time they had before the witnesses appeared and obscured everything!

But just then the Captain waved off Schubal, who—seeing that his concern had been postponed for a little while—immediately stepped aside and, joined right away by the attendant, began a quiet conversation, which was neither lacking sidelong glances towards the stoker and Karl nor the most convincing hand gestures. Schubal seemed to be practicing his next big speech.

"Didn't you want to ask the young man something, Herr Jakob?" said the Captain amid general silence to the gentleman with the bamboo cane.

"Indeed," said the latter with a slight bow of thanks for his attentiveness. And then asked Karl again: "So what is your name?"

Karl, who believed it was in the best interest of the main cause for this persistent inquirer's inquiry to be dealt with soon, answered curtly, without, as was his custom, introducing himself by way of his passport, which he would have had to find first: "Karl Rossmann."

"But," said the man addressed as Jakob, and stepped back, initially almost in disbelief, with a smile. Also the Captain, the chief purser, the ship's officer, yes even the attendant clearly showed excessive astonishment at Karl's name. Only the gentlemen from the harbor authority and Schubal remained indifferent.

"But," repeated Herr Jakob, approaching Karl with somewhat stiff steps, "then I am your uncle Jakob and you are my dear nephew. I suspected it all along!" he said to the Captain before he hugged and kissed Karl, who let all this happen in silence.

"And what is your name?" asked Karl, as soon as he felt he had been released, very politely but entirely unmoved, and strained himself to foresee the consequences that this new development may have for the stoker. For the time being, there was no indication that Schubal could profit from this event.

"Realize your good luck, young man," said the Captain, who believed that Karl's questions had wounded the personal dignity of Herr Jakob, who now stood at the window, apparently to avoid showing the others his excited face, which he kept dabbing at with a handkerchief. "It is the Senator Edward Jakob who has just announced himself to be your uncle. A brilliant career is now awaiting you, no doubt entirely contrary to your previous expectations. Try to grasp this, as well as you can at the moment, and collect yourself!"

"I do indeed have an Uncle Jakob in America," said Karl turning to the Captain, "but if I understood correctly, Jakob is merely the Senator's surname."

"So it is," said the Captain expectantly.

"But my Uncle Jakob, who is my mother's brother, bears the first name Jakob, while his surname would naturally have to be identical to that of my mother, whose maiden name is Bendelmayer."

"Gentlemen!" called the Senator, returning cheerfully from his recuperative post by the window, in response to Karl's explanation. Everyone, with the exception of the harbor authorities, broke out in laughter, some due to emotion, some for reasons unknown.

"By no means could my statement have been that ridiculous," thought Karl.

"Gentlemen," the Senator repeated, "you are participating, against your and my intention, in a little family scene and I can therefore not avoid providing you an explanation, because I believe that only the Captain"—this reference led to reciprocal bows—"is fully informed."

"Now I must really pay attention to every word," said Karl to himself and was pleased, as he noticed during a sideways glance, to notice that life had begun to return to the figure of the stoker.

"I have spent the many years of my American visit—though the word visit is hardly suitable for an American citizen, which I am with all my soul—so during all these long years, I have been living entirely detached from my European relatives, for reasons which, firstly, do not belong here and, secondly, would really be too painful for me to explain. I even fear the moment that I may be forced to explain them to my dear nephew, when frank words about his parents and their kin will unfortunately be unavoidable."

"He is my uncle, no doubt," said Karl to himself and listened. "He probably had his name changed."

"And now my dear nephew was—let's just use the word that truly describes the issue—simply thrown out, like one throws a cat out the door when it is bothersome. I certainly do not wish to excuse what my nephew did to be punished in this way, but his fault is such that simply naming it already contains enough absolution."

"That sounds good enough," thought Karl, "but I don't want him to tell it to everyone. And anyway, he can't possibly know about it. How could he?"

"He was namely," continued his uncle, rocking a little on the bamboo cane that he had fixed before him, whereby he actually succeeded in preventing the unnecessary ceremony that the situation would otherwise certainly have had, "he was namely seduced by a maid servant, Johanna Brummer, approximately 35 years of age. I definitely do not wish to offend my nephew with the word 'seduce,' but it is difficult, after all, to find another, equally suitable word."

Karl, who had already moved rather close to his uncle, turned around at this point to read the impression the story had made on the faces of those present. No one was laughing; everyone was listening patiently and earnestly. After all, one doesn't laugh at the nephew of a Senator at the first opportunity that presents itself. It was more accurate to say that the stoker was smiling at Karl, even if just slightly, which was firstly good news, as it was a new sign of life, and secondly forgivable, because Karl had wanted to make a secret out of this issue that had now become so public.

"Now this Brummer woman," his uncle went on, "has had my nephew's child, a healthy boy, who was given the name Jakob at his baptism, no doubt in commemoration of my humble self, who, despite certainly only being mentioned incidentally by my nephew, must have made a great impression on the girl. Fortunately, I might add. For his parents, in order to avoid having to pay alimony or being otherwise drawn further into this scandal—I am familiar, I must emphasize, with neither the local laws nor any further details about his parents' circumstances—so, in order to avoid paying alimony and their son's scandal, they had him, my dear nephew, transported to America with irresponsibly insufficient equipment, as one can see, and the boy would have been left to his own devices, if it were not for the signs and wonders that have not quite ceased in America, and would probably have deteriorated in some alley of the New York harbor if that maid servant had not informed me of the entire story, including a personal description of my nephew and, sensibly, also the name of the ship, in a letter directed at me, which, after a long odyssey, came into my possession the day before yesterday. If my intention was to entertain you, gentlemen, I could certainly read you several passages of this letter"—he pulled two enormous, densely written sheets of paper from his pocket and waved them back and forth—"it would certainly make an impression, for it was written with a somewhat simple, although always well-intentioned cleverness and with much love for the child's father. But I wish neither to entertain you more than necessary for the purpose of clarification, nor as a welcome to potentially hurt any feelings harbored by my nephew, who can read the letter, if he desires, for his own instruction in the privacy of the room that is already awaiting him."

Karl, however, had no feelings for that girl. In the surging crowd of a continuously receding past, she sat in her kitchen next to the kitchen cupboard, upon whose surface she had propped her elbows. She looked at him when he came into the kitchen now and then to get a glass of water for his father or pass on instructions from his mother. Sometimes she wrote a letter in a contorted position beside the kitchen cupboard and drew inspiration from Karl's face. Sometimes she held her hand over her eyes, then no words could get through to her. Sometimes she kneeled in her cramped little room beside the kitchen and prayed to a wooden cross; Karl then observed her shyly in passing through the crack in the slightly opened door. Sometimes she bustled about in the kitchen and shrank back laughing like a witch when Karl got in her way. Sometimes she closed the kitchen door when Karl had entered and held the handle in her hand until he demanded to leave. Sometimes she bought things that he didn't even want and pressed them silently in his hands. But once she said "Karl" and led him, who was still amazed at the unexpected familiarity, sighing and making grimaces into her little room, which she locked. Nearly choking him, she embraced his neck, and while she asked him to undress her, she actually undressed him and laid him in her bed as though she would never leave him to anyone from now on and stroke him and care for him until the end of the world. "Karl, oh my Karl!" she cried, as though she were seeing him and having her ownership of him confirmed, while he saw not the slightest thing and felt uncomfortable in the many warm bed clothes that she seemed to have piled up specially on his behalf. Then she laid herself down beside him and wanted him to tell her some secrets, but he couldn't tell her any and she was annoyed either in jest or in earnest, shook him, listened to his heartbeat, offered her chest for him to do the same, which she could not bring him to do, pressed her bare stomach against his body, groped with her hand between his legs so repulsively that Karl shook head and neck from the pillows, then thrust her stomach against him several times. He felt as though she were part of him and, perhaps for this reason, was overcome by a dreadful helplessness. In tears, and after many requests on her part to meet again, he finally reached his bed. That was all that had happened and his uncle had still managed to make a big story out of it. And the cook had also thought of him and informed his uncle of his arrival. She had dealt with that nicely and he would have to return the favor.

"And now," cried the Senator, "I would like to hear from you publicly whether I am your uncle or not."

"You are my uncle," said Karl and kissed his hand and was kissed on the forehead in return. "I am very glad that I have met you, but you are mistaken if you believe that my parents only speak ill of you. Aside from that, your speech contained several mistakes, that is to say, I mean, everything didn't really happen in that way. Indeed, you are truly not able to judge things very well from here, and furthermore, I believe that it would do no particular damage if the gentlemen are slightly misinformed about the details of an issue that could hardly be of much interest to them."

"Well spoken," said the Senator, who led Karl before the visibly sympathizing Captain and asked: "Do I not have a splendid nephew?"

"I am happy," said the Captain with a bow that can only be achieved by those with military training, "to have met your nephew, Herr Senator. It is a particular honor for my ship that it was able to provide the setting for such a meeting. But the journey in the steerage must have been quite terrible; after all, who knows for sure who's riding along down there? Of course, we do everything possible to alleviate the journey for the people on the steerage as much as possible, much more than the American liners, for example, but we have still not managed to succeed in making such a journey a pleasure."

"It did me no harm," said Karl.

"It did him no harm!" repeated the Senator, laughing loudly.

"Only, I'm afraid I lost my trunk while—" and with this he reminded himself of everything that had happened and what remained to be done, looked around and beheld all those present, silent with deference and amazement in their former places, their eyes directed at him. Only the harbor officials—insofar as their stringent, complacent faces allowed any insight—showed their regret at having come at such an inconvenient time. The pocket watch, which they now had lying before them, was probably more important than everything that had happened and might still happen in this room.

The first one to express his good wishes after the Captain was strangely enough the stoker. "I congratulate you wholeheartedly," he said, and shook Karl's hand, by which he also intended to express something like appreciation. As he then intended to address the Senator with the same words, the Senator stepped back as though the stoker had thereby exceeded his rights; the stoker desisted immediately.

But the others now understood what was to be done and at once formed a tumult around Karl and the Senator. So it happened that Karl even received congratulations from Schubal, which he accepted, and thanked him for. Finally the harbor officials came up to them in the restored calm and said two English words, which made a ridiculous impression.

The Senator was entirely inclined to remind himself and the others of more marginal moments, in order to fully savor this enjoyment, which was, of course, not only tolerated by everyone but also accepted with interest. So he pointed out that he had entered Karl's most distinctive features, as mentioned in the cook's letter into his notebook, should he possibly need them at any moment. And then, during the stoker's unbearable rambling, he had taken out his notebook for no other purpose than to distract himself and tried, as a game, to connect the cook's observations, which were of course lacking a detective's precision, to Karl's appearance. "And that is how to find one's nephew!" he concluded, in a tone as though he wished to be congratulated again.

"What will become of the stoker?" asked Karl, passing over his uncle's last story. In his new position, he believed he could articulate everything that came to mind.

"The stoker will get what he deserves," said the Senator, "and what the Captain considers to be right. I think we have heard enough and more than enough from the stoker, as I'm sure each of the gentlemen here will agree."

"But that's not the point, in a matter of justice," said Karl. He stood between his uncle and the Captain and believed, perhaps influenced by this position, that the decision was in his hands.

But the stoker still seemed to have lost all hope. He held his hands halfway behind his belt, which, due to his excited movements, had been exposed along with a strip of his checkered shirt. This didn't trouble him in the least; now that he had lamented all his suffering, one should also see the few rags covering his body before carrying him away. He devised that the attendant and Schubal, as the two lowest in rank, should render this final act of kindness. Schubal would have his peace and quiet then and no longer be brought to despair, as the chief purser had put it. The Captain would not be able to hire anyone but Romanians, Romanian would be spoken everywhere, and then maybe everything really would run better. No stoker would chatter away in the purser's office anymore; only his final chatter would be kept in quite fond memory, for, as the Senator had explicitly stated, it had indirectly provided the occasion for the recognition of his nephew. This nephew, by the way, had previously tried to be of use to him quite often and had received more than enough thanks in return by his service during the recognition; it would not even occur to the stoker to demand anything more from him now. Besides, even if he was the Senator's nephew, he was far from being a captain, and it was from the Captain's mouth that the harsh verdict would ultimately fall.—So, in accordance with his conviction, the stoker also attempted to avoid looking over at Karl, but unfortunately, there was no other place left in this room full of enemies for him to rest his eyes.

"Don't misunderstand the situation," said the Senator to Karl. "It may be a matter of justice, but it is simultaneously a matter of discipline. Both, and particularly the latter, underlie the Captain's judgment."

"So it is," muttered the stoker. Those who noticed it and understood smiled uneasily.

"We, on the other hand, have already hindered the Captain in fulfilling his official duties, which surely accumulate incredibly, especially upon arrival in New York, so much that it is high time for us to leave the ship, and not to exacerbate things by making an event out of this marginal squabbling between two engineers through our highly unnecessary interference. I understand your course of action, dear nephew, completely, by the way, but that is exactly what gives me the right to lead you away from here in a hurry."

"I shall have a boat lowered for you at once," said the Captain, without, to Karl's amazement, raising even the slightest objection to his uncle's words, although this could doubtlessly be seen as self-abasement on the part of his uncle. The chief purser rushed hastily to the desk and telephoned the Captain's order to the boatswain.

"Our time is running out," Karl said to himself, "but I can't do anything without offending everyone. I can't leave my uncle, now that he's only just found me again. The Captain is in fact polite, but that's the end of it. His politeness stops when it comes to discipline, and my uncle certainly spoke from the Captain's heart. I don't want to speak to Schubal; I'm even sorry that I shook hands with him. And all the other people here are inconsequential."

And with these thoughts in mind, he walked over to the stoker, pulled his right hand from behind his belt, and held it playfully in his own. "Why don't you say anything?" he asked. "Why do you put up with it all?"

The stoker only wrinkled his brow, as though he were searching for the expression for what he had to say. Incidentally, he looked down at Karl's and his hand.

"You've been wronged like no one else on this ship, this I know for sure." And Karl drew his finger back and forth between those of the stoker, who looked around with gleaming eyes as though a joy had been bestowed upon him that no one could resent him for.

"You must defend yourself, say yes and no, otherwise people will have no idea of the truth. You must promise me that you will do as I say, for I myself, I have good reason to fear, will not be able to help you anymore." And now Karl wept as he kissed the stoker's hand and took the cracked and almost lifeless hand and pressed it to his cheeks, like a treasure that one must relinquish.—But Uncle Senator was already there at his side and pulled him, albeit with the slightest force, away.

"The stoker appears to have charmed you," he said and glanced meaningfully over Karl's head at the Captain. "You were feeling abandoned and then you found the stoker, and are now grateful to him; that is surely quite laudable. But don't take it too far, at least for my sake, and learn to realize your position."

Outside the door there was a racket, shouts could be heard, and it was even as though someone were being thrown brutally against the door. A sailor entered, somewhat disheveled, with a girl's apron tied around his waist. "There are people outside," he cried and thrust his elbow around once, as though he were still in the crowd. He finally came to his senses and wanted to salute the Captain when he noticed the apron, tore it off, threw it on the floor, and cried: "That's disgusting, they've put a girl's apron on me." And then he clicked his heels together and saluted. Someone was about to laugh, but the Captain said sternly: "That's what I call a good mood. Just who is outside?"

"They are my witnesses," said Schubal, stepping forward, "My sincerest apologies for their inappropriate behavior. When the crew has the voyage behind them, they are sometimes quite mad."

"Call them in right away!" ordered the Captain, and immediately turning around to the Senator, he said politely but quickly: "Please, Herr Senator, be so good as to take your nephew and follow this sailor, who will take you to your boat. I need hardly say what a pleasure and honor it has been to personally make your acquaintance, Herr Senator. I only hope that we will soon have the opportunity to continue our interrupted conversation about the state of the American fleet and perhaps be interrupted again in such a pleasant manner as today."

"One nephew is enough for the time being," said the uncle laughing. "And now please accept my thanks for your kindness and farewell. It would not be entirely impossible, by the way,"— he took Karl in his arm affectionately—"for us to spend a longer period of time together on our next journey to Europe."

"That would be a great pleasure," said the Captain. The two men shook hands. Karl could only manage to briefly shake the Captain's hand in silence, for the Captain was already preoccupied with the perhaps fifteen people who moved in under Schubal's lead in a concerned, albeit very loud manner. The sailor asked the Senator's permission to lead the way and then parted the crowd for him and Karl, who easily passed through the rows of bowing people. It appeared that these otherwise good-natured people regarded Schubal's quarrel with the stoker as a joke that did not even cease to be amusing in front of the Captain. Karl noticed among them the kitchen maid Line, winking at him playfully as she tied around her waist the apron that had been thrown down by the sailor, for it was hers.

Still following the sailor, they left the office and turned into a short passageway that led them, after a few steps, to a little door, from which a short ladder led down to the boat that had been prepared for them. The sailors in the boat, into which their leader jumped with a single bound, rose and saluted. The Senator was just warning Karl to be careful climbing down, when Karl, still on the topmost rung, broke into heavy tears. The Senator placed his right hand under Karl's chin and held him tightly, stroking him with his left hand. Closely linked, they slowly descended step by step and entered the boat, where the Senator chose a good seat for Karl directly opposite him. At the Senator's signal, the sailors pushed off from the ship and were immediately working at full force. They were hardly a few meters from the ship when Karl made the unexpected discovery that they were on the same side of the ship as the windows of the purser's office. All three windows were filled with Schubal's witnesses, who greeted and winked in the most friendly way; even his uncle thanked them, and a sailor accomplished the feat of blowing them a kiss without actually interrupting the rhythm of his rowing. It was truly as though the stoker no longer existed. Karl considered his uncle, whose knees were almost touching his own, more closely, and began to doubt whether this man would ever be able to replace the stoker. His uncle also avoided his eyes and looked at the waves, as they surged around their boat.

In the Penal Colony

"It is a remarkable apparatus," said the officer to the researching traveler as he surveyed the apparatus, which was quite familiar to him, with some measure of admiration. It seemed that it was only out of courtesy that the traveler had accepted the invitation of the commandant, who had called upon him to attend the execution of a soldier who had been condemned for insubordination and insulting a superior. The interest in this execution also did not seem to be very great within the penal colony. Present here, at least, in the deep, sandy little valley enclosed on all sides by barren slopes, in addition to the officer and the traveler, were only he who had been condemned, a dull-witted, wide-mouthed man with unkempt hair and face, and a soldier, who was holding the heavy chain in which all the small chains that fettered the condemned man at his ankles, wrists, and neck were linked to one another with connecting chains. Incidentally, the condemned man looked so doggishly submissive that it appeared as though one could let him run freely around the slopes and would only need to whistle when the execution began for him to return.

The traveler was not particularly interested in the machine and paced with almost visible indifference back and forth behind the condemned man, while the officer attended to the final preparations, one moment crawling under the apparatus, which was deeply embedded in the ground, the next climbing a ladder to examine the upper parts. These were tasks that could actually have been left to a mechanic, but the officer performed them with great enthusiasm, perhaps because of his particular admiration for this apparatus, perhaps because they could not be entrusted to anyone else for other reasons. "Now everything is ready!" he finally called out and climbed down from the ladder. He was extraordinarily exhausted, breathing with his mouth wide open, and had forced two delicate ladies' handkerchiefs behind the collar of his uniform. "These uniforms are surely too heavy for the tropics," said the traveler, instead of inquiring about the apparatus as the officer had expected. "Indeed," said the officer and washed his hands, which had been soiled with oil and grease, in a nearby bucket of water, "but they mean home; we don't want to lose our home.— Now have a look at this apparatus," he added quickly, as he dried his hands on a towel and pointed simultaneously to the apparatus. "Until now, work by hand had been necessary, but from now on the apparatus operates entirely on its own." The traveler nodded and followed the officer, who sought to prepare himself for all eventualities and then said: "Disturbances do occur, of course; even though I hope it will not happen today, one must nevertheless allow for it. The apparatus should operate continuously for twelve hours, after all. If disturbances do occur, however, they will only be quite minor and repaired immediately."

"Won't you have a seat?" he asked finally, pulled one cane chair from a stack, and offered it to the traveler, who could not refuse. He was now sitting on the edge of a pit, into which he threw a fleeting glance. It was not very deep. On one side of the pit, the excavated earth had been piled up to form a parapet, on the other side stood the apparatus. "I don't know," said the officer, "whether the commandant has already explained the apparatus to you." The traveler made an uncertain gesture with his hand; the officer could not ask for more, for now he could explain the apparatus himself. "This apparatus," he said, grasping a crankshaft and leaning himself against it, "is the invention of our former commandant. I myself participated in the very first experiments and was also involved in all work leading to its completion. The credit for the invention, however, is his alone. Have you heard of our former commandant? No? Well, it is not an overstatement for me to say that the organization of the entire penal colony is his work. We, his friends, already knew at the time of his death that the colony's organization was so self-contained that his successor, even if he had a thousand new plans in mind, would not be able to alter a thing for at least many years to come. And our prediction has come true; the new commandant was forced to acknowledge as much. It's such a shame that you did not meet the former commandant!—But," the officer interrupted himself, "I am rambling while his apparatus is right here before us. It consists, as you see, of three parts. In the course of time, each of these parts has acquired a somewhat vernacular name. The lower part is called the Bed, the upper one is the Scribe, and this hovering part in the middle is called the Harrow." "The Harrow?" asked the traveler. He had not been listening very attentively; the sun was trapped so intensely by the shadeless valley, it was difficult to gather one's thoughts. The officer seemed to him all the more admirable, in his fitted, parade-dress uniform, weighted with epaulettes, draped with braids, as he explained his subject with such enthusiasm, and also managed to tighten a few screws here and there with his screwdriver as he spoke. The soldier appeared to be in much the same condition as the traveler. He had wound the chain around both of the condemned man's wrists, leaned with one hand on his rifle, let his head hang down, and concerned himself with nothing. The traveler was not surprised at this, for the officer was speaking French, and surely neither the soldier nor the condemned man was able to understand French. It was therefore all the more remarkable that the condemned man was nevertheless making an effort to follow the officer's explanations. With a sort of drowsy tenacity, he always directed his eyes to wherever the officer was pointing, and when he was interrupted by the traveler's question, he, like the officer, looked at the traveler.

"Yes, the Harrow," said the officer. "The name fits. The needles are arranged in a harrowlike fashion and the whole thing is operated like a harrow, although only in one place and much more skillfully. Anyway, you will understand how in a moment. The condemned man is laid here on the Bed.—You see, I shall first describe the apparatus before having the procedure itself carried out. You will then be able to follow it better. One of the cogwheels in the Scribe is badly worn; it screeches quite a lot when it is running; one can hardly make oneself understood; unfortunately, replacement parts are difficult to acquire here.—Now, as I said, this is the Bed. It is covered entirely with a layer of padding, the purpose of which you will learn later. The condemned man is laid on his stomach onto this padding, naked, of course; to bind him there are straps, here for the hands, here for the feet, here for the neck. Here at the head of the Bed, where the man, as I said, is at first lying face-down, is this little felt gag that can be easily regulated so that it just fits into the man's mouth. Its purpose is to prevent screaming and biting of the tongue. Of course the man must take the felt in his mouth or else his neck will be broken by the neck strap." "That's padding?" asked the traveler and leaned forward. "Yes, certainly," said the officer smiling, "feel it for yourself." He took the traveler's hand and guided it over the Bed. "It is a specially treated padding, which is why it looks so strange; I'll get to its purpose in a moment." The traveler's interest in the apparatus had already been won a little; his hand protecting his eyes from the sun above, he looked up at the apparatus. It was a large structure. The Bed and the Scribe were the same size and looked like two dark chests. The Scribe was mounted about two meters above the Bed; both were connected at the corners by four brass rods, which were almost radiating in the sunlight. Between the chests, the Harrow was suspended on a steel band.

The officer had hardly noticed the traveler's previous indifference, but was certainly aware of his growing interest now; hence he paused in his explanations to allow the traveler time for undisturbed inspection. The condemned man imitated the traveler; as he could not place his hand above his eyes, he squinted with his eyes unshaded.

"So now the man is lying down," said the traveler, leaned back in his chair, and crossed his legs.

"Yes," the officer said, pushed his cap back a bit and ran his hand across his hot face. "Now listen! Both the Bed and the Scribe have their own electric battery; the Bed needs it for itself, the Scribe for the Harrow. As soon as the man is strapped in, the Bed is set in motion. It vibrates with minute, very rapid convulsions simultaneously from side to side and up and down. You will have seen similar apparatuses in sanatoriums; only with our Bed all movements are calculated exactly; that is to say, they must correspond precisely to the movements of the Harrow. This Harrow, however, has the actual task of executing the sentence."

"And what is the sentence?" asked the traveler. "You don't know that either?" said the officer with astonishment and bit his lip: "Forgive me if my explanations are perhaps disorganized; I beg your pardon. The explanations always used to be given by the commandant, you see; now the new commandant has evaded this honorable duty. But such an esteemed visitor,"—the traveler sought to fend off this distinction with both hands, but the officer insisted on the expression—"such an esteemed visitor not even being informed about the form of our sentence is another new development that—." He had a curse on his lips, but he composed himself and said only: "I was not informed about it; I am not at fault. I am, by the way, certainly the most qualified to explain the types of sentences we pass, for I carry here"—he patted his breast pocket—"the relevant drawings from the hand of our former commandant."

"Drawings from the hand of the commandant himself?" asked the traveler: "Was he everything all in one man? Was he soldier, judge, engineer, chemist, and draftsman?"

"Indeed," said the officer, nodding his head with a fixed, pensive gaze. Then he scrutinized his hands; they didn't seem clean enough to him to be handling the drawings; he went to the bucket and washed them again. Then he pulled out a small leather folder and said: "Our sentence does not sound harsh. The order that the condemned man has violated will be inscribed with the Harrow on his body. Using this man as an example,"—the officer pointed at the man—"his body will be inscribed with 'Honor thy superior!'"

The traveler took a fleeting look at the man; he had bowed his head as the officer had pointed at him and seemed to have gathered all his hearing strength in order to gain some information. But the movements of his thick lips as he pressed them together evidently showed that he could understand nothing. The traveler had wanted to ask several things, but at the sight of the man he asked only: "Does he know his sentence?" "No," said the officer and was about to continue his explanation when the traveler interrupted him: "He doesn't know his own sentence?" "No," said the officer again and hesitated for a moment as though he required the traveler to further justify his question, and then said: "It would be pointless to announce it to him. After all, he will experience it on his own body." The traveler wanted to remain silent when he felt the condemned man directing his gaze at him; he seemed to be asking if he could condone the described procedure. So the traveler, who had already leaned back, leaned forward again and also asked: "But he does know that he has been condemned, doesn't he?" "Nor that either," said the officer and smiled at the traveler as though he were expecting another strange disclosure from him. "No?" said the traveler and wiped his brow, "So then the man still doesn't know how his defense was received?" "He had no opportunity to defend himself," said the officer, looking to the side as though he were talking to himself and did not want to embarrass the traveler by telling him these things that were, to him, so obvious. "But he must have had an opportunity to defend himself," said the traveler, rising from his chair.

The officer realized that his explanation of the apparatus was in danger of being delayed for a long time, so he went over to the traveler, took him by the arm, gestured with his hand to the condemned man, who, now that attention was so clearly focused on him, stood up straight—the soldier also pulled at the chain—and said: "The situation is as follows: I have been appointed as judge here in the penal colony. Despite my youth. For I assisted the former commandant in all criminal matters as well and am also the most familiar with the apparatus. The basic principle according to which I make decisions is: Guilt is always beyond doubt. Other courts cannot bide by this principle, for they consist of many people and also have higher courts above them. That is not the case here, or at least it wasn't with the former commandant. The new one, however, has already revealed his desire to interfere in my court, but so far I have succeeded at holding him off and I shall continue to succeed.—You wanted to have this case explained; it is as simple as all the others. A captain filed charges this morning that this man, who was assigned to him as his servant and sleeps outside of his door, had been asleep on duty. He is obligated, you see, to get up at the stroke of every hour and salute outside the captain's door. Certainly not a difficult task, but a necessary one, for he is supposed to stay fresh for security as well as service. Last night, the captain wanted to see if his servant was fulfilling his duty. He opened the door at the stroke of two and found him bent over sleeping. He fetched his riding whip and struck him across the face. Instead of standing up and begging for forgiveness, the man grabbed his master by the legs, shook him and shouted: 'Throw the whip away or I'll eat you.'—Those are the facts of the case. The captain came to me an hour ago, I wrote down his statement, and the sentence directly afterwards. Then I had the man put in chains. It was all very simple. If I had first summoned the man and questioned him, it would only have led to confusion. He would have told lies, and if I had succeeded in refuting these lies, he would have replaced them with new lies, and so on. But as it is, I have got him and will not let him go.—Has everything been explained now? But time is passing, the execution ought to have started by now, and I still haven't finished my explanation of the apparatus." He forced the traveler into his seat, stepped up to the apparatus again and began: "As you see, the Harrow corresponds to the human shape; here is the harrow for the torso, here are the harrows for the legs. Only this small needle is intended for the head. Is that clear?" He bent toward the traveler, poised to give the most comprehensive explanations.

The traveler looked at the Harrow with a furrowed brow. The account of the legal procedures had not pleased him. All the same, he had to tell himself that this was a penal colony, that special measures were necessary here, and that military procedures were necessary to the last. Furthermore, he placed some hopes in the new commandant, who apparently, albeit slowly, intended to introduce a new procedure, which this officer's narrow mind was incapable of absorbing. From this train of thought, the traveler asked: "Will the commandant be attending the execution?" "It's not certain," said the officer, embarrassed by the unexpected question, and his friendly expression contorted: "That is exactly why we must hurry. As much as I regret it, I will even have to curtail my explanations. But tomorrow, of course, when the apparatus has been cleaned— its only flaw is that it gets so dirty—I can add more detailed explanations. So for now, only that which is most necessary.—Once the man is lying on the Bed and it has started to vibrate, the Harrow is lowered onto the body. It adjusts itself on its own so that the spikes only just touch the body; once this adjustment is complete, this steel rope tightens at once into a rod. And now the performance begins. The uninformed observer will not notice any external difference in the punishments. The Harrow appears to work uniformly. As it vibrates, it stabs its spikes into the body, which is also vibrating from the Bed. Now in order to allow everyone to observe the sentence being carried out, the Harrow is made out of glass. Fixing the needles into it created several technical difficulties, but after many attempts we succeeded. We spared no effort, as you see. And now everyone can see through the glass how the inscription on the body is carried out. Wouldn't you like to come closer and have a look at the needles?"

The traveler got up slowly, walked up to the Harrow, and bent over it. "You see," said the officer, "two kinds of needles in multiple arrangements. Each long one has a short one next to it. Namely, the long one inscribes and the short one sprays water to wash away the blood and keep the inscription clear at all times. The bloody water is then channeled into these small gutters and finally flows into this main gutter, whose drainpipe leads into the pit." The officer indicated with his finger the precise path that the bloody water had to follow. When, in order to make it as demonstrative as possible, he actually collected it in both hands at the drainpipe's outlet, the traveler lifted his head and, with his hand feeling the way behind him, moved to return to his seat. He then saw to his horror that the condemned man had also followed the officer's invitation to inspect the mechanism of the Harrow up close. He had dragged the drowsing soldier forward a little with the chain and also leaned over the glass. One could see that he was also searching with uncertain eyes for that which the two gentlemen had just been observing, but that he could not succeed because he was lacking the explanation. He bent over here and over there. He ran his eyes over the glass again and again. The traveler wanted to force him back, for what he was doing was probably punishable. But the officer held the traveler back with one hand, took a clod of earth from the parapet with the other, and threw it at the soldier. With a start, the soldier looked up, saw what the condemned man had dared to do, dropped his rifle, dug his heels into the ground, jerked the condemned man back in such a way that he fell down at once, and then looked down at him as he writhed and rattled his chains. "Stand him up!" shouted the officer, for he noticed that the traveler was being overly distracted by the condemned man. The traveler even leaned right over the Harrow without concerning himself with it, only wanting to find out what was happening to him. "Handle him with care!" shouted the officer again. He ran around the apparatus, grasped the condemned man himself under the arms, and, although his feet slipped several times, managed to stand him up with the soldier's help.

"Now I know everything," said the traveler when the officer returned to him again. "Except for that which is most important," said the latter, taking the traveler by the arm and pointing upwards: "There, in the Scribe, is the machinery that determines the movements of the Harrow, and this machinery is arranged according to the design that the sentence requires. I still use the drawings of the former commandant. Here they are,"—he drew several pages from the leather folder—"I'm afraid I cannot let you handle them; they are my most precious possessions. Have a seat. I will show them to you from this distance, so you will be able to see them well." He showed the first page. The traveler would have liked to have said something approving, but he saw only labyrinth-like lines that crossed one another repeatedly and covered the paper so densely that it required some effort to recognize the white spaces in between. "Read it," said the officer. "I can't," said the traveler. "But it's quite clear," said the officer. "It is very elaborate," said the traveler, evading him, "but I can't decipher it." "Yes," said the officer with a laugh and put the folder away again, "it is no handwriting exercise for school children. It takes a long time to read it. Surely you would also be able to understand it in the end. It cannot be a simple script, of course; it is not supposed to kill right away, after all, but within an average interval of twelve hours; the turning point is calculated for the sixth hour. So the actual script must be surrounded by many, many elaborations; the real script encircles the body only in a narrow band; the rest of the body is intended for decoration. Can you now appreciate the work of the Harrow and the entire apparatus?—Just watch!" He sprang onto the ladder, turned a wheel, called down: "Watch out, step aside!" and everything got underway. If the wheel had not screeched, it would have been magnificent. The officer shook his fist at the disruptive wheel as though he had been surprised by it, then spread his arms out toward the traveler in apology and climbed down hastily to observe the operation of the apparatus from below. Something that only he had noticed was still not in order; he climbed up again, reached with both hands into the interior of the Scribe, slid down one of the poles instead of using the ladder to get down faster, and in order to be understood among all the noise, he now screamed with extreme tension into the traveler's ear: "Do you understand the procedure? The Harrow is beginning to write; once it has finished the first layout of the script on the man's back, the padding rolls and turns the body slowly onto its side to provide the Harrow with more space. In the meantime, the places that have been written raw are laid on the padding, which due to its special treatment stops the bleeding right away and prepares for deeper inscription. As the body is rotated further, these teeth here at the edge of the Harrow then rip the padding from the wounds, sling it in the pit, and the Harrow sets to work again. In this way it inscribes deeper and deeper for the entire twelve hours. For the first six hours the condemned man lives almost as before, only suffering pain. After two hours, the felt is removed, for the man no longer has the strength to scream. Here in this electrically heated bowl at the head end, warm rice porridge is placed, and if he wishes, he can take whatever he can lap up with his tongue. No one misses the chance. I know of none who has, and my experience is great. Only around the sixth hour does he lose his desire to eat. I usually kneel down at this point and observe this phenomenon. The man rarely swallows the last bite, he only turns it around in his mouth and spits it into the pit. I have to duck then, otherwise it will hit me in the face. But how still the man becomes at the sixth hour! Even the stupidest man begins to understand. It starts around the eyes. From here it spreads further. It's a sight that almost tempts you to lie down beside him under the Harrow. Nothing else happens, the man just begins to decipher the text, he purses his lips as though he is listening. As you have seen, it is not easy to decipher the text with your eyes; but our man deciphers it with his wounds. But it is nevertheless hard work; he needs six hours to accomplish it. But then the Harrow pierces through him entirely and throws him in the pit, where he is slapped down onto the bloody water and the padding. Then the sentence is concluded and we, the soldier and I, bury him."

The traveler had inclined his ear to the officer and, with his hands in his coat pockets, watched the machine as it worked. The condemned man also watched it, but without understanding. He bent forward a little and was following the vibrating needles when the soldier, at a sign from the officer, cut through his shirt and trousers with a knife from behind so that they fell off of him; he tried to catch his clothes as they fell to cover his nakedness, but the soldier lifted him up and shook the last shreds from him. The officer switched off the machine, and in the silence that then emerged, the condemned man was laid under the Harrow.

The chains were removed and the straps were fastened in their place; at first, this appeared to be almost a relief for the condemned man. And now the Harrow sank a bit lower, for he was a thin man. When the needles touched him, a shudder ran through his skin; he stretched his left hand out blindly, while the soldier was busy with his right one; but it was in the direction where the traveler was standing. The officer watched the traveler continuously from the side, as though he were trying to read on his face the impression that the execution, which he had now at least superficially explained, was making on him.

The strap intended for the wrist snapped; the soldier had probably pulled it too tight. The officer was supposed to help; the soldier showed him the torn part of the strap. And the officer went over to him and said with his face turned toward the traveler: "The machine is very complex, so something is bound to snap or break now and again; but one must not let that deter one's overall assessment. A replacement for the strap, by the way, can be provided right way; I will use a chain; the sensitivity of the vibration will be inhibited, however, for the right arm." And while he was putting on the chains, he added: "Resources for the machine's maintenance are now very limited. Under the former commandant, funds that I had free access to were reserved solely for this purpose. There was a depot in which all kinds of replacement parts were stored. I admit, I was almost wasteful with them, I mean previously, not now, as claimed by the new commandant, for whom everything is merely a pretext to combat old institutions. Now he manages the funds himself, and if I send for a new strap, the torn one will be demanded as evidence, the new one won't arrive for another ten days, and then it will be of poor quality and not much use. But no one is concerned with how I am to operate the machine in the meantime without a strap."

The traveler pondered: it is always precarious to intervene decisively in the affairs of others. He was neither citizen of the penal colony, nor citizen of the state that it belonged to. If he were to try to condemn or even obstruct the execution, they could tell him: you are a foreigner; be quiet. He would be unable to respond to this and could only add that he did not understand his own behavior in this case, for he was traveling solely with the intention of observing, and in no way of altering foreign legal constitutions. But the present situation was nevertheless very tempting. The injustice of the procedure and the inhumanity of the execution were beyond a doubt. No one could assume any self-interest on the part of the traveler, for the condemned man was a stranger to him, he was not a fellow countryman, and not at all the sort of person to arouse one's sympathy. The traveler himself had recommendations from high officers, was received here with great courtesy, and his invitation to this execution even seemed to indicate that his assessment was being requested. And this was all the more probable since the commandant, as he had heard all too clearly, was not a proponent of this procedure and almost hostile in his behavior toward the officer.

The traveler then heard a shout of rage from the officer. He had just managed, not without difficulty, to push the felt gag into the condemned man's mouth, when the man closed his eyes in an uncontrollable fit of nausea and vomited. The officer hastily lifted him up away from the gag and tried to turn his head toward the pit; but it was too late, the vomit was already running down the machine. "It's all the commandant's fault!" shouted the officer, senselessly shaking the front brass poles. "The machine is being befouled like a pigsty." He showed the traveler with shaking hands what had happened. "Did I not spend hours trying to make it clear to the commandant that no food should be given the day before the execution. But the new mild course is of another opinion. Before the man is led away, the commandant's ladies stuff him full of sweets. His whole life he has subsisted on stinking fish and now he must eat sweets! It would be possible after all, I would not object—but why can't the new gag be acquired that I have been requesting for the past three months. How can one not be disgusted taking this gag in one's mouth that has been sucked and bitten on by more than a hundred dying men?"

The condemned man had lowered his head and looked peaceful. The soldier was busy cleaning the machine with the man's shirt. The officer approached the traveler, who took a step back out of some kind of intuition, but the officer seized his hand and pulled him aside. "I would like to have a word with you in confidence," he said. "I am allowed to, am I not?" "Certainly," said the traveler and listened with lowered eyes.

"This procedure and this execution that you now have the opportunity to admire no longer have any open supporters in our colony. I am its sole advocate and simultaneously the only advocate of the old commandant's legacy. I can no longer think of developing the procedure any further; I use up all my strength preserving that which exists. When the old commandant was alive, the colony was full of his followers. I possess part of the old commandant's persuasiveness, but I entirely lack his power. As a result, his supporters have gone into hiding. They are still numerous, but no one will admit to it. If you go to a teahouse today, on an execution day that is, and keep your ears open, you will perhaps hear only ambiguous statements. These are all supporters, but under the current commandant and with his current views they are entirely useless to me. And so I ask you: should a life's work such as this"—he pointed to the machine—"perish due to this commandant and the women who influence him? Can one allow that to happen? Even if one is only visiting our island for a few days as a foreigner? But there is no time to lose. Plans are already being made to undermine my judicial authority; discussions are already taking place in the commandant's headquarters that I am not being consulted about; even your visit seems to me to be indicative of the entire situation; they are cowardly and send you, a foreigner, ahead.—How different the executions were in earlier times! A day beforehand, the entire valley would already be overflowing with people, they all came just to watch; early in the morning, the commandant would appear with his ladies; fanfares would wake the entire encampment; I would make the announcement that everything was prepared; the company—no high official could be absent—would arrange themselves around the machine. This stack of cane chairs is a pathetic remnant from that time. The machine was freshly cleaned and shining; I used new replacement parts for nearly every execution. Before hundreds of eyes—all spectators stood on their tiptoes all the way to those hills over there—the condemned man was laid under the Harrow by the commandant himself. That which a common soldier is allowed to perform today used to be my duty as presiding judge, and it was an honor. And then the execution began! No dissonance disturbed the machine's work. Some no longer watched but lay with their eyes closed in the sand; everyone knew: justice is now being done. In the silence, one could only hear the condemned man's groans, muffled by the gag. Today the machine is no longer able to force a groan out of the condemned man that is too loud for the gag to stifle; but back then, a corrosive liquid dripped from the needles as they wrote that we are no longer allowed to use today. And then the sixth hour arrived! It was impossible to fulfill all the requests to watch up close. The commandant, wise as he was, ordered that children were to be given particular preference; I, however, by virtue of my office, was always allowed to stand by; I often crouched there, two little children in my arms to the left and the right. How we all took in the expression of transfiguration on the martyred face, how we bathed our cheeks in the glow of the justice that was achieved at last and already fading! What times they were, my comrade!" The officer had apparently forgotten who was standing before him; he had embraced the traveler and laid his head upon his shoulder. The traveler was deeply embarrassed; he looked impatiently past the officer. The soldier had finished cleaning and was now pouring rice porridge from a tin into the bowl. No sooner had the condemned man, who seemed to have already recovered entirely, noticed this, than he began to snap at the porridge with his tongue. The soldier kept pushing him away, for the porridge was apparently intended for a later time, but it was certainly also improper for the soldier to dig into the bowl with his filthy hands and eat from it in front of the ravenous man.

The officer composed himself quickly. "I didn't intend to unsettle you," he said, "I know it is impossible to make someone understand those times today. Besides, the machine still works and is effective on its own. It is effective on its own, even if it stands alone in this valley. And the corpse still ultimately falls with an incomprehensibly gentle flight into the pit, even if hundreds no longer gather like flies, as they did back then, around the pit. Back then we had to install a strong fence around the pit, but it has long since been torn away."

The traveler tried to turn his face away from the officer and looked around aimlessly. The officer thought he was contemplating the valley's bleakness; he therefore grasped his hands, moved around him to catch his eye, and asked: "Do you see the disgrace?"

But the traveler said nothing. The officer let him be for a moment; with his legs apart and his hands on his hips, he stood still and looked at the ground. He then smiled at the traveler encouragingly and said: "I was nearby yesterday when the commandant invited you. I heard his invitation. I know the commandant. I understood immediately what he intended with the invitation. Even though his power would be great enough to intervene against me, he does not yet dare to, but he certainly wants to expose me to your judgment, that of a respected foreigner. He has worked it out carefully; this is your second day on the island, you were not familiar with the old commandant and his way of thinking, you are biased by your European point of view, perhaps you are fundamentally opposed to the death penalty in general, and this kind of mechanical execution method in particular, and moreover you can see how an execution takes place without public participation, sadly, on a machine that is already somewhat damaged. So wouldn't it be possible, taking all this into account (this is how the commandant thinks), that you do not consider my procedure to be right? And if you think it is not right, (I am still speaking as the commandant) you will not keep silent about it, for you surely trust your tried and tested convictions. Of course, you have seen and learned to respect many peculiar customs in many nations, and will therefore probably not speak out against the procedure as vigorously as you might in your native country. But the commandant doesn't need you to. One fleeting, indiscreet word will suffice. It must not even conform to your convictions, as long as it appears to fulfill his aim. He will question you very cunningly, of this I am certain. And his ladies will sit around in a circle and prick up their ears: you will say something like: 'Criminal procedures are different where I come from,' or 'The defendant is interrogated before sentencing where I come from,' or 'Torture existed only in the Middle Ages where I come from.' These are all remarks that are just as correct as they seem self-evident to you, innocent remarks that do not question my procedure. But how will the commandant receive them? I see him now, the good commandant, immediately pushing his chair aside and hurrying to the balcony; I see his ladies, pouring after him; I hear his voice—the ladies call it a thundering voice—as he says: 'A great Western scholar, appointed to study criminal procedure in all countries, has just declared our procedure according to old custom to be an inhumane one. Given this verdict from such a distinguished person, it is of course no longer possible for me to tolerate this procedure. I therefore decree that starting today—and so on.' You try to intervene, you didn't say that which he proclaimed, you didn't call my procedure inhumane, on the contrary, according to your deep insight you find that it is the most humane and most humanly dignified, you also admire this machinery—but it is too late; you can't even get onto the balcony, which is already full of ladies; you try to make yourself noticeable; you want to scream; but a lady's hand covers your mouth—and I and the work of the old commandant are lost."

The traveler had to suppress a smile; so easy was the task that he had thought to be so difficult. He said evasively: "You overestimate my influence; the commandant has read my letter of recommendation, he knows that I am not knowledgeable in criminal procedure. If I were to express my opinion, it would be the opinion of a private person and no more significant than the opinion of anyone else, and in any case it is far more insignificant than the opinion of the commandant, who has, as I understand, quite extensive rights in this penal colony. If his opinion about this procedure is as certain as you believe it to be, however, then I'm afraid the end has come for the procedure without requiring my modest assistance."

Had the officer understood it yet? No, he had not yet understood. He shook his head vigorously, looked back briefly toward the condemned man and the soldier, who flinched and let the rice porridge be, walked up quite closely to the traveler, not looking him in the face, but at someplace on his coat and said more softly than before: "You don't know the commandant; your view of him and all of us is—pardon the expression—somewhat naïve; believe me, your influence cannot be overestimated. Indeed I was elated when I heard that you alone were to attend the execution. This order of the commandant was intended to strike me, but now I am turning it to my advantage. Undistracted by false insinuations and contemptful glances—which could not have been avoided if more people had attended the execution—you listened to my explanations, saw the machine and are now about to view the execution. Your decision has surely already been made; should small insecurities remain, they will be eliminated by the sight of the execution. And now I will make my appeal to you: help me and not the commandant!"

The traveler did not let him speak further. "How could I do that?" he cried out. "That is entirely impossible. I can't help you any more than I can harm you."

"Yes, you can," said the officer. The traveler saw with some fear that the officer was clenching his fists. "Yes you can," the officer repeated even more urgently. "I have a plan that is certain to succeed. You believe that your influence is inadequate. I know that it is adequate. But even if you are right, isn't it necessary to try everything to preserve this procedure, even that which may be insufficient? So listen to my plan. To carry it out, it is above all necessary for you to restrain yourself as much as possible in the colony today with your judgment of the procedure. Unless you are asked directly, you may not say anything at all; your statements, however, must be brief and vague; one should notice that it is difficult for you to talk about it, that you are resentful, that if you were to speak openly, you would literally have to break out cursing. I am not asking you to lie; not at all; you should only answer briefly, like: 'Yes, I saw the execution,' or 'Yes, I heard all the explanations.' Only this, nothing further. As for the resentment that one is supposed to observe, there is enough cause for that, after all, even if it is not as the commandant understands it. He will misunderstand it entirely, of course, and interpret it according to his views. This is what my plan is based on. Tomorrow an important conference with all the senior administrators is being chaired by the commandant and taking place in the commandant's headquarters. The commandant of course knows how to make a display out of such conferences. A gallery was built that is always full of spectators. I am obliged to take part in the meetings, but the reluctance agitates me. Now you are sure to be invited to the meeting in any case; if you behave according to my plan today, the invitation will turn into an urgent request. But should you for some incomprehensible reason not be invited, you must by all means request an invitation; that you will then receive it is beyond doubt. So tomorrow you will be sitting with the ladies in the commandant's box. He reassures himself frequently with upward glances that you are there. After various indifferent, ridiculous agenda items intended solely for the benefit of the spectators—it is usually harbor construction, always harbor construction!—the question of criminal procedure will be raised. If the commandant fails to raise it, or fails to raise it soon enough, I will see to it. I will rise and report on today's execution. Very briefly, only this report. Such a report is not customary there, but I will do it anyway. The commandant will thank me, as always, with a friendly smile, and then, not being be able to restrain himself, he will seize the good opportunity. 'We have just heard the report about the execution,' he will say, or something similar. 'I would only like to add to this report that this execution was attended by the great scholar, whose exceptionally honorable visit to our colony you all know about. Today's meeting has also increased in significance due to his presence. Shall we not ask this great scholar how he has judged the execution, according to old custom, and the procedure that preceded it?' There is applause all around, of course; general approval, I am the loudest.

The commandant bows to you and says: 'Then I ask the question in everyone's name.' And now you step up to the balustrade. Place your hands on it for everyone to see, otherwise the ladies will grab them and play with your fingers.—And now you speak at last. I don't know how I will bear the suspense of the hours until then. In your speech, you must not restrain yourself at all, make a racket with the truth, lean over the balustrade, shout, yes, shout your opinion at the commandant, your unshakable opinion. But perhaps you don't want to, it doesn't suit your character. Perhaps you behave differently in such situations in your home country; that is also correct, that also suffices completely, don't stand up at all, say only a few words, whisper them so that they are barely heard by the administrators beneath you, that will suffice. You yourself must not speak of the lack of attendance at the execution, of the screeching wheel, the torn strap, the disgusting gag. No, I will take care of everything else and, believe me, if my speech does not chase him out of the room, then it will force him to his knees so that he will have to confess: Old commandant, I bow before you.—That is my plan; would you like to help me carry it out? But of course you would, more than that, you must." And the officer grabbed the traveler by both arms and looked at him, breathing heavily in his face. He had screamed the last sentences so that even the soldier and the condemned man had become attentive; although they could understand nothing, they stopped eating and looked over at the traveler as they chewed.

The answer that the traveler had to give had been clear to him from the start; he had experienced too much in his life to waver here; he was fundamentally honest and was not afraid. But even so, he hesitated now for one breath of air under the gaze of the soldier and the condemned man. Finally, however, he said, as he had to say: "No." The officer blinked his eyes several times, but did not take his eyes off him. "Would you like an explanation?" asked the traveler. The officer nodded silently. "I am an opponent of this procedure," the traveler continued. "Even before you took me into your confidence—I will not betray this confidence, of course, under any circumstances—I had already considered whether I would be justified in intervening against this procedure and whether my intervention could have even the slightest chance of success. It was clear to me who I should turn to first: to the commandant, of course. You made it even clearer for me but without having made my decision any stronger; on the contrary, I am touched by your honest conviction, even if it cannot divert me."

The officer remained silent, turned to the machine, grasped one of the brass poles, and then, leaning back a little, looked up at the Scribe as though he were checking to see if everything was in order. The soldier and the condemned man appeared to have befriended one another; the condemned man was making signs to the soldier, difficult though this was being so tightly strapped in; the soldier bent down toward him; the condemned man whispered something, and the soldier nodded.

The traveler followed the officer and said: "You don't yet know what I intend to do. I will give the commandant my view of the procedure, not in a conference, but in private; I am also not going to stay here long enough to be called into any conference; I will depart early tomorrow morning, or at least board my ship."

It did not appear that the officer had been listening. "So the procedure did not convince you," the officer said to himself and smiled, like an old man smiles at the nonsense of a child and conceals his own true thoughts behind his smile. "The time has come then," he said finally and suddenly looked at the traveler with bright eyes that held some kind of challenge, some kind of call to participate.

"What time has come?" asked the traveler uneasily, but received no answer.

"You are free," said the officer to the condemned man in his own language. The man did not believe it at first. "You're free to go," said the officer. For the first time, the condemned man's face had some real life in it. Was it true? Was it only a whim of the officer that could pass? Had the foreign traveler obtained a pardon for him? What was it? His face seemed to be asking these questions. But not for long. Whatever it may be, he wanted to be truly free, if they were letting him, and began to shake around as much as the Harrow permitted.

"You are breaking my straps," shouted the officer, "be still! We're going to undo them." And he gave the soldier a sign and they set to work. The condemned man laughed quietly to himself without saying a word, turning his face back and forth between the officer to his left and the soldier to the right, not forgetting to include the traveler.

"Pull him out," the officer ordered the soldier. This had to be done with great caution due to the Harrow. Due to his impatience, the condemned man already had several small lacerations on his back.

From now on, however, the officer hardly tended to him anymore. He walked up to the traveler, pulled out the leather folder again, leafed through it, finally found the page he was looking for, and showed it to the traveler. "Read," he said. "I can't," said the traveler. "I told you before, I can't read these papers." "Take a close look at this page," said the officer and stood next to the traveler to read it with him. When this also didn't help, he moved his little finger across the paper at a great height, as though the paper were under no circumstances to be touched, in order to make it easier for the traveler to read. The traveler also made an effort, to at least be able to oblige the officer in this, but it was impossible. The officer then began to spell out the inscription letter by letter, and then read it again cohesively. "'Be just!'—it says. Now you can read it after all," he said. The traveler bent down so far over the paper that the officer moved it farther away out of fear that he would touch it; although the traveler said nothing further, it was clear that he had still not been able to read it. "'Be just!'—it says," repeated the officer. "Perhaps," said the traveler, "I believe that is what it says." "Well good," said the officer, at least partially satisfied, and climbed onto the ladder with the page in hand; he embedded it with great care into the Scribe and appeared to entirely rearrange the machinery; it was very strenuous work and also must have involved very small wheels, for sometimes the officer's head disappeared inside the Scribe completely, so close was his examination of the machinery.

The traveler followed his work continuously from below; his neck became stiff and his eyes hurt from the sky flooded with sunlight. The soldier and the condemned man were only concerned with one another. The condemned man's shirt and trousers, which were already lying in the pit, were pulled out by the soldier with the tip of his bayonet. The shirt was terribly dirty and the condemned man washed it in the bucket of water. As he then put on his shirt and trousers, the soldier as well as the condemned man had to laugh out loud, for his clothing had been cut in two at the back. Perhaps the condemned man believed he was obligated to entertain the soldier, for he turned in circles in his cut up clothes before the soldier, who was squatting on the ground, and striking his knee as he laughed. Even so, they still restrained themselves out of consideration for the gentlemen's presence.

When the officer had finally finished his work above, he surveyed the whole machine with all its parts once again with a smile, slammed the lid of the Scribe shut this time that had until now been open, climbed down, looked into the pit and then at the condemned man, noted with satisfaction that he had retrieved his clothing, went to the bucket of water to wash his hands, recognized the disgusting filth too late, was unhappy that he was unable to wash his hands, finally plunged them—the alternative was inadequate, but he had to resign himself—into the sand, stood up, and began to unbutton the coat of his uniform. In doing so, the two ladies' handkerchiefs that he had forced behind his collar fell into his hands. "Here, you can have your handkerchiefs," he said and threw them to the condemned man. And to the traveler he explained: "Gifts from the ladies."

Despite the apparent haste with which he removed his uniform coat and then undressed completely, he still handled each article of clothing very carefully, even running his fingers over the silver lacing on his tunic and shaking a tassel into place. It hardly suited this diligence, however, that as soon as he finished handling each article, he immediately threw it with a reluctant jerk into the pit. The last thing that remained was his short sword with its sling. He pulled his sword from its sheath, broke it, then gathered everything together—the pieces of the sword, the sheath, and the sling—and threw them away so violently that they clanked together down in the pit.

Now he stood there naked. The traveler bit his lip and said nothing. He knew what was going to happen, but had no right to prevent the officer from doing anything. If the criminal procedure to which the officer was so attached really was so close to being abolished—possibly as a result of the traveler's intervention, to which, for his part, he had felt obligated—then the officer was now acting entirely correctly; in his place, the traveler would not have acted any differently himself.

The soldier and the condemned man understood nothing at first; initially they were not even watching. The condemned man was delighted to have his handkerchiefs back, but could not delight in them for long because the soldier snatched them away with a quick, unpredictable movement. The condemned man then tried in turn to pull the handkerchiefs out from the soldier's belt, behind which they had been tucked, but the soldier was alert. And so they squabbled, half in play. Not until the officer was completely naked did they become attentive. Especially the condemned man seemed struck by the notion of some great reversal. What had happened to him was now happening to the officer. Perhaps it would be carried out like this to the very end. The foreign traveler had probably given the order for it. So it was revenge. Without having suffered to the end, he was being avenged to the end. A broad, inaudible smile now appeared on his face and did not disappear.

The officer, however, had turned to the machine. If it was already clear before how well he understood the machine, it was now almost astounding to see how he handled it and how it obeyed him. His hand only needed to approach the Harrow for it to raise and lower itself several times until it had reached the right position to receive him; he touched only the edge of the

Bed and it already began to vibrate; the felt gag came to meet his mouth, but although one saw that the officer actually did not want to have it, the hesitation lasted only a moment; he soon resigned himself and accepted it. Everything was ready. Only the straps hung down on the sides, but they were obviously unnecessary, as the officer did not need to be strapped in. The condemned man then noticed the loose straps; in his opinion, the execution was not complete if the straps were not fastened. He beckoned eagerly to the soldier, and they ran over to strap the officer in. The officer had already stretched out a foot to kick the crank that was to set the Scribe in motion, then he saw that the two had come, so he pulled his foot back and let himself be strapped in. But now he could no longer reach the crank. Neither the soldier nor the condemned man would find it, and the traveler was determined not to move. It was not necessary; the straps had hardly been fastened when the machine already began to work; the Bed vibrated, the needles danced on his skin, the Harrow hovered up and down. The traveler had already been staring at it for a while when he remembered that a wheel in the Scribe should have been screeching, but everything was silent, not the slightest humming was to be heard.

The machine was working so quietly that it almost became unnoticeable. The traveler looked over at the soldier and the condemned man. The condemned man was the livelier one; everything about the machine interested him; one moment he was bending down, the next he was stretching up; he constantly had his index finger stretched out to show the soldier something. The traveler found it awkward. He was determined to stay here until the end, but he would not have stood the sight of those two for much longer. "Go home," he said. Maybe the soldier would have been willing, but the condemned man perceived the order as outright punishment. He begged imploringly with folded hands to be allowed to stay and as the traveler shook his head refusing to concede, he even knelt down. The traveler saw that orders were futile here, and was about to go over and chase the two away when he heard a noise up in the Scribe. He looked up. Was the cogwheel causing problems after all? But it was something else. The Scribe's lid rose slowly and then opened completely. The teeth of a cogwheel appeared and rose, and soon the entire wheel was visible; it was as though some great force was pressing the Scribe together, so that there was no room left for this wheel. The wheel rolled to the edge of the Scribe, fell to the ground, rolled upright for a while in the sand, and then fell over. But another one was already rising up above, and after it were many more—large, small, and hardly distinguishable ones—and the same thing happened to all of them. One always thought the Scribe must already be empty when a new, especially numerous group appeared, rose, fell to the ground, rolled in the sand, and fell over. This process caused the condemned man to completely forget the traveler's order; the cogwheels thoroughly delighted him. He kept trying to catch one, simultaneously urging the soldier to help him, but withdrew his hand in fright, for the new wheel that immediately followed it frightened him, at least as it first began to roll.

The traveler, on the other hand, was quite disturbed. The machine was obviously collapsing; its quiet operation was an illusion; he had the feeling that he must now see to the officer, who could no longer take care of himself. But while the falling cogwheels were claiming all of his attention, he had failed to oversee the rest of the machine; and now, after the last cogwheel had left the Scribe, he bent over the Harrow to find a new, even more terrible surprise. The Harrow was not writing, but only stabbing; the Bed was not turning the body, but only vibrating and lifting it into the needles. The traveler wanted to intervene, to possibly bring the whole thing to a standstill. This was not the torture, after all, that the officer was aiming for; this was outright murder. He stretched out his hands. The Harrow, however, was already rising with the impaled body to one side, as it usually did only after the twelfth hour. The blood flowed in a hundred streams, not mingled with water; this time, the little water pipes had also failed. And now the final part failed as well; the body did not detach itself from the needles, blood was streaming from it, but it hung above the pit without falling. The Harrow was trying to return to its old position, but as if it realized itself that it was not free of its load, it remained above the pit after all. "Help me, won't you!" shouted the traveler to the soldier and the condemned man, himself grabbing hold of the officer's feet. He wanted to push against the feet on this side, while the other two took hold of the officer's head on the other side, and in this way slowly lift him off the needles. But the two of them could not make up their minds to come; the condemned man even turned his back; the traveler had to go over to them and urge them toward the officer's head by force. In doing so, he saw the corpse's face almost against his will. It was as it had been in life; no sign of the promised redemption was to be found. Whatever all the others had found in the machine, the officer had not found; his lips were firmly pressed together, his eyes were open, had the expression of life, his gaze was calm with conviction, his brow was pierced by the point of the great, iron spike.

When the traveler, followed by the soldier and the condemned man, reached the first houses of the colony, the soldier pointed to one of them and said: "Here is the teahouse."

On the ground floor of one house was a deep, low, cavernous room, its walls and ceiling blackened by smoke. Along its entire width, it was open toward the street. Although the teahouse differed very little from the other houses in the colony, which, aside from the palatial buildings of the commandant's headquarters, were all very dilapidated, it nevertheless gave the traveler the impression of an historical memory, and he felt the power of earlier times. He approached more closely, walking, followed by his companions, among the unoccupied tables that stood on the street in front of the teahouse, and breathed in the cool, dank air that came from within. "The old man is buried here," said the soldier. "He was denied a place in the cemetery by the priest. For a time, they were undecided about where to bury him; in the end they buried him here. Surely the officer didn't tell you anything about that, for of course that was what he was most ashamed of. He even tried several times to dig up the old man at night, but he was always chased away." "Where is the grave?" asked the traveler, who couldn't believe the soldier. At once, both the soldier and the condemned man walked in front of him with outstretched hands pointing to the grave's supposed location. They led the traveler all the way to the back wall, where guests were sitting at a few tables. They were probably dockworkers—strong men with short, shining black beards. All were without coats; their shirts were torn, they were a poor, humiliated people. As the traveler approached, several of them rose, pressed themselves against the wall, and looked at him. "He is a foreigner," they whispered around the traveler. "He wants to see the grave." They pushed one of the tables aside, under which a gravestone could be seen. It was a simple stone, low enough to be hidden under a table. It bore an inscription with very small letters; the traveler had to kneel down in order to read it. It read: "Here rests the old commandant. His followers, who may no longer carry a name, have dug him this grave and raised this stone. There is a prophecy that the commandant will arise after a certain number of years and lead his followers in recapturing the colony. Have faith and wait!" As the traveler had read this and risen, he saw all around him the men standing and smiling as though they had read the inscription with him, found it ridiculous, and challenged him to share their opinion. The traveler acted as though he hadn't noticed, distributed a few coins among them, waited until the table had been pushed over the grave, then left the teahouse and went to the harbor.

The soldier and the condemned man had found acquaintances in the teahouse who had held them back. They must have torn themselves away soon, however, for they were already running behind the traveler when he had only reached the middle of the long flight of stairs leading to the boats. They probably wanted to force the traveler at the last minute to take them with him. While the traveler was down below negotiating the ferry to the steamer with a boatman, the two raced down the stairs in silence, for they did not dare to shout. But by the time they reached the bottom, the traveler was already in the boat, and the boatman was just casting off from the bank. They might still have been able to leap into the boat, but the traveler lifted a heavy, knotted rope from the floor and threatened them with it, thereby preventing them from leaping.

A COUNTRY DOCTOR

I WAS IN A QUANDARY: I HAD AN URGENT JOURNEY AHEAD OF ME;
a gravely ill patient was waiting for me in a village ten miles away;
a great flurry of snow filled the wide space between him and me;
I had a light carriage with large wheels, just the kind entirely
suited to our country roads; wrapped up in my fur coat, my instrument bag in hand, I stood ready to depart in the courtyard; but
the horse was missing. My own horse, as a result of the strain of
this icy winter, had perished the night before; my servant girl was
now running around the village looking for a horse to borrow;
but I knew it was in vain, and, with more and more snow piling
upon me as I became more and more rigid, I stood there uselessly. The girl appeared at the gate, alone, swinging the lantern;
of course, who would lend someone his horse now for such a
journey? I crossed the courtyard once again; I saw no possibility;
absentminded, distressed, I kicked at the battered door of a
pigsty that had been unused for years. It opened and swayed
back and forth on its hinges. Warmth and a smell like that of
horses emerged. A dim stable lantern swung inside from a rope.
A man, crouching in the low shed, showed his open blue-eyed
face. "Shall I harness up?" he asked, crawling out on all fours. I
didn't know what to say and bent down only to see what else was
in the sty. The servant girl stood next to me. "One never knows
what kind of things one has in one's own house," she said and we

both laughed. "Hey brother, hey sister!" called the groom, and two horses—powerful animals with strong flanks—forced themselves through the doorway, which they filled completely, solely with the strength of their twisting haunches, one after another, their legs tucked closely against their bodies, lowering their well-formed heads like camels. But they stand upright at once, with long legs and heavily steaming bodies. "Help him," I say, and the willing girl hurries to pass the groom the harness for the carriage. But hardly had she reached him, when the groom grabs her and thrusts his face against hers. She screams out and seeks refuge with me; on her cheek are two rows of teeth impressed in red. "You brute," I shout angrily, "are you asking for a whipping?" but I remind myself right away that he is a stranger; that I don't know where he is from, and that he is helping me of his own free will, whereas everyone else has failed me. As if he knows of my thoughts, he is not offended by my threat, but, still busied with the horses, he turns around only once to look at me. "Climb in," he says then, and indeed: everything is ready. I have never traveled with such a fine horse and carriage, I realize, and climb in cheerfully. "But I shall drive; you don't know the way," I say. "Certainly," he says, "I am not even coming along; I am staying with Rose." "No," Rose screams and runs into the house, rightly anticipating the inevitability of her fate; I can hear the clanking of the door chain as she fastens it; I can hear the lock catching into place; I can see her as she also extinguishes all lights in the hallway, and rushes further through the rooms, to make it impossible to be found. "You're coming along," I say to the groom, "or I shall forgo the journey, urgent though it is. I wouldn't think of handing over the girl to you as payment for the journey." "Gee up!" he says and claps his hands; and the carriage is swept away like wood in the current. I can still hear the door to my house bursting and splintering under the groom's onslaught, my eyes and ears are then filled with a roaring that equally pervades all my senses. But this is only for a moment; I have arrived already, as though my patient's yard were directly before the gate to my courtyard; the horses are standing calmly; it has stopped snowing; moonlight all around; the patient's parents hurry out of the house; his sister behind them; I am almost lifted out of the carriage; from their confused words, I can gather nothing; in the sickroom, the air is barely breathable; the neglected oven is smoking; I will push the window open; but first I want to see the patient. Gaunt, without fever, not cold, not warm, with empty eyes, shirtless, the boy pulls himself up from his feather-bed, flings his arms around my neck, and whispers in my ear: "Doctor, let me die." I look around; no one heard it; the parents are bent forward in silence awaiting my judgment; the sister has brought a chair for my handbag. I open the bag and search among my instruments; the boy continues to reach out toward me from his bed to remind me of his plea; I take a pair of tweezers, check them in the candlelight, and put them back down. "Well," I think blasphemously, "the gods help in such cases; send the missing horse, add a second one due to urgency, and, as though that weren't enough, even donate a groom." Only now did I remember Rose; what can I do, how can I save her, how can I pull her from beneath that groom, ten miles away from her, with uncontrollable horses in front of my carriage? These horses, who have now loosened their straps somehow, push the windows open, I don't know how, from the outside; each one sticking its head through a window, observing the patient, undeterred by the family's cries. "I'll drive back right away," I think, as though the horses were summoning me for the journey, but I allow the sister, who believes that I am dazed by the heat, to take my fur coat. I am provided with a glass of rum; the old man pats me on the shoulder, as though surrendering his treasure justifies this familiarity. I shake my head; I become nauseous in the old man's circle of thought; this is my only reason for refusing to drink. The mother is standing by the bed and beckoning me; I follow her and, while one horse whinnies loudly at the ceiling, I lay my head on the chest of the boy, who shivers beneath my wet beard. What I know is confirmed: the boy is healthy; his circulation is somewhat weak, soaked in coffee by his doting mother, but healthy and best turned out of bed with a shove. I am no world reformer and let him lie. I am appointed by the district authorities and fulfill my duty to the limit; up to where it is almost too much. Poorly paid, I am nevertheless generous and willing to help the poor. I must take care of Rose and then the boy may be right and I too will wish to die. What am I doing here in this endless winter! My horse has perished and there is no one in the village who will lend me his. I have to drag my team out of the pigsty; had they not happened to be horses, I'd have to travel with swine. That's the way it is. And I nod to the family. They know nothing about it and if they did, they wouldn't believe it. Writing prescriptions is easy, but otherwise it is difficult to communicate with people. Well, my visit would be over at this point; once again I have been troubled unnecessarily, I am used to that; the entire district torments me with the help of the night bell; but that I also have to hand over Rose this time—that lovely girl, who has lived in my house for years, whom I have hardly noticed—this sacrifice is too great and I must somehow figure it out in my head temporarily with subtleness in order to avoid taking it out on this family, who cannot give Rose back to me with the best will in the world. But as I close my handbag and wave for my fur coat, the family stands together; the father sniffing the rum glass in his hand; the mother, whom I have probably disappointed—well, what do these people expect?—tearfully biting her lips; and the sister waving a blood-soaked towel. I am somehow possibly willing to admit that the boy may be sick after all. I go to him; he welcomes me with a smile, as though I were bringing him the heartiest of soups,—oh, now both horses are whinnying; perhaps the noise, ordained by a higher authority, is supposed to make the examination easier—and now I find: yes, the boy is sick. In his right side, in the area of his hips, a wound the size of the palm of my hand has opened. Rose-colored, in many different shades; dark in the depths, growing light towards the edges; softly granulated, with irregularly accumulating blood, open like a mine at the pithead. So it looks from a distance. Up close, a complication also becomes apparent. Who can look at this without whistling softly? Worms, as thick and long as my little finger, rosy on their own and also splattered with blood, hold tight on the inside of the wound, with little white heads and many little legs, squirming towards the light. Poor boy, there is nothing to be done for you. I have discovered your great wound; this blossom in your side will destroy you. The family is happy, they see me being active; the sister tells the mother about it, the mother tells the father, the father tells several guests, who come in through the moonshine of the open door, on the tips of their toes, balancing with outstretched arms. "Will you save me?" the boy whispers sobbing, entirely dazed by the life in his wound. That's what the people in my area are like; always demanding the impossible of their doctor. They have lost their old faith; the pastor sits at home and picks his vestments apart, one by one; but the doctor is supposed to accomplish everything with his soft surgeon's hand. Well, as they please: I did not volunteer; if you are using me for holy purposes, I'll even allow that to happen to me; what more do I want, old country doctor, robbed of my servant girl! And they come, the family and the village elders, and undress me; a school choir with their teacher at the head stands before the house and sings an utterly simple melody to the text:

> "Undress him, then he will heal,
> And should he not heal, then kill him!
> 'Tis only a doctor, 'tis only a doctor."

Then I am undressed and, with my fingers in my beard and my head tilted, I take a calm look at the people. I am thoroughly composed and above them all, and I also remain so, although it is no help to me, for they are now taking me by the head and feet and carrying me to the bed. They lay me down by the wall on the side of the wound. Then they all leave the room; the door is closed; the singing falls silent; clouds move in front of the moon; warm are the bedclothes around me; the horseheads sway like shadows in the open windows. "You know," said a voice in my ear, "I have very little faith in you. You were only thrown off here, after all; didn't come here on your own feet. Instead of helping, you are crowding me in my deathbed. I'd love nothing better than to scratch your eyes out." "That's right," I said, "it's a disgrace. But I'm a doctor. What am I to do? Believe me, it's not easy for me either." "Am I supposed to be content with that excuse? Oh, I suppose I have to be. I always have to content myself. I came into the world with a fine wound; that was all I was given." "My young friend," I say, "your mistake is that you are lacking an overview. I, who have been in all sickrooms far and wide, can tell you: your wound is not all that bad. Made at an acute angle with two strokes of an ax. Many offer their sides and can hardly hear the ax in the forest, let alone that it is coming closer to them." "Is it really so, or are you deceiving me in my fever?" "It is really so; take the district doctor's word of honor with you on your way." And he takes it and grows still. But now it is time to think of saving myself. The horses are still standing faithfully in their places. Clothing, fur coat, and bag are quickly gathered together; I don't want to hold myself up by getting dressed; if the horses are to race like they did on the journey here, I would jump, so to speak, from this bed into my own. Obediently one horse withdraws from the window; I throw the bundle into the carriage; the fur coat flies too far, catching on a hook by only one sleeve. Good enough. I swing myself onto the horse. The straps dragging loosely, one horse hardly connected to the other, the carriage sways behind them, the fur coat trailing in the snow. "Gee up!" I say, but they do not gallop; we cross the snow desert as slowly as old men; for a long time, the children's new, but mistaken song sounds after us:

> "Rejoice, ye patients, rejoice,
>   The doctor's been laid in bed with you!"

I'll never get home this way; my flourishing practice is lost; a successor is stealing from me, but to no avail, for he cannot replace me; in my house, that revolting groom is raging; Rose is his victim; I can't bear to think of it. Naked, exposed to the frost of this ill-fated age, with an earthly carriage and unearthly horses, I, an old man, roam about. My fur coat is hanging on the back of the carriage, but I cannot reach it, and no one in that agile mob of patients lifts a finger. Betrayed! Betrayed! Once you have followed the false toll of the night bell—it can never be put right.

A HUNGER ARTIST

IN RECENT DECADES, INTEREST IN HUNGER ARTISTS HAS DECLINED
significantly. Whereas it was once profitable to organize large performances of this kind on your own, today it is entirely impossible.
Those were different times. Then, entire cities paid attention to
the hunger artist; the interest grew from hunger-day to hunger-day;
everyone wanted to see the hunger artist at least once a day; on
the later days, there were subscribers who sat before the little
wire cage for days; there were even visits at night, by torchlight to
enhance the effect; on pleasant days the cage was brought out-
doors and then it was especially the children that the hunger
artist was shown to; whereas he was often just an amusement to
the adults, who took part in it because it was fashionable, the
children would watch in amazement, with open mouths, holding
one another's hands for safety, as he sat on scattered straw,
spurning even a chair, pale, in a black leotard, with starkly jutting
ribs, nodding once politely before answering questions with a
strained smile, also stretching his arm through the bars to allow
his leanness to be felt, before sinking entirely into himself again,
concerning himself with no one, not even with the striking of the
clock, the only piece of furniture in his cage, that was so important to him, but merely staring ahead with his eyes almost closed,
and sipping now and then from a tiny glass of water to moisten
his lips.

Apart from the changing spectators, permanent watchmen, selected by the audience, were also there, often butchers, strangely enough, who, always three at a time, had the task of observing the hunger artist day and night to make sure that he didn't consume food in some secret way. But it was simply a formality, introduced to appease the masses, for insiders knew that the hunger artist would never, under any circumstances, not even under duress, eat the slightest thing during the hunger period; the honor of his art forbade it. Of course, not every watchman could fathom this; sometimes groups of night watchmen were formed who carried out their duty very laxly; they intentionally sat together in a distant corner and delved into a card game with the apparent intention of allowing the hunger artist a little refreshment, which he, in their opinion, could remove from some secret stock. Nothing was more torturous to the hunger artist than such watchmen; they made him miserable; they made the hungering dreadfully difficult. Sometimes he overcame his weakness and sang during their watch, as long as he could bear it to show the people how unjustly they were suspecting him. But that didn't help much; they were then only surprised at his ability to eat even while singing. He much preferred the watchmen who sat close by the cage, who, because they were not satisfied with the dim nighttime lighting in the hall, illuminated him with the electric flashlights that the impresario had provided them with. The glaring light didn't bother him; he couldn't sleep at all in any case, and he was always able to doze a little with any lighting and at any hour, even in an overfilled, clamorous hall. He was very content to spend the entire night with such watchmen entirely without sleep; he was content to joke with them, to tell them stories from his life as a traveler, to then listen to their stories, everything just to keep them awake, to be able to show them again and again that he had nothing edible in his cage and that he was hungering, like none of them could. But he was the happiest when morning came and they were served a lavish breakfast at his expense, on which they flung themselves with the appetites of healthy men after a hard night of keeping watch. Indeed, there were even people who wanted to see this breakfast as an improper manipulation of the watchmen, but that was going rather too far, and when they were asked to take on the night watch merely for the sake of the cause without breakfast, they made themselves scarce, but they still kept their suspicions.

Indeed, this was among those suspicions that are an inextricable part of hungering. No one, of course, was capable of continuously spending all their days and nights with the hunger artist as watchman; so no one could know from their own experience whether the hungering had truly been without interruption or fault; only the hunger artist himself could know this, so at the same time he could be the only fully satisfied spectator of his own hungering. But there was another reason that he was never satisfied; perhaps it was not the hungering at all that had made him so emaciated that many, to their regret, had to stay away from the performances because they could not bear the sight of him, but rather that he was so emaciated out of his own dissatisfaction with himself. He alone, however, knew what no insider knew: how easy it was to hunger. It was the easiest thing in the world. He made no secret of it but no one believed him; at best they thought him to be modest, but mostly they thought he craved publicity or was even a swindler, for whom hungering was indeed easy because he knew how to make it easy, and then even had the nerve to half admit it. He had to accept all of this, had become accustomed to it over the years, but on the inside this dissatisfaction always gnawed at him, and never, after no hunger period—this they had to grant him—had he left the cage voluntarily. The impresario had determined that the maximum amount of time for hungering was forty days; he never allowed hungering to go beyond that, not even in the great cities, and this was for a good reason. From experience, he knew that a city's interest could be stirred up for about forty days by gradually increasing advertisements, but then the public would lose interest and a significant decrease in popularity was noted; in this respect of course, there were small differences between one town or country and another, but as a rule, forty days was the maximum time. So on the fortieth day when the door to the flower-crowned cage was opened, an ecstatic audience filled the amphitheater, a military band played, two doctors entered the cage to carry out the necessary measurements on the hunger artist, the results were announced to the hall through a megaphone, and finally, two young ladies, delighted that their names were drawn, came and attempted to lead the hunger artist out of the cage and down a few steps where, on a little table, a carefully selected invalid's meal had been served. And at this moment, the hunger artist always resisted. Although he voluntarily laid his bony arms in the helpfully outstretched hands of the ladies who were bending down toward him, he would not stand up. Why stop now after forty days? He would have held out longer, for an unlimitedly long time; why stop now, when he was doing his best, indeed not even his best, hungering? Why did they want to rob him of the fame of continuing to hunger, of not only becoming the greatest hunger artist of all time, which indeed he probably already was, but also of surpassing himself beyond all comprehension, for he felt no limits in his ability to hunger. Why had this crowd, who pretended to admire him so much, have so little patience with him; if he could continue to endure the hunger, why couldn't they endure it? He was also tired; he was sitting comfortably in the straw and was now supposed to stand up straight and tall and walk to the food, the very thought of which made him nauseous, the expression of which he refrained from demonstrating out of consideration for the ladies. And he looked up into the eyes of these ladies, who appeared to be so kind, but in reality were so cruel, and shook his overly heavy head on his weak neck. But then there happened what always happened. The impresario came forward, raised his arms silently—the music made it impossible to speak—above the hunger artist as though he were inviting heaven to behold his work here, this pitiful martyr, which the hunger artist certainly was, only in an entirely different sense; he grasped the hunger artist around his thin waist, doing so with exaggerated caution to show what a frail thing he had to do with here; and he handed him over—not without secretly shaking him a little, so that the hunger artist swayed uncontrollably with his legs and torso—to the ladies who had meanwhile become deathly pale. Now the hunger artist endured everything; his head lay on his chest, as though it had rolled away and was mysteriously lingering there; his body was hollowed out; his legs, in an instinct of self-preservation, were tightly pressed together, but they still scraped along the ground as if it were not the real one and the real one were still being sought; and the entire, albeit very slight, weight of his body rested on one of the ladies, who, seeking help and panting—this was not how she had imagined her honorary post—first craned her neck as far as possible to keep her face at least from touching the hunger artist, but then, because this didn't work, and her more fortunate companion did not come to her aid but contented herself with carrying the hunger artist's hand, that little bundle of bones, she burst into tears amid rapturous laughter in the hall and had to be relieved by an attendant who had been positioned there for this purpose. Then came the food, a little of which the impresario had managed to pour into the hunger artist's mouth during a spell of unconscious half-sleep as he chatted cheerfully in an attempt to draw attention away from the hunger artist's condition; then a toast was raised to the public, which, as the impresario claimed, was prompted by something the hunger artist had whispered into his ear; the orchestra reinforced everything with a great fanfare, people dispersed, and no one was justified in being dissatisfied with what they had seen, no one, only the hunger artist, always only the hunger artist.

He lived this way, with regular short rest intervals, for many years, in apparent glory, honored by the world, but mostly in a miserable mood, which was made even more miserable due to the fact that no one knew how to take him seriously. But what were they to console him with? What more could he wish for? And if some good-natured person turned up who felt sorry for him and tried to explain that his sadness was probably due to the hunger, it could happen, especially at an advanced stage in hungering process, that the hunger artist responded with an outburst of anger and, to everyone's horror, by starting to shake at the bars of his cage like an animal. But for such fits, the impresario had a means of punishment that he was fond of using. He would make excuses for the hunger artist before the assembled audience, admitting that the irritability, which was induced by the hunger and not readily comprehensible for satiated people, excused the hunger artist's behavior; in this context, he would then refer to the hunger artist's claim that he was able to hunger much longer than he hungered now, which could also be explained in this way; he would praise the noble aspiration, the good will, the great self-denial that were surely also contained in this assertion; but then he would attempt to refute the assertion by simply displaying photographs, which were simultaneously being sold, for in the pictures, one saw the hunger artist on his fortieth day of hungering, in bed, almost extinguished by exhaustion. This distortion of the truth, well known to the hunger artist but nevertheless always unnerving, was too much for him. The consequence of prematurely ending the hungering was being portrayed here as the cause! Combating this ignorance, this world of ignorance, was impossible. Again and again he had listened eagerly and in good faith to the impresario, clinging to the bars, but every time the photographs appeared, he would let go of the bars, sink back into the straw, and the reassured public could come forward again and observe him.

When those who witnessed such scenes thought back to them a few years later, they often failed to comprehend themselves. For in the meantime, the aforementioned change had set in; it happened almost abruptly; the reasons may have been deeper, but who could be bothered to discover them; in any case, one day the pampered hunger artist found himself abandoned by the pleasure-seeking crowd, which preferred to flock to other spectacles. The impresario sped through half of Europe once more to see if here or there the old interest might not be rediscovered; all in vain; as if by some secret agreement, an outright aversion to hungering displays had developed everywhere. Of course, this could not really have come about so abruptly, and in hindsight, they now recalled some warning signs that were neither heeded nor suppressed sufficiently in the throes of success, but it was now too late to do anything about it. Although the time for hungering was sure to come again, this was no consolation to those living now. So what was the hunger artist to do? He who had been celebrated by thousands could not show himself in show booths at little village fairs, and the hunger artist was not only too old, but also too fanatically devoted to hungering to learn a new profession. So he dismissed the impresario, companion of an unparalleled career, and began an engagement with a large circus; to spare his own sensibility, he did not even look at the terms of contract.

A large circus, constantly replacing and supplementing its countless number of people and animals, can always use anyone at any time, even a hunger artist, with his modest demands, of course; and besides, it was not only the hunger artist who was being engaged, but also his old famous name. In fact, one could not even say, given the peculiarity of this art form, which had not diminished with increasing age, that a worn-out artist, who was no longer at the height of his ability, was trying to take refuge in a quiet circus job. On the contrary, the hunger artist ensured that he hungered just as well as before, which was entirely credible; indeed, he even claimed that if they would let him have his way—and this they promised without further ado—he would actually now, for the first time, give the world cause for justified astonishment; a claim that, in consideration of the sentiment of the times, which the hunger artist in his eagerness easily forgot, only made the professionals smile.

Deep down, however, the hunger artist had not lost his sense of the real situation and took it for granted that he would not be placed with his cage as a highlight in the middle of the ring, but outside in a quite accessible spot near the stalls. Large, colorfully painted signs framed the cage announcing what was to be seen there. When the audience surged to the stalls during the shows' intervals to see the animals, they would almost inevitably pass by the hunger artist and pause there for a moment; they might have spent more time with him if the throng of people, pushing through the narrow path and not understanding this stop on the way to the eagerly awaited stalls, had not made longer, peaceful observation impossible. And that was the reason why the hunger artist, who had of course been looking forward to these visiting hours as the main achievement of his life, began instead to shrink from them. In the early days, he could hardly wait for the intervals; he had looked forward to the thronging masses with delight until only too soon—even the most stubborn, almost conscious self-deception could not withstand his experience—he became convinced that most of them were, at least according to their actions, again and again, without exception, nothing more than stall visitors. And this view of them from a distance still remained the best one. For when they came all the way up to him, he was immediately surrounded by the shouts and curses of the groups that were constantly shifting: those who wanted to have a look at him in peace—the hunger artist soon found these to be the more embarrassing ones—and who did so not out of understanding, but just to be whimsical and stubborn; and the others, who primarily wanted to go to the stalls. Once the big horde had passed, the stragglers came, but although these were no longer prevented from stopping as long as they liked, they hurried past with long strides, almost without a side glance in order to get to the animals in time. And it was a none-too-frequent stroke of luck when a father came with his children, pointing at the hunger artist with his finger, explaining extensively what it was all about, talking about earlier times when he had been to similar, but incomparably more impressive performances; and although the children, lacking sufficient education from school and life, were still incapable of understanding—what was hunger to them?—they still revealed something of the new, impending, more merciful times in the sparkle of their exploring eyes. Perhaps, the hunger artist would sometimes tell himself, everything would be a bit better if he were not located so close to the stalls. This made the choice too easy for people, not to mention the stench from the stalls, the restlessness of the animals at night, the raw pieces of meat carried by for the beasts of prey, the howling at feeding time, which offended and continuously depressed him. But he did not dare to approach the management; he had the animals to thank, after all, for the crowd of visitors, among which here and there one could be found who was meant for him. And who knew where they would hide him if he were to remind them of his existence and thereby also that he was, in fact, nothing more than a hindrance on the way to the stalls.

A small hindrance, indeed, a diminishingly small hindrance. People became familiar with the peculiarity of requesting in this day and age that attention be paid to a hunger artist, and with this familiarity, his verdict had been delivered. He wanted to hunger as well as he could, and he did it, but nothing could save him anymore, people passed him by. Just try to explain to someone the art of hungering! To someone who does not feel it, it cannot be made conceivable. The beautiful signs grew dirty and incomprehensible; they were torn down; no one thought of replacing them; the little board displaying the number of hungering days completed, which had initially been carefully renewed on a daily basis, had long since remained unchanged, for after the first weeks the attendants had even become tired of this small task; and so the hunger artist continued to hunger, just as he had once dreamt of, and he succeeded effortlessly, just as he had predicted back then, but no one was counting the days; no one, not even the hunger artist himself knew how great his achievement already was, and his heart became heavy. And if once in a while someone strolled idly by, stopping to make fun of the old number and speak of fraud, it was in this sense the stupidest lie that apathy and innate malice could invent, for it was not the hunger artist who was cheating—he worked honestly—but the world that was cheating him of his reward.

But many more days passed, and then that too came to an end. One day an overseer noticed the cage and asked the attendants why this perfectly good cage had been left standing here unused with rotten straw inside; no one knew, until someone, with the help of the little board, remembered the hunger artist. They stirred up the straw with sticks and found the hunger artist inside. "Are you still hungering?" asked the overseer. "When will you finally stop?"

"Please forgive me, everyone," whispered the hunger artist; only the overseer, who was holding his ear to the cage, understood him. "Certainly," said the overseer, pointing his finger to his forehead as a sign to the personnel indicating the hunger artist's condition, "We forgive you." "I always wanted you to admire my hungering," said the hunger artist. "And we do admire it," the overseer said obligingly. "But you shouldn't admire it," said the hunger artist. "Well then we don't admire it," the overseer said. "And why shouldn't we admire it?" "Because I have to hunger; I can't help it," said the hunger artist. "Well, you don't say," said the overseer, "why can't you help it?" "Because," said the hunger artist, raising his frail head slightly and speaking with lips puckered as if for kissing right into the overseer's ear so that nothing was lost, "because I could not find food that I liked. Had I found it, believe me, I would have not have caused a scene, and would have eaten my fill like you and everyone." These were his last words, but in his broken eyes remained the firm, though no longer proud, conviction that he was continuing to hunger.

"Now put this in order," said the overseer, and the hunger artist was buried along with the straw. Into the cage they put a young panther. It was refreshing for even the dullest of senses to see this wild animal throwing itself about the cage that had been desolate for so long. It lacked for nothing. The food, which it liked, was brought to him by the keepers without lengthy deliberation; it didn't even seem to miss freedom; this noble body, equipped almost to the bursting point with all that he needed, also seemed to carry freedom around with it; it seemed to be hiding somewhere in its teeth; and its joy in life came with such strong fervor from his throat that it was not easy for the spectators to withstand it. But they endured it, crowded around the cage, and didn't want to stir from their spot at all.

A Report to an Academy

Honored Gentlemen of the Academy!

You have done me the honor of inviting me to submit a report about my past life as an ape.

In this sense, I am unfortunately not able to fulfill your request. Nearly five years separate me from apedom, a period of time that is perhaps short measured by the calendar, but infinitely long to gallop through as I have done, accompanied for stretches by excellent humans, advice, applause, and orchestral music, but basically alone, for the company remained—to maintain the metaphor—far behind the barrier. This achievement would have been impossible had I wished to stubbornly hold on to my origins, to memories of my youth. In fact, renouncing all stubbornness was the supreme commandment that I imposed upon myself; I, free ape, submitted to this yoke. As a result, the memories closed themselves off to me more and more. Although I initially would have been free to return—had the humans permitted it—through the vast gateway formed by the sky above the earth, this gate became lower and narrower, the more my development was compelled forward. I felt more comfortable and determined in the human world; the storm that blew after me from my past subdued; today, it is merely a draft of air that cools my heels; and the hole in the distance that it comes through, and through which I once came, has grown so small that, even if I had sufficient strength and will to walk back there, I would have to flay the skin from my body to get through. To speak frankly, however much I like to choose metaphors for these things, to speak frankly: your apedom, Gentlemen, insofar as you have something like that in your background, cannot be further removed from you than mine. But everyone who walks here upon earth feels a tickle at their heel: the little chimpanzee and the great Achilles alike.

However, in a limited sense I can maybe answer your question after all, and I even do so with great pleasure. The first thing that I learned was to shake hands; a handshake shows frankness; I hope that today, now that I am standing at the height of my career, the first handshake may also be followed by frank words. They will not contribute anything essentially new to the Academy, and will fall far short of that which has been requested of me and which I am unable to say with the best will in the world—all the same, it should indicate the guideline according to which a former ape entered the human world and established himself there. Of course, I would certainly not mention the trivialities that follow if I were not completely sure of myself, and if my position on all of the great variety theater stages of the civilized world had not been established to the point of invincibility.

I am from the Gold Coast. For the story of how I was captured, I must rely on the reports of others. A hunting expedition from the Hagenbeck firm—I have since emptied many a good bottle of red wine with its leader, by the way—was lying in wait on the raised hide in the bankside brush when I ran down amongst a troop of apes in the evening to the watering hole. They shot; I was the only one to be hit; I took two bullets.

One in the cheek—that one was slight, but it left a large, bare red scar, that earned me the name of Red Peter, a disgusting, entirely inappropriate name, literally invented by an ape, as if the red patch on my cheek were the only thing distinguishing me from Peter, the performing ape, well known here and there, who kicked the bucket not long ago. This as a side note.

The second bullet struck me beneath the hip. It was severe; it's the reason that I still have a slight limp. I recently read an article by one of the ten thousand windbags who go on about me in the newspapers: my ape nature is not yet entirely suppressed; his proof is that I like to remove my trousers when guests come to show them where the bullet entered. Each little finger on that fellow's writing hand should be shot off one by one. As for me, I may remove my trousers before whomever I please; there is nothing to be found there other than a well-groomed coat and the scar left by—let us use for this specific purpose a specific word, which is not to be misunderstood—the scar left by an outrageous gunshot. Everything has been brought to light; there is nothing to hide; if it is a matter of truth, everyone of noble mind discards their finest manners. On the other hand, if that writer were to remove his trousers when visitors came, this would have an entirely different appearance, and I am willing to accept it as a sign of reason that he does not do so. But in return, he can get off my back with his sensitive feelings.

After those shots I woke up—and here is where my own memories gradually begin—in a cage on the steerage of the Hagenbeck steamer. It was not a four-sided wire cage; rather there were three sides fastened to a crate; so the crate formed the fourth wall. The whole thing was too low for me to stand up straight and too narrow for me to sit down. I therefore crouched with turned-in, continuously trembling knees, and, because I probably didn't want to see anyone at first and only wanted to be in the dark, I turned to face the crate while the bars behind me cut into my flesh. It is considered beneficial to keep wild animals like this initially, and, after my experience, I cannot deny today that this is, in a human sense, truly the case.

But I didn't think of that then. For the first time in my life, I had no way out; or no direct one, at least; direct before me was a crate, board fit tightly into board. True, there was a gap that ran through the boards, which I greeted with a blissful howl of ignorance when I first discovered it, but this gap was not nearly wide enough to even stick my tail through, and could not even be widened with all my ape strength.

I was later told that I had made unusually little noise, which led them to conclude that I was sure to die soon or, if I survived the first critical period, to become quite trainable. I survived this period. Muffled sobbing, painful flea-hunting, tiredly licking a coconut, banging the crate with my skull, sticking out my tongue if someone came near—these were the first activities in my new life. In all of it, however, only the one feeling: no way out. Of course, I can only retrace the apelike feelings I had back then with human words and distort them as a result, but even though I can no longer reach the old ape truth, it lies at least in the direction of my description. Of this there is no doubt.

I had had so many ways out until then, and now I had none. I was trapped. If I had been nailed down, my freedom would not have grown any smaller. Why is that? Scratch open the flesh between your toes and you won't find the reason. Press yourself against the bar behind you until it nearly divides you in two and you won't find the reason. I had no way out, but I had to make one for myself, for I could not live without it. Always against that crate—I would inevitably have done myself in. But at Hagenbeck, apes belong against the crate—so I stopped being an ape. A nice, clear line of thought that I must have somehow come up with in my belly, for apes think with their bellies.

I'm afraid that you do not entirely understand what I mean by a way out. I use this term in its fullest and most common sense. I deliberately do not say freedom. I do not mean that great feeling of freedom on all sides. I may have known it as an ape, and I have known humans who long for it. But in my case, I demanded freedom neither then nor today. By the way: humans deceive themselves all too often with freedom. And just as freedom counts among the noblest of feelings, the corresponding deception is also among the noblest. Often, before my performances in the variety shows, I have observed a pair of performers on their trapeze high up under the ceiling. They swung, they swayed, they sprung, they glided into one another's arms, one carried the other by the hair with his teeth. "This too is human freedom," I thought, "arbitrary movement." What a mockery of sacred nature! No structure could withstand the laughter of apedom at this sight.

No, it was not freedom that I wanted. Only a way out; to the right, left, wherever; I made no other demands; even if the way out were only to be a deception; the demand was small, the deception would not be greater. Move forward, move forward! To not always stand here with raised arms pressed against a crate.

Today I see it clearly: without the greatest inner calm I would never have been able to escape. And I quite possibly owe everything that I have become to the calmness that overcame me after the first days there on the ship. The calmness, in turn, I probably owed to the people on the ship.

They are good people, in spite of everything. Even today I am glad to remember the sound of their heavy footsteps, which used to resonate in my half-sleep. They were in the habit of tackling everything extremely slowly. If one of them wanted to rub his eyes, he raised his hand like a hanging weight. Their jokes were crude, but affectionate. Their laughter was always mixed with a dangerous-sounding but meaningless cough. They always had something in their mouths to spit out, and where they spit it out was irrelevant. They always complained that my fleas jumped over onto them; however they were never seriously angry with me because of it; they knew, after all, that fleas thrived in my fur and that fleas are jumpers; they accepted it. When they were off-duty, some of them sometimes sat down in a semicircle around me; hardly spoke, but simply grunted at one another; smoked a pipe, stretched out on crates; slapped their knees as soon as I made the slightest movement; and here and there one of them would take a stick and tickle me where I liked it. If I were invited today to take part in a voyage on that ship, I would be certain to refuse the invitation, but it is just as certain that there are not only ugly memories from the steerage that I could dwell on.

The calmness that I acquired among these people is primarily what held me back from any attempt to escape. From today's perspective, it seems that I had at least sensed that I must find a way out if I wanted to live, but that this way out was not to be achieved through flight. I can't recall whether flight was possible, but I believe it was; for an ape, flight should always be possible. With the current state of my teeth, I already have to be careful with ordinary nut cracking, but back then, I could have managed to gradually bite through the lock on the door. I didn't do so. What would have been gained by it? I would have been recaptured as soon as I had stuck my head out, and locked up in an even worse cage; or I would have fled unnoticed to other animals, such as the giant snakes opposite me, and breathed my last breath in their embrace; or I would have succeeded in stealing up on deck and jumping overboard, after which I would have rocked for a little while on the ocean and drowned. Acts of desperation. I did not calculate in such a human fashion, but under the influence of my surroundings, I behaved as though I had calculated.

I wasn't calculating, but I was observing calmly. I watched these people going back and forth, always the same faces, the same movements; often it seemed that there was only one of them. So this human, or these humans, walked without disturbance. A great purpose dawned upon me. No one promised me that the gate would be lifted if I were to become like them. Such promises, apparently impossible to fulfill, are not made. But if they are fulfilled, the promises will also appear retrospectively in exactly the place where one had previously looked for them in vain. Now there was nothing about these humans that I found particularly appealing. Had I been a believer in the freedom I mentioned, I would certainly have preferred the ocean to the way out that presented itself to me in these humans' dull eyes. But in any case, I had already been observing them for a long time before I began thinking of such things; indeed it was the accumulated observations that urged me in this particular direction to begin with.

It was so easy to imitate these people. I could already spit in the very first days. Then we spat in each other's faces; the difference was only that while I licked my face clean afterwards, they didn't lick theirs. Soon I was smoking the pipe like an old man; if I then also pressed my thumb into the bowl, the whole steerage cheered; only it was a long time before I understood the difference between a pipe that was empty and one that was filled.

The brandy bottle gave the most trouble. The smell tormented me; I forced myself with all my strength, but weeks passed before I overcame myself. Strangely enough, people took this inner struggle more seriously than anything else about me. I don't distinguish between people even in my memories, but there was one who came again and again, alone or with comrades, by day, by night, at all kinds of hours; he positioned himself before me with a bottle and gave me lessons. He didn't understand me; he wanted to solve the mystery of my being. He slowly uncorked the bottle and then looked at me to see if I had understood; I admit, I always looked at him with wild, excessive attentiveness; such a human student could not find a human teacher on the whole round earth. Once the bottle is uncorked, he raises it to his mouth; I follow him with my eyes right into his gullet; he nods, satisfied with me, and sets the bottle to his lips; I, delighted by gradual understanding, screech as I scratch myself up and down and wherever it happens to itch; he is pleased, raises the bottle and takes a drink; I, impatient and desperate to emulate him, soil myself in my cage, which again gratifies him enormously; and then, holding the bottle far from himself and raising it up again with a swing and leaning back with didactic exaggeration, he empties it in one draught. I, exhausted from far too much eagerness, can't follow any longer and hang weakly on the bars while he ends the theoretical lesson by stroking his belly and grinning.

Now the practical exercises begin. Am I not already far too exhausted by the theoretical part? Certainly, far too exhausted. This is part of my destiny. And yet I reach as best I can for the bottle that is extended to me; uncork it trembling; with my success, new strength gradually emerges; I raise the bottle, hardly to be distinguished from the original; put it to my lips—and throw it with disgust, with disgust, although it is empty and only filled with the smell, throw it with disgust to the floor. To the sorrow of my teacher, to the greater sorrow of myself; it is no conciliation for him or myself that, after throwing the bottle away, I don't forget to stroke my belly magnificently, grinning as I do so.

All too often, this was how the lesson went. And to my teacher's credit, he wasn't angry with me; true, he did sometimes hold his burning pipe to my fur until it started to smolder somewhere that was difficult for me to reach, but then he put it out again himself with his huge, kind hand; he wasn't angry with me; he realized that we were fighting on the same side against my ape nature and that I had the more difficult part.

But what a victory it was for him as well as for me when one evening, in front of a large circle of spectators—perhaps it was a celebration, a gramophone was playing, an officer was walking among the people—when on this evening, unnoticed at the moment, I grabbed a brandy bottle that had accidently been forgotten in front of my cage, uncorked it as I had been taught amid the growing attention of the company, put it to my mouth, and, without hesitation, without turning up my mouth, like an expert drinker, with eyes rolling and throat swashing, really and truly emptied the bottle; threw the bottle down, no longer in desperation but as an artist; indeed, forgetting to stroke my belly. But for that, because I couldn't help it, because I felt an urge, because my senses were surging, I called out a brief "Hello!" breaking out into human speech, sprang with this call into the human community, and its echo—"Listen, he's speaking!"—felt like a kiss on my entire sweat-drenched body.

I repeat: I did not find it appealing to imitate humans; I imitated them because I was looking for a way out, for no other reason. And little had been achieved by that victory. My voice failed me immediately; it only came back months later; the aversion to the brandy bottle returned even stronger. My course, however, had been set once and for all.

When I was handed over to my first trainer in Hamburg, I quickly realized that two possibilities were available to me: the Zoological Gardens or variety theater. I didn't hesitate. I told myself: make every effort to get to the variety theater; that is the way out; Zoological Garden is only a new cage; if you are put in that, you are lost.

And I learned, gentlemen. Oh, you learn when you must; you learn when you want a way out; you learn ruthlessly. You oversee yourself with the whip; you lash yourself at the slightest resistance. My ape nature hurtled out of me, rolling over itself and away, so that my first teacher almost became apish himself, soon had to give up our lessons and be brought into a mental institution. Fortunately he came out again soon.

But I used up many teachers, indeed several teachers at the same time. When I had become more sure of my abilities, when the public followed my progress, when my future began to look bright, I hired my own teachers, had them situated in five adjoining rooms, and studied with all of them simultaneously by constantly jumping from one room to the next.

The progress I made! Those rays of knowledge penetrating my awakening brain from all sides! I won't deny that it delighted me. But I also admit that I did not overestimate it, not even then, much less now. With an exertion that has not yet been repeated anywhere on earth, I have attained the average education of a European. In itself, that would perhaps be nothing, but it is something after all insofar as it helped me out of the cage and provided me with this particular way out, this human way out. There is an excellent German figure of speech: to disappear into the bushes; this I have done, I have disappeared into the bushes. I had no other way, assuming always that freedom was not an option.

When I review my development and its purpose thus far, I neither complain nor am I satisfied. My hands in my pockets, the bottle of wine on the table, I half lie, half sit in my rocking chair and look out the window. If a visitor comes, I receive him with propriety. My impresario sits in the anteroom; if I ring, he comes and listens to what I have to say. I almost always have performances in the evenings, and I could hardly be more successful. When I come home late at night from banquets, from scientific societies, from social gatherings, a small half-trained chimpanzee awaits me and I indulge myself in the apelike fashion. I do not wish to see her by day; you see, she has the insanity of the confused, trained animal in her eyes; I am the only one who sees it, and I find it unbearable.

All in all, I have in any case achieved what I wanted to achieve. You can't say it wasn't worth the effort. Otherwise, I don't want any human judgment; all I want is to spread insight; I am only reporting; to you as well, honored Gentlemen of the Academy, I have only been reporting.

CHILDREN ON THE COUNTRY ROAD

I HEARD THE WAGONS PASSING BY THE GARDEN FENCE, SOMETIMES I also saw them through the slightly swaying gaps in the leaves. How the wood of their spokes and shafts creaked in the hot summer! Workers came from the fields and laughed, so that it was a disgrace.

I was sitting on our little swing, I was resting among the trees in my parents' garden.

Beyond the fence, it didn't stop. Children ran past in the blink of an eye; grain wagons with men and women on the sheaves and all around the darkened flower beds; toward evening, I saw a gentleman with a cane taking a leisurely stroll and a couple of girls, approaching him arm in arm, stepped aside into the grass with a greeting.

Then birds flew up like sparks; I followed them with my eyes, saw how they rose in one breath, until I no longer believed they were rising but that I was falling, and holding myself tight on the ropes out of faintness, began to swing a little. Soon I was swinging higher; as the air blew cooler, and in place of the flying birds, quivering stars had appeared.

By candlelight, I received my supper. Often I had both arms on the wooden counter, already tired, I bit into my buttered bread. The intricately embroidered curtains billowed in the warm wind, and sometimes someone passing by outside would hold them in their hands if they wanted to see me better and talk to me. Usually the candle would go out quickly and the mosquitoes would hang about in the dark candle smoke for a while. If someone interrogated me from the window, I would look at him as though I were gazing at the mountains or the plain air, and he was also not very eager for an answer.

If someone then leapt over the windowsill and announced that the others were already in front of the house, I would, of course, get up with a sigh.

"Come on, what are you sighing about? What happened? Something especially tragic that can never be made right? Will we never be able to recover from it? Is all really lost?"

Nothing was lost. We ran out to the front of the house. "Thank God, there you are at last!"—"You're just always late."—"Why me?"—"Especially you, stay at home if you don't want to come along."—"No mercy!"—"What? No mercy? That's no way to talk!"

We broke through the evening headfirst. There was no day or nighttime. Soon the buttons on our waistcoats were grinding together like teeth; soon we were running at a steady distance, fire in our mouths, like animals in the tropics. Like cuirassiers in old wars, stamping and high in the air, we goaded one another down the short alley and with this momentum in our legs, further on up the country road. Some stepped into the roadside ditch, hardly had they vanished before the dark escarpment when they appeared up on the path, standing like strangers, and looked down.

"Why don't you come down here?"—"Come up here first!"—"So you can push us down? Wouldn't cross our minds, we're too clever for that."—"You're too cowardly, you meant to say. Come on, come!"—"Really? You? You of all people are going to push us down? I'd like to see you try!"

We attacked, took a blow to the chest and laid ourselves down in the grass of the roadside ditch, falling willingly. Everything was evenly warm, we did not feel warmth, not coldness in the grass, one just grew tired.

If you turned onto your right side, placing a hand under your ear, you would want to fall asleep. You would want to rouse yourself again with your chin raised high, but instead you would fall into a deeper ditch. Then you would want to throw yourself against the air, holding your arm crosswise, your legs blown askew, and surely fall again into an even deeper ditch. And you would not want to stop.

How to stretch out fully in the last ditch, especially in the knees, was hardly something you thought about and you lay, ready to cry, like an invalid, on your back. You blinked when a boy, elbows at his hips, once leapt over us with dark soles from the escarpment to the road.

You could already see the moon quite high in the sky, a mail coach drove by in its light. A slight wind rose all around, also in the ditch it could be felt, and nearby the forest began to rustle. It was then no longer so important to be alone.

"Where are you?"—"Come here!"—"All together!"—"Why are you hiding, stop messing around!"—"Didn't you know that the mail already passed?"—"No! It's already past?"—"Of course, it passed by while you were sleeping."—"I was sleeping? Imagine that!"—"Be quiet, one can see it on your face."—"Surely not."— "Come on!"

We ran closer together, some joined hands, we could not hold our heads high enough because we were going downhill. One of us let out an Indian war cry, we got a gallop in our legs like never before, as we leapt, the wind lifted us by the hips. Nothing could have held us back; we were so much in stride that we could cross our arms and have a look around even as we passed one another.

We stopped on the bridge over the wild stream; those who had run farther turned back. The water below pounded at stones and roots as if it were not already late evening. There was no reason why one of us did not leap onto the bridge's railing.

A train drove out from behind bushes in the distance, all its compartments were lit up, the glass windows certainly lowered. One of us began to sing a street song, but we all wanted to sing. We sang far more quickly than the train was traveling, we swung our arms because our voices were not enough, with our voices we entered a crowd that we felt good in. If you mix your voice among others, you are trapped like one who has been caught with a fishhook.

So we sang, the forest behind us, in the distant passengers' ears. The adults were still awake in the village, the mothers were preparing the beds for the night.

It was time. I kissed the one standing next to me, held out my hands to the next three, began to walk back, no one called me. At the first crossing where they could no longer see me, I turned and followed the paths back into the forest. I was headed for the city in the south, of which they said in our village:

"The people there! Just imagine, they don't sleep!"

"And why not?"

"Because they don't get tired."

"And why not?"

"Because they are fools."

"Don't fools get tired?"

"How could fools get tired!"

OUTING IN THE MOUNTAINS

"I DON'T KNOW," I CRIED SOUNDLESSLY. "I JUST DON'T KNOW. If nobody comes, then nobody comes. I've done nobody any harm, nobody has done me any harm, but nobody wants to help me. Absolutely nobody. But that's not really the way it is. Only that nobody is helping me—otherwise absolutely nobody would be quite nice. I would very much like—and why not, after all?—to go on an outing with a group of nobodies. To the mountains, of course, where else? How these nobodies press against one another, all the many arms stretched across and linked together, the many feet, separated by tiny steps! Naturally, everyone is in tailcoats. We stroll along, the wind blowing through the gaps that we and our limbs leave open. Throats become free in the mountains! It is a miracle that we are not singing."

A Message from the Emperor

THE EMPEROR—SO THEY SAY—HAS SENT TO YOU, THE SINGLE, pathetic subject, the miniscule shadow that has fled the imperial sun to the most distant distance. To you of all people the Emperor has sent a message from his deathbed. He had the messenger kneel down at his bedside and whispered the message into his ear; it was so important to him that he had it repeated back into his ear again. With a nod of his head he confirmed the accuracy of that which was said. And before the entire spectatorship of his death—all obstructing walls are broken down and in a circle on the wide, high swinging flights of stairs the empire's great men are standing—before all of them he had given the messenger his instructions. The messenger sets off at once; a strong, untiring man; stretching one arm, then the other out before him, he creates a path through the crowd; if he meets resistance, he points to his chest, which bears the sign of the sun; and he advances with more ease than anyone else. But the crowd is so vast; their dwellings never come to an end. How he would fly if open fields were to emerge before him, and you would soon hear the glorious pounding of his fists on your door. But instead, he labors uselessly; he is still forcing himself through the chambers of the inner palace; he will never get through them; and if he does manage this, nothing would be gained; he would have to fight his way down the stairs; and if he manages this, nothing would be gained;

the courtyards would have to be crossed; and after the courtyards, the second outer palace; and again steps and courtyards; and again a palace; and so on through millennia; and were he to finally stumble through the outermost gate—but this can never, never happen—the royal city will still lie before him, the center of the world, piled high with its own dregs. No one gets through here even with a message from a dead man.—But you, you will sit at your window and dream it up for yourself, as evening falls.

THE WINDOW TO THE STREET

HE WHO LIVES A LONELY LIFE AND WOULD STILL LIKE TO MAKE some kind of contact from time to time, he who simply wants, in consideration of the changes in the time of day, the weather, the job circumstances, and the like, to have an arm that he can hold on to,—he will not last long without a window to the street. And if his state is such that he isn't looking for anything at all, and only walks up to his windowsill as a tired man, whose eyes move up and down between the crowd and the sky, and who refuses and has bent his head back a little,—even then the horses below will draw him down into their entourage of carts and noise and thereby finally into human unity.

Unmasking a Con Man

Finally, at about ten in the evening, and in the company of a man whom I had once met only fleetingly, and who this time had unexpectedly joined me again and spent two hours dragging me around the streets, I arrived at the stately house to which I had been invited for a social gathering.

"Well then!" I said and clapped my hands to signal the absolute necessity for us to part. I had already made several less determined attempts. I was feeling very tired.

"Are you going up now?" he asked. In his mouth I heard a sound like the clashing of teeth.

"Yes."

I had been invited, after all; I had told him straightaway. But I had been invited to come upstairs, where I would very much have liked to have already been, and not standing down here at the door and staring over the ears of the man opposite me. Nor standing silent with him as well, as though we were set to stay at this spot a long time. The surrounding houses were also taking part in this silence, as was the darkness above them up to the stars. And the footsteps of invisible passersby, whose path no one cared to guess, the wind, pressing persistently against the opposite side of the street, a gramophone, singing against the closed windows of some room,—they let themselves be heard in this silence, as though it had always been their property and always would be.

And my companion acquiesced on his own behalf and—after a smile—also on mine, stretched his right arm up along the wall and leaned his face against it, closing his eyes.

But I didn't see this smile quite to the end, for shame suddenly turned me around. For it was not until this smile that I realized that he was a con man, and nothing more. And having been in this city for months already, I thought I knew these con men through and through; how they emerge from the side streets at night to confront us with outstretched hands, like innkeepers; how they slink about the advertising pillars near where we stand as though to play hide-and-seek and spy with at least one eye from behind the pillar's curve; how at the crossroads, when we become anxious, they suddenly hover before us on the edge of the sidewalk! I thought I understood them so well. After all, they had been my first city acquaintances in the little taverns, and I have them to thank for my first glimpse of that relentlessness that I am now so incapable of imagining the world without that I have already begun to feel it within myself. How could they still stand before you, even when you had long since escaped them, when there had long since been nothing left for them to con? They didn't sit down, they didn't fall over, but looked at you with eyes that were, even if only from a distance, still persuasive! And their means were always the same: they planted themselves before us, as broadly as they could; sought to keep us from reaching the place we were aiming for; prepared instead a room for us in their own chest, and if the accumulated emotions reared up within us, they would take it as an embrace into which they would throw themselves face first.

And this time I only recognized these old pranks after we had been together for such a long time. I rubbed my fingertips together to undo the disgrace.

My man, however, leaned here just as before, still thinking himself to be a con man, and his satisfaction with his fate reddened his free cheek.

"Exposed!" I said and tapped him lightly on the shoulder. Then I hurried up the stairs and the blindly devoted faces of the servants up in the hallway delighted me like a pleasant surprise. I looked at them all, one after the other, as they took my coat and dusted off my boots. With a breath of relief and stretched to full height, I then entered the hall.

RESOLUTIONS

To RISE FROM A MISERABLE STATE MUST BE EASY, EVEN WITH forced energy. I wrest myself from my armchair, run around the table, loosen my head and neck, bring fire to my eyes, tighten the muscles around them. Counteract every feeling, greet A. vehemently should he arrive now, kindly tolerate B. in my room, with C. take in everything that is said, despite the pain and effort, with long drafts.

But even if that works, the whole thing, the easy and the difficult, will falter with each mistake, which cannot be avoided, and I will have to turn myself back in the circle.

Thus it remains that the best advice is to accept everything, behave like an inert mass and if you feel yourself being blown away, not let yourself be lured into taking a single unnecessary step, look at the others with an animal's gaze, feel no remorse, in short, to oppress with your own hand that which remains from life as a ghost, i.e. to augment the final gravelike silence and allow nothing else to exist.

A characteristic movement in such a condition is the small finger traveling along the eyebrows.

The Bachelor's Misery

It seems so hard to remain a bachelor, to struggle as an old man to preserve your dignity while pleading for admittance when you wish to spend an evening in human company, to be ill and spend weeks staring at the empty room from the corner of your bed, to always take leave at the front door, to never push your way upstairs with your wife at your side, to have only side doors in your room that lead to other apartments, to carry your supper home in one hand, to be forced to marvel at other people's children and not be allowed to constantly repeat, "I have none," to model your appearance and demeanor on one or two bachelors from memories of your youth.

This is how it will be, only that in reality you yourself will be standing there, today and in the future, with a body and a real head, and therefore also a forehead to hit with your hand.

THE BUSINESSMAN

IT IS POSSIBLE THAT SOME PEOPLE PITY ME, BUT I DON'T NOTICE it at all. My small business fills me with worries that make my forehead and temples ache, but without giving me any prospect of contentment, for my business is small.

For hours in advance I have to make decisions, keep the caretaker's memory alert, warn him of feared mistakes, and assess during one season the fashions of the next, not as they will be followed by people in my own circles, but by inaccessible communities in the countryside.

My money is in the hands of strangers; the state of their affairs cannot be clear to me; I cannot anticipate the misfortune that could strike them; how could I avert it! Perhaps they have grown extravagant and are hosting a feast in some tavern garden, while others, on their flight to America, stop and visit them for a while.

Now when the business is closed on a weekday evening and I suddenly see the hours before me in which I will not be able to work to fulfill its incessant needs, the agitation that I pushed far away in the morning rises in me like a returning tide, but it cannot be contained and it floods out aimlessly, carrying me along.

And yet I am unable to use this mood at all and can only go home, for my face and hands are filthy and sweaty, my clothes stained and dusty, the work cap on my head and boots scratched by crate nails. I walk then as though carried by waves, snapping the fingers on both hands and tousling the hair of the children approaching me.

But my path is too short. Soon I am in my building, opening the elevator door and stepping inside.

I realize that I am now and suddenly alone. Others, who have to climb stairs, become a little tired when doing so, and have to wait with panting breaths until someone comes to open the apartment door. They have a reason for irritation and impatience, because they must enter the hallway where they hang their hat, and not until they have walked through the hallway past several glass doors and entered their own room are they alone.

I, however, am alone right away in the elevator and look, leaning on my knees, into the narrow mirror. As the elevator begins to rise, I say:

"Be quiet, back with you all, head for the shade of the trees, behind the windows' draperies, in the vault of the arcade!"

I speak through my teeth and the stair banisters slide past the panes of frosted glass like plunging water.

"Fly away; may your wings, which I have never seen, carry you to the valley village or to Paris, if that's where you want to be.

"But enjoy the view from the window when the processions emerge from all three streets, not evading one another but weaving through one another, and letting free space emerge again between their last ranks. Wave your handkerchiefs, be appalled, be moved, praise the beautiful lady as she passes by.

"Cross the stream on the wooden bridge, nod to the bathing children, and marvel at the hooray of the thousand sailors on the distant battleship.

"Only follow that inconspicuous man and when you have pushed him into a doorway, rob him and then watch him, each of you with your hands in your pockets, as he sadly makes his way to the street on the left.

"The police, scattered on their galloping horses, restrain their animals and force you back. Let them, the empty streets will make them unhappy, I know it. You see? They are already riding away in pairs, slowly around the street corners, flying across the squares."

Then I must exit, send the elevator back down, ring the door-bell, and the maid opens the door as I greet her.

ABSENTMINDED GAZING

WHAT SHALL WE DO DURING THESE SPRING DAYS THAT ARE COMING so quickly upon us? Early this morning the sky was gray, but if you go to the window now, you will be surprised and lean your cheek against the window's handle.

Down below, you can see the light of the sun that is surely already sinking on the face of the little girl who is just walking and looking about, and at the same time, you see the shadow of the man falling upon her who is approaching more quickly from behind.

Then the man has already passed by and the child's face is again quite bright.

THE NEW ADVOCATE

WE HAVE A NEW ADVOCATE, DR. BUCEPHALUS. THERE IS LITTLE about his outward appearance to remind one of the time when he was Alexander of Macedon's battle charger. Those familiar with his background, however, will notice quite a bit. Just recently, I even saw a very simple court servant on the stairs outside marveling at the advocate with the expert eye of a small frequenter of the races, as he mounted the stairs with thighs raised high and steps that rang against the marble.

In general, the bar approves of Bucephalus' admission. With astonishing insight, people say to themselves that, under the current social order, Bucephalus is in a difficult situation, and that for this reason, as well as his significance in world history, he by all means deserves to be accommodated. Today—no one can deny it—there is no great Alexander. Although many know how to murder; and there is no lack of agility in striking a friend with a lance across the banquet table; and for many, Macedon is too crowded, making them curse Philip, the father—but nobody, nobody can lead the way to India. Even back then, India's gates were unreachable, but the royal sword indicated their direction. Today the gates are somewhere else entirely; carried off higher and further away; no one indicates their direction; many hold swords, but only to wave them about; and the gaze that aims to follow them becomes confused.

So perhaps it is really best to do as Bucephalus has done and immerse oneself in statute books. Free, his flanks unconfined by the thighs of a rider, reading by quiet lamplight, far from the clamor of Alexander's battle, turning the pages of our ancient tomes.

The Passersby

If you take a walk down a street at night and a man, already visible from afar—for the street before us ascends and the moon is full—runs toward us, we will not seize him, even if he is weak and ragged, even if someone is running behind him shouting, but we will let him run on.

For it is night, and we can't help it if the street ascends before us in the full moon, and besides, perhaps the two have staged the chase for their amusement, perhaps a third man is pursuing them both, perhaps the first is being unjustly pursued, perhaps the second wants to murder him and we would be accessories to murder, perhaps the two know nothing of each other and each is only running on his own account to his bed, perhaps they are sleepwalkers, perhaps the first one has weapons.

And after all, shouldn't we be tired, haven't we drunk so much wine? We are relieved that we can also no longer see the second man now.

THE PASSENGER

I AM STANDING ON THE PLATFORM OF THE ELECTRIC TRAM AND am entirely uncertain as to my status in this world, in this city, in my family. I could not even say offhand which claims I could rightly make in any direction. I cannot justify at all that I am standing on this platform, holding on to this strap, letting myself be carried by this tram, that people get out of the tram's way, or walk silently, or rest in front of the shop windows. No one is demanding it of me, but that is irrelevant.

The tram is approaching a stop, a girl goes and stands near the stairs ready to get off. She appears as distinct to me as though I had felt her with my hands. She is dressed in black, the pleats of her skirt barely move, her blouse is tight and has a collar of white finely-meshed lace, her left hand is placed flat against the wall, the umbrella in her right rests on the second highest step. Her face is brown, her nose, slightly pressed on the sides, and it finishes round and wide. She has a lot of brown hair, wisps of which are strewn across her right temple. Her small ear lies close to her head, but because I am standing near, I can see the entire back of her right ear and the shadow beneath it.

I asked myself at the time: How is it that she is not amazed by herself, that she keeps her mouth closed and says nothing of the sort?

In the Gallery

If some frail, consumptive circus rider were being driven in circles around the ring by her whip-wielding, merciless boss for months without interruption, on a faltering horse, before a tireless audience, whirring on her horse, throwing kisses, swaying from the waist, and if this performance were to continue among the incessant roaring of the orchestra and the ventilators into the constantly expanding gray future, accompanied by the fading and swelling of clapping hands, which are actually steam hammers—perhaps then a young visitor in the gallery would rush down the long flight of stairs, through all the circles, plunge into the ring, and call out: Stop! through the fanfares of the ever accommodating orchestra.

But as it is not so, a lovely lady, white and red, flies in between the curtains that are opened before her by proud liveried attendants; the ringmaster, devotedly seeking her gaze, breathes towards her with an animal's posture; lifts her up carefully onto the dapple gray, as though she were his most beloved granddaughter setting off on a perilous journey; hesitates to give the signal with his whip; finally overcomes himself and gives it with a crack; runs alongside the horse with an open mouth; follows the rider's leaps with a sharp eye; is hardly able to grasp her virtuosity; tries to warn her by calling out in English; angrily warns the grooms holding the hoops to be painstakingly attentive; implores the orchestra with raised hands to be silent before her great death-defying somersault; finally lifts the little one from her trembling horse, kisses both her cheeks, and deems no homage from the audience to be sufficient; while she herself, supported by him, high on the tips of her toes, surrounded by a cloud of dust, with arms outstretched and head thrown back, wants to share her joy with the entire circus—since it is so, the visitor to the gallery lays his face on the railing and, sinking into the final march as though into a heavy dream, he weeps, without knowing it.

THE REJECTION

IF I ENCOUNTER A PRETTY GIRL AND BEG HER: "BE SO KIND, AS TO come with me" and she passes by silently, she means to say:

"You are no duke with a famous name, no broad-shouldered American with the build of a Red Indian, with calm steady eyes, with skin massaged by the air of the meadows and the rivers flowing through them, you have taken no journeys to the great seas or upon them, the whereabouts of which I do not know. So I ask, why should I, a pretty girl, go with you?"

"You forget, no automobile is carrying you in long, swaying thrusts through the streets; I see no gentlemen, pressed into their suits, comprising your entourage, and mumbling your blessings as they walk in a perfect semicircle behind you; your breasts are arranged nicely laced up in your bodice, but your thighs and hips make up for that restraint; you are wearing a taffeta dress with gathered pleats, such as those that certainly delighted us all last autumn, and yet—with this risk of death upon your body—you smile from time to time.

"Yes, we are both right, and to keep us from becoming irrefutably aware of this, it would be better, I'm sure, if we each went home alone."

FOR GENTLEMEN RIDERS TO THINK ABOUT

NOTHING, IF YOU THINK ABOUT IT, COULD TEMPT ONE TO WANT to be first in a race.

The fame of being recognized as a country's best rider brings too much pleasure as the band strikes up, so that we can't help regretting it the morning after.

The envy of opponents—cunning, rather influential people—is bound to hurt you in the narrow chute that you must now ride through after that racecourse, which before had been empty except for a few riders left behind from the last round, small figures riding against the edge of the horizon.

Many of your friends hurry to collect their winnings and only shout their "Hurray" to you over their shoulders from the distant booths; your best friends, however, didn't even bet on your horse, as they feared losses that would make them angry with you, but now that your horse was first and they didn't win anything, they turn away when you pass by, preferring to look along the grandstands.

Your rivals behind you, firm in the saddle, try to grasp the tragedy that has befallen them, and the injustice that has been somehow done to them; they assume a fresh demeanor, as though a new race must be started, and a serious one, after this child's play.

To many ladies, the winner seems ridiculous because he swells with pride but isn't sure how to handle the endless handshaking, saluting, bowing down, and waving-into-the-distance, while the defeated keep their mouths closed and lightly pat the necks of their usually whinnying horses.

And finally, rain even begins to fall from the now gloomy sky.

THE SUDDEN STROLL

IF IN THE EVENING YOU SEEM TO HAVE DEFINITELY DECIDED TO
stay home, and have put on your house coat, and are sitting at
an illuminated table after supper, and have taken in hand the
activity or game upon whose completion you usually go to sleep;
if the weather outside is inhospitable, making staying at home
inevitable; if you have already been sitting quietly at the table
for so long that departure would be certain to elicit general
astonishment; if the stairway is already dark and the front door
locked; and if, despite all of this, you get up with a sudden
unease, change your coat, appear at once dressed for the street,
explaining that you must go out, doing so after a brief goodbye,
suspecting that you have more or less left behind aggravation,
according to the swiftness with which you slammed the front
door; if you then find yourself again out in the street, with limbs
that respond with particular agility to this unexpected freedom
you have granted them; if you feel all decisiveness gathered
within you through this one decision; if you realize with greater
than usual importance that your strength more than suffices to
effect the quickest change with ease and to bear it; and if you
stroll down the long side streets in this way,—then for this evening, you have completely seceded from your family, which is
veering off into insubstantiality, while you yourself, quite solid,

black with delineation, slapping your thighs behind you, rise to your true form.

All this will be reinforced by going to see a friend at this late evening hour, to see how he is doing.

Wish to Become a Red Indian

OH TO BE A RED INDIAN, INSTANTLY PREPARED, AND ON A GALLOPING horse, leaning into the air, feeling a brief tremor, again and again, over the trembling ground, until you let go of the spurs, for no spurs were needed, until you threw away the reins, for no reins were necessary, and you barely saw the land before you as a smoothly mown heather, without horse's neck and horse's head.

JACKALS AND ARABS

WE WERE CAMPING IN THE OASIS. MY COMPANIONS WERE SLEEPING.
An Arab, tall and white, came past me; he had attended to the
camels and was going to his sleeping quarters.

I flung myself backwards into the grass; I tried to sleep; I
couldn't; the lamenting howl of a jackal in the distance; I sat up
again. And that which was so far away was suddenly so near. A
swarm of jackals all around me; eyes of opaque gold gleaming,
vanishing; lean bodies, moved obediently and nimbly, as if driven
by a whip.

One came from behind, pushing itself through beneath my
arm, closely, as though it needed my warmth, then stepped before
me and spoke to me, almost eye to eye:

"I am the oldest jackal far and wide. I am glad to still be able to
greet you here. I had almost given up hope, for we have been waiting for you for an eternity; my mother waited, and her mother, and
all their mothers back to the mother of all jackals. Believe me!"

"That is surprising," I said and forgot to light the woodpile
lying ready to deter jackals with its smoke, "that is quite surprising
to hear. It is only by chance that I have come here from the far
north; I am on a short journey. So what do you want, jackals?"

And as if encouraged by my perhaps all too friendly words,
they drew their circle closer around me; all were breathing short,
snarling breaths.

"We know," began the eldest, "that you have come from the north, that is precisely what we have built our hopes on. Reason can be found there, which is not to be found here among the Arabs. Not a spark of reason, you see, can be struck from this cold arrogance. They kill animals, in order to eat them, and despise carrion."

"Don't speak so loudly," I said, "Arabs are sleeping nearby."

"You really are a foreigner," said the jackal, "otherwise you would know that not once in the history of the world has a jackal feared an Arab. So we should fear them, should we? Is it not misfortune enough that we've been cast out among such people?"

"Perhaps, perhaps," I said, "I am not in a position to judge things that I know so little about; this appears to be a very old quarrel; it probably runs in your blood; so it will perhaps only end in blood."

"You are very clever," said the old jackal; and they all breathed even faster; their lungs racing, although they were standing still; an acrid smell, at times only to be endured with clenched teeth, streamed from the open mouths, "You are very clever; what you say complies with our old teachings. So we will take their blood and the quarrel will be over."

"Oh!" I said, wilder than I had intended, "they will fight back; they will shoot you down in packs with their rifles."

"You misunderstand us," he said, "in the human manner, which apparently still persists in the far north. We are not going to kill them. The Nile would not have enough water to wash us clean. We already run away at the mere sight of their living bodies, to cleaner air, to the desert, which is therefore our home."

And the jackals all around, who had meanwhile been joined by many others who had come from far away, lowered their heads between their front legs and cleaned them with their paws; it was as though they wanted to conceal an aversion that was so terrible that I would have most liked to leap up high and escape from their circle.

"So what do you intend to do?" I asked and started to get up; but I couldn't; two young animals had bitten tightly into my coat and shirt; I had to stay seated. "They are holding your train," the old jackal explained earnestly, "a mark of honor." "They are to let go of me!" I cried, turning first to the old jackal and then to the young ones. "They will, of course," said the old one, "if you wish. But it will take a little while, for they have bitten in deep, as is our custom, and can only slowly detach their jaws from one another. In the meantime, listen to our request." "Your behavior hasn't made me very receptive," I said. "Don't make us pay for our lack of grace," he said, now resorting for the first time to the lamenting tone of his natural voice. "We are poor creatures; all we have is our teeth. For everything that we want to do, good or bad, the only thing we have is our teeth." "So what do you want?" I asked, only slightly appeased.

"Sir," he cried, and all the jackals howled; in the most distant distance, it seemed to me to be a melody. "Sir, you are to end this quarrel that is dividing the world. You are just as our ancestors described the man who will do so. We must have peace from the Arabs; breathable air; the view all around the horizon cleansed of them; no cries of lament as the Arab stabs the ram to death; the death of all animals should be calm; it should be emptied by us and cleansed to the bones undisturbed. Purity, we want nothing but purity," and now they all cried and sobbed—"How can you bear to live in such a world—you of noble heart and sweet intestines? Filth is their white; filth is their black; their beard is a horror; you must vomit when you see the corner of their eyes; and when they lift their arms, hell opens before you in their armpits. Therefore, Sir, oh my dear Sir, with the help of your all-capable hands, cut through their throats with these scissors!" And following the jerk of his head, a jackal came forward dangling from one fang a small, rust-covered pair of sewing scissors.

"The scissors at last, and that's the end of it!" cried the Arab leader of our caravan, who had stolen up on us against the wind and was now swinging a gigantic whip.

They all scattered in haste, but stopped at a distance, huddled together; the many animals so close together and motionless looked like a narrow pen, surrounded by flickering will-o-the-wisps.

"So, Sir, you have also seen and heard this spectacle," said the Arab and laughed as cheerfully as permitted by the restraint of his people. "So you know what the animals are demanding?" I asked. "Of course, Sir," he said. "That is known to us all; as long as there have been Arabs, those scissors have been wandering through the desert and will wander with us to the end of our days. Every European is asked to do the great deed; every European is exactly the one who seems to them to be called on to carry it out. It's an absurd hope that these animals have; they are fools, real fools. We love them for it; they are our dogs; more beautiful than yours. Just look, a camel died during the night, I've had it brought here."

Four bearers came and threw the heavy cadaver down before us. It was hardly lying there when the jackals raised their voices. Each one drawn irresistibly as if by ropes, they came forward, hesitatingly, with their bodies grazing the ground. They had forgotten the Arabs, forgotten the hatred; the all-obliterating presence of the heavily steaming corpse enchanted them. One was already hanging on the throat and found the artery with its first bite. Like a small frantic pump trying just as desperately as hopelessly to extinguish an overwhelming fire, every muscle in the jackal's body tugged and twitched in its place. And soon all of them lay working at the same task, mounted up high on top of the corpse.

Then the leader struck his sharp whip vigorously back and forth above them. They raised their heads, half intoxicated, half conscious; saw the Arab standing before them; felt the whip now with their muzzles; withdrew with a leap and ran backwards for a stretch. But the camel's blood was already lying there in pools, steaming aloft; in several places, the body was torn wide open. They couldn't resist; again they were there; again the leader raised his whip; I grasped his arm.

"You are right, Sir," he said. "We'll leave them to their calling; and it is also time for us to leave. You've seen them now. Wonderful animals, don't you agree? And how they hate us!"

UNHAPPINESS

W HEN IT HAD ALREADY BECOME UNBEARABLE—ONCE TOWARD
evening in November—and I was pacing along the narrow carpet
in my room as though on a racecourse, startled by the sight of
the illuminated street, I turned around again, and found at the
far end of the room, in the depths of the mirror, a new goal
after all, and I screamed out, in order to just hear that scream
that is answered by nothing and from which nothing can take its
strength, and which therefore rises without a counterweight and
cannot stop, even when it has fallen silent, when the door in the
wall opened, so hastily because haste was necessary, after all, and
even the carthorses down on the cobbles reared up like wild horses
in battle, their throats revealed.

A small ghost of a child emerged from the entirely dark corridor in which the lamp was not yet shining and stopped, standing
on its tiptoes on an imperceptibly trembling floor beam. Blinded
at once by the twilight in the room, it tried quickly to bury its face
in its hands, but suddenly calmed itself with a glance to the window, where, before its crossbars, the haze forced up from the
streetlights finally settled below the darkness. With its right elbow,
it held itself upright against the wall in front of the open door and
let the draft of air from outside drift around its ankles, also along
its throat, its temples.

I watched for a while, then I said "Good Day" and took my coat from the fire screen, for I didn't want to just stand there half-naked. For a little while, I kept my mouth open so that the excitement would leave me through my mouth. I had a bad taste in my mouth, my eyelashes quivered on my cheeks, in short, the last thing I needed was this admittedly expected visitor.

The child was still standing against the wall in the same place, its right hand pressed against the wall, which was coarsely grained, and, quite rosy-cheeked, it rubbed with its fingertips. I said: "Are you really looking for me? Is it not a mistake? Nothing easier than a mistake in this large house. My name is So-and-so. I live on the third floor. So am I the one you want to visit?"

"Hush, hush!" said the child over its shoulder, "Everything is all right."

"Then come further into the room, I'd like to close the door."

"I've just closed the door. Don't worry. Just calm down."

"It's no trouble. But a lot of people live on this corridor, all of them my acquaintances, of course; most of them are coming home from work now; if they hear talking in one of the rooms, they simply believe they have the right to open the door and see what's going on. That's just the way it is. These people have their daily work behind them; who would they subjugate themselves to in their provisional evening freedom! Anyway, you know this as well. Let me close the door."

"What is it? What's the matter? The whole house can come in, as far as I'm concerned. And once again: I have already closed the door, or do you believe that only you can close the door? I have even locked it with the key."

"Alright then. That's all I wanted anyway. You didn't have to lock it with the key, though. And now make yourself comfortable, since you're here. You are my guest. Trust me entirely. Make yourself at home without fear. I will neither force you to stay here, nor to go away. Must I actually say this? Do you know so little about me?"

"No. You really didn't need to say it. Even more, you shouldn't have said it at all. I am a child; why go to such effort on my account?"

"It's not as bad as that. A child, of course. But you're not that small. You are already quite grown up. If you were a girl, you would not be able to simply lock yourself up with me in a room."

"We don't have to worry about that. I just wanted to say: the fact that I know you so well does little to protect me, but simply relieves you of the effort of lying to me. But you pay me compliments nevertheless. Stop it, I ask you to stop it. And on top of that, I don't recognize you everywhere and always, especially not in this darkness. It would be better if you turned on the light. No, rather not. In any case, I shall remember that you have already threatened me."

"What? I'm supposed to have threatened you? Please! After all, I am so delighted that you are finally here. I say 'finally' because it is already so late. It is incomprehensible to me why you have arrived so late. It is therefore possible that in my delight I spoke incoherently and that you understood it that way. I admit ten times over that I spoke in such a way, yes that I threatened you with anything you like.—Just no arguing, for heaven's sake!—But how could you believe it? How could you offend me so? Why are you set on ruining the brief little duration of your visit here? A stranger would be more forthcoming than you."

"I believe you; that requires no particular insight. By nature, I am already as close to you as any stranger could become. And you know as much, so why the melancholy? Tell me if you wish to put on an act and I will leave this minute."

"Oh really? You also dare to say that to me? You are a little too bold. After all, you are in my room. You are rubbing your fingers like mad on my wall. My room, my wall! And anyway, what you're saying is ridiculous, not only impudent. You say your nature compels you to speak to me in this way. Really? Your nature compels you? That is nice of your nature. Your nature is mine, and if it is my nature to behave kindly towards you, you are not allowed to behave otherwise."

"Is that kind?"

"I'm talking about earlier."

"Do you know what I will be like later?"

"I know nothing."

And I went over to the bedside table, on which I lit the candle. At the time, I had neither gas nor electric light in my room. I then sat for a while longer at the table, until I grew tired of that as well, put on my overcoat, took my hat from the sofa, and blew out the candle. As I went out, I tangled myself up in the leg of an armchair.

On the stairs I met a tenant from the same floor.

"You're going out again, you rascal?" he asked, resting upon his legs spread out across two steps.

"What should I do?" I asked. "This time I had a ghost in my room."

"You say that with the same dissatisfaction as if you had found a hair in your soup."

"You're joking. But remember, a ghost is a ghost."

"Very true. But what if one doesn't believe in ghosts at all?"

"Well do you think that I believe in ghosts? But what good does this disbelief do me?"

"Very easy. You must simply not be afraid anymore when a ghost really visits you."

"Yes, but that is just the incidental fear. The real fear is the fear of the origin of the apparition. And that fear remains. I have a great deal of it within me." Out of nervousness, I began to search through all my pockets.

"But since you were not afraid of the apparition itself, you could have gone ahead and asked what its cause was!"

"You have apparently never spoken with ghosts. You can never get a clear answer out of them. It is a back-and-forth. These ghosts seem to be more in doubt of their existence than we are, which is no wonder, by the way, considering their frailty."

"But I heard, you can feed them."

"Then you are well informed. You can. But who would do such a thing?"

"Why not? If it's a female ghost, for example," he said and swung himself onto the top stair.

"I see," I said, "but even then, it's not worth it."

I thought for a moment. My acquaintance was already so high up, that he had to lean forward under an arch in the stairwell to see me. "But still," I called, "if you take my ghost away from me up there, then it's over between us, forever."

"But I was just joking," he said and pulled his head back.

"Alright then," I said and could have actually gone for a walk now. But because I felt so utterly forlorn, I went upstairs instead and lay down to sleep.

THE WAY HOME

SEE THE PERSUASIVENESS OF THE AIR AFTER THE THUNDERSTORM! My merits are apparent to me and overwhelm me, even though I don't resist.

I march, and my pace is the pace of my side of the street, this street, this neighborhood. I am rightly responsible for every strike against the doors and on the tabletops, for all toasts that are spoken, for the lovers in their beds, in the scaffolding of new buildings, pressed against the walls in the dark alleys or on the ottomans of brothels.

I weigh my past against my future, but find both to be excellent, am unable to prefer one over the other, and I must only reprimand the injustice of the destiny that has thus favored me.

But when I enter my room, I am a little contemplative, although I did not find anything worthy of contemplation as I climbed the stairs. It doesn't help me much that I open the window wide and that music is still playing in someone's garden.

AN OLD MANUSCRIPT

IT SEEMS AS THOUGH MUCH HAS BEEN NEGLECTED IN THE DEFENSE
of our fatherland. We haven't bothered about it until now, and
have gone about our daily work; recent events, however, are trou-
bling us.

I have a shoemaker's shop in the square in front of the Imperial Palace. No sooner do I open my shop at dawn than I see the
entrances to all streets leading to the square occupied by armed
men. But they are not only our soldiers, but evidently also nomads
from the north. In some way that is unfathomable to me, they
have pushed through all the way to the capital, which is very far
from the border. In any case, they are there; it seems that every
morning there are more of them.

As is their nature, they camp beneath the open sky, for they
detest dwelling houses. They busy themselves by sharpening their
swords, honing their arrows, with exercises on horseback. They
have turned this quiet square, which is always kept anxiously
clean, into a real sty. Although we do try to sometimes run out of
our shops and drag away at least the worst of the filth, this happens less and less frequently, for the effort is pointless, and furthermore, it puts us in danger of falling beneath the wild horses
or being injured by the whips.

Speaking to the nomads is impossible. They do not know our
language; indeed, they barely have one of their own. They

communicate among themselves rather like jackdaws. Again and again, that jackdaw cry can be heard. Their inability to fathom our way of life, our institutions, is just as great as their indifference to them. As a result, they also respond to any kind of sign language with rejection. You can even dislocate your jaw and twist your hands out of your wrists and they will not have understood you and never will understand you. They often contort their faces; the white of their eyes turns and foam emerges from their mouth, but they neither wish to say anything, nor to frighten anyone; they do it because it is in their nature to do so. What they need, they take. You can't say that they use force. Before they seize something, you step aside and relinquish everything to them.

They have also taken several good things from my supplies. I can't complain about it, however, when I see how things are for the butcher across from me, for example. As soon as he has fetched his wares, they are already snatched from him and devoured by the nomads. Their horses also eat meat; a rider often lies next to his horse and both feed on the same piece of meat, one at each end. The butcher is afraid and does not dare to discontinue the meat deliveries. But we understand this, pool our money together, and support him. If the nomads did not get their meat, who knows what they would think of doing; although, who knows what they would think of even if they do get their daily meat.

Only recently, the butcher thought he could at least spare himself the trouble of slaughtering and brought a live ox one morning. He mustn't ever do that again. I must have lain flat on the floor, all the way at the back of my workshop for an hour, with all my clothes, blankets, and cushions piled on top of me, just to keep from hearing the bellowing of the ox, which the nomads had leapt on from all sides, ripping pieces out of its warm flesh with their teeth. It had been still for some time before I dared to go out; like drinkers around a wine barrel, they lay tiredly around the remains of the ox.

That was the time when I thought I saw the Emperor himself in the palace window; he never comes to these outer chambers otherwise; he always lives only in the innermost garden; but this time he was standing there at one of the windows—so it seemed to me, at least—watching the goings-on in front of his palace with a lowered head.

"How will it end?" we all ask ourselves. "How long will we bear this burden and torment? The Imperial Palace has attracted the nomads, but doesn't know how to drive them away again. The gate remains locked; the guards, who used to always be marching in and out ceremoniously, remain behind barred windows. We craftsmen and traders have been entrusted with the salvation of our fatherland; but we are not equal to such a task; and we have never boasted that we were capable of it either; it is a misunderstanding and it will be our ruin."

CLOTHING

OFTEN, WHEN I SEE CLOTHING WITH MULTIPLE PLEATS, RUFFLES and decorations lying beautifully on beautiful bodies, I think that they do not remain this way for long, but will get wrinkles that can no longer be ironed smooth, gather dust so thick in the ornaments that it can no longer be removed, and that no one would want to make themselves so sad and ridiculous as to put the same precious gown on every morning and take it off in the evening.

And yet I see girls, who are certainly beautiful and have multiple charming muscles and little bones and taut skin and masses of fine hair, who nonetheless appear daily in the same natural costume, always resting the same face on the same hands and looking in their mirror.

Only sometimes in the evening, when they come home late from a party, that face in the mirror appears to be worn out, puffy, dusty, already seen by everyone, and hardly wearable any longer.

A VISIT TO THE MINE

TODAY THE TOP ENGINEERS CAME DOWN BELOW TO VISIT US. Some sort of order was issued by the management to make new galleries and the engineers came to conduct the first measurements. How young these people are and already so different! They have all developed freely, and their precise character already shows itself without restraint in their early years.

One of them, black-haired, lively, lets his eyes roam in all directions.

A second, with a notebook, records things as he walks, looks around, compares, takes notes.

A third, with his hands in his coat pockets, making everything about him tense, walks upright; he preserves his dignity; only his perpetual lip-biting reveals his impatient, irrepressible youth.

A fourth is giving the third explanations that he has not asked for; smaller than the third, and running along beside him like a tempter, he seems to be reciting a litany to him, his index finger constantly in the air, about everything to be seen here.

A fifth, perhaps the highest in rank, tolerates no accompaniment; he is at the front one moment, at the back the next; the group conforms to his pace; he is pale and weak; responsibility has hollowed out his eyes; often, in contemplation, he presses his hand against his forehead.

The sixth and seventh walk slightly bowed, head close to head, arm in arm, in intimate conversation; if this was not obviously our coalmine and our workplace in the deepest gallery, one could believe that these bony, beardless, button-nosed gentlemen were young clerics. One is laughing to himself, usually with a catlike purr; the other, also laughing, is doing the talking and adding some sort of rhythm with his free hand. How sure these two gentlemen must be, indeed, what service must they already have rendered our mine despite their youth, that they are allowed to occupy themselves so resolutely, during such an important inspection and before the eyes of their superior, only with their own concerns, or at least with concerns that are unrelated to the current task. Or might it be possible that they, despite all their laughter and inattentiveness, are perceiving that which is necessary after all? One hardly wishes to risk a certain judgment about such gentlemen.

On the other hand, there is no doubt that the eighth, for example, is incomparably more attentive that they are, indeed than all the other gentlemen. He has to touch everything and tap it with a little hammer that he is constantly taking out of his bag and constantly stashing there again. Sometimes he even kneels down in the dirt despite his elegant clothing and taps on the floor, and then again, as he is walking along, taps the walls or the roof above his head. Once he lay down at full length and lay there still; we almost thought an accident had occurred; but then he jumped up with a little twitch of his lean body. So he'd only been carrying out another inspection. We think we know our mine and its stones, but what this engineer is constantly inspecting in this way is beyond our comprehension.

A ninth pushes a kind of baby buggy in front of him in, in which measuring instruments lie. Extremely valuable instruments, laid deeply in the softest cotton. This cart should actually be pushed by an attendant, but it is not entrusted to him; an engineer had to be called, and he is glad to do it, as one can see. He is probably the youngest; perhaps he doesn't even understand all the instruments, but he keeps his eyes on them constantly, almost putting him in danger of bumping the cart into the wall.

But there is another engineer who walks along next to the cart and prevents it. He obviously understands the instruments thoroughly and seems to be their true guardian. From time to time he takes some part of the equipment out of the cart without stopping it, looks it over, screws it open or closed, shakes and taps, holds it to his ear and listens. And finally, while the cart driver is usually standing still, he lays the little thing, hardly visible from a distance, with the utmost caution back into the cart. This engineer is rather domineering, but only on the instruments' behalf. Ten steps before the cart, at a wordless finger signal, we are already supposed to step aside, even where there is no room to do so.

The idle attendant walks behind these two gentlemen. As is to be expected given their great knowledge, these gentlemen have long since discarded any arrogance; the attendant, on the other hand, seems to have collected it all within himself. With one hand on his back, the other in front above the gilt buttons or the fine cloth of his liveried coat, he nods frequently to the right and left, as though we had greeted him and he were responding, or as though he had assumed that we had greeted him but was unable to verify it from his great height. Of course we do not greet him, although the sight of him almost makes you believe that it is a huge thing to be office attendant to the management of the mines. Admittedly, we laugh behind his back, but because not even a crack of thunder could prompt him to turn around, he still remains as something incomprehensible in our estimation.

Today, not much more work will get done; the interruption was too extensive; such a visit takes all thought of work away with it. It's far too tempting to look after the gentlemen in the darkness of the trial gallery into which they have all disappeared. Our shift will also be ending soon; we'll not be watching the gentlemen when they return.

The Next Village

My grandfather used to say: "Life is astonishingly short. Now, in my memory, it is so compressed that I can hardly fathom, for example, how a young man can decide to ride to the next village, without being afraid that—quite apart from unfortunate accidents—even the timespan of an ordinary, fortunately passing life is far from sufficient for such a ride."

THE CARES OF A HOUSEHOLD FATHER

SOME SAY THE WORD ODRADEK IS OF SLAVONIC ORIGIN AND attempt to account for the word's formation on this basis. Others believe that its origin is German, and that it is only influenced by the Slavonic. The uncertainty of both interpretations, however, probably allows us to rightly conclude that neither applies, especially because neither one can offer any help in finding the word's meaning.

No one, of course, would concern themselves with such studies if a creature named Odradek did not really exist. Initially, it looks like a flat, star-like bobbin, and it does in fact appear to be covered with twine; although it seems they are only torn, old, knotted, or matted together pieces of twine of the most various types and colors. But it is not only a spool; a small rod sticks out from the middle of the star and another one then fits into this rod at a right angle. With the help of this last little rod on the one side, and one of the rays of the star on the other side, the entire thing can stand upright as if on two legs.

One would be tempted to believe that this construction used to have some sort of functional shape and is now only broken. But this does not seem to be the case; at least no indication for this can be found; no signs or fractures are to be seen that would indicate as much; although the entire thing appears to be useless, it is complete in its own way. More cannot be said about it, incidentally, because Odradek is extraordinarily agile and impossible to catch.

He is alternatively located in the attic, the stairwell, the corridors, the hall. Sometimes he is not to be seen for months; then he has probably moved to other houses; but inevitably he returns to our house again. Sometimes, if you step out of the door and he happens to be leaning against the banister, you feel like approaching him. Of course, you don't ask him any difficult questions, but treat him—alone, his tininess tempts you to do so—like a child. "So what's your name?" you ask him. "Odradek," he says. "And where do you live?" "No fixed address," he says and laughs; but is only the kind of laugh that can be generated without lungs. It sounds rather like the rustling of fallen leaves. With that the conversation is usually over. These answers, by the way, are not always given; often he is silent for a long time, like the wood that he appears to be.

I ask myself in vain what will become of him. Can he even die? Everything that dies used to have some kind of purpose, some kind of function, and it has worn itself out doing it; this does not apply to Odradek. So will he one day tumble down the stairs, perhaps before the feet of my children and my children's children, with his threads of twine trailing behind him? Apparently he doesn't harm anyone; but the thought that he should also outlive me is almost a painful one.

The Trees

FOR WE ARE LIKE TREE TRUNKS IN THE SNOW. THEY SEEM TO BE resting on the smooth surface, and you should be able to push them away with a little nudge. But, no, you can't, for they are firmly attached to the ground. So you see, even this is only illusory.

Eleven Sons

I have eleven sons.

The first is quite unsightly on the outside, but earnest and clever; nevertheless, although I love him as I do all my other children, I do not think very highly of him. His way of thinking seems to me too simple. He looks neither to the right, nor to the left, nor far into the distance; he constantly runs, or rather rotates, around in his little circle of thought.

The second is handsome, slender, well built; it is delightful to see him in a fencing pose. He too is clever, but he has experience of the world as well; he has seen a lot, and so it seems that even the natural landscape itself speaks more intimately to him than those who have stayed home. Although this asset is certainly not due solely, or even essentially, to his travels; rather it belongs to his inimitable nature, which is, for example, acknowledged by everyone who tries to imitate him as he dives acrobatically, and with multiple somersaults and an almost wild restraint, into the water. The courage and enthusiasm last until the end of the diving board, but instead of jumping, the imitator suddenly sits down and raises his arms in apology.—And despite all this (I should actually be happy to have such a child, after all), my relationship to him is not unclouded. His left eye is slightly smaller than the right one and blinks a lot; a little flaw, certainly, that makes his face even more dashing than it would have been otherwise, and considering how unapproachably self-contained he is by nature, no one would take disapproving notice of this smaller blinking eye. I, his father, do so. Of course, it is not this physical flaw that pains me, but a slight irregularity in his soul that somehow corresponds to it; some poison infecting his blood, some inability to perfect his natural disposition that is only visible to me. On the other hand, this especially makes him my own true son, for this flaw of his is also the flaw of our entire family and only particularly evident in this son.

The third son is equally handsome, but it is not the kind of handsomeness that pleases me. It is the handsomeness of a singer: the curved lips; the dreamy eyes; the head that requires a drapery behind it to have an effect; the excessively arching breast; the hands that are quick to rise up and far too quick to be lowered; the legs that act coyly because they can carry no weight. And furthermore: the sound of his voice is not full; it deceives for a moment, allows the expert to prick up his ears, but runs out of breath soon thereafter.—Although everything in general tempts me to show this son off, I prefer to keep him hidden; he does not impose himself, not because he is aware of his shortcomings, but out of innocence. Also, he feels strange in these times, as though he belongs to my family, but also to another one lost to him forever; he is often listless, and nothing can cheer him up.

My fourth son is perhaps the most sociable of all. Truly a child of his time, he can be understood by everyone, he stands on common ground with all, and everyone is inclined to give him a nod. Perhaps from this general recognition, his nature gains a kind of lightness, his movements a kind of freedom, his judgments a kind of carelessness. You may wish often to repeat some of his sayings, but only some, for in general, he suffers from too much lightness. He is like someone who jumps admirably, cutting the air like a swallow, only to land dismally in the bleak dust, a nothing. Such thoughts sour the sight of this child for me.

The fifth son is kind and good. He promised far less than he fulfilled and was so insignificant that one literally felt alone in his presence, but he still managed to achieve some standing. If someone were to ask me what happened, I could hardly answer. Perhaps innocence is still able to cut through the raging elements of this world most easily after all. And innocent he is— perhaps all too innocent. Kind to everyone—perhaps all too kind. I confess: I become uncomfortable when someone praises him to me. After all, they say that praising is made somewhat too easy when one praises someone so obviously praiseworthy as my son.

My sixth son seems, at least at first glance, to be the most pensive of all. He hangs his head, but is still a chatterer. This is why it is not easy to reach him. If he loses, he falls into unconquerable sadness; if he gains the upper hand, he maintains it by chattering. But I don't deny that he has a certain self-forgotten passion; in broad daylight he often struggles his way through his thoughts as though in a dream. Without being ill—in fact his health is very good—he staggers at times, particularly during nightfall, but needs no help, does not fall. Perhaps his physical development is responsible for this phenomenon; he is far too tall for his age. This makes him generally unattractive, despite strikingly attractive details such as his hands and feet. His forehead is also unattractive, by the way; somehow shrunken in the skin as well as the bone structure.

The seventh son belongs to me perhaps more than all the others. The world does not know how to appreciate him; it doesn't understand his particular sort of humor. I do not overestimate him; I know, he is limited enough; if the world had no other flaw other than its inability to appreciate him, it would still be perfect. But within the family, I would never want to do without this son. He brings unrest as well as a deep respect for tradition, and joins both, at least as I see it, into an incontestable whole, although he himself knows less than anyone about what to do with this whole. He will not be the one to set the wheel of the future in motion, but his nature is so cheery, so hopeful, I would wish for him to have children, and for them to have children in turn. Unfortunately, it doesn't seem that this wish is going to be fulfilled. With a complacence that is as comprehensible to me as it is undesirable, and which also happens to stand in stark contrast to the judgment of those around him, he roams around alone, is not concerned with girls, and will still never lose his good humor.

My eighth son is my child of sorrow, and I really know no reason for it. He looks at me as though I am a stranger, although I feel a strong fatherly bond to him. Time has healed many things; but before, a shiver used to overcome me at the mere thought of him. He has gone his own way, has broken all ties to me; and with his hard head, his small, athletic body—only his legs were rather weak as a boy, but this may have already righted itself in the meantime—he will certainly make his way wherever he chooses. I often felt the urge to call him back, to ask him how he is faring, why he has cut himself off from his father, and essentially what his intentions are, but now he is so far away and so much time has already passed, now it can stay as it is. I hear that he's the only one of my sons to wear a full beard; that is not so attractive, of course, on such a short man.

My ninth son is very elegant and has that sweet look that is intended for women. So sweet that he can even seduce me on occasion, although I know that literally a wet sponge would suffice to wipe away all that unearthly radiance. But the curious thing about this boy is that he is not out to seduce; he would be satisfied spending his whole life lying on the sofa and wasting his eyesight looking at the ceiling, or, better still, letting it rest beneath his eyelids. If he is in this favorite position of his, then he likes to talk and is not bad at it; concise and vivid; but only within narrow boundaries. If he exceeds them, which is unavoidable considering their narrowness, his talking becomes entirely empty. One would wave for him to stop, if there were any reason to hope that those sleep-filled eyes would take any notice.

My tenth son is considered to have an insincere character. I will not fully dispute this flaw, nor fully confirm it. What is certain is that he who sees him approaching with a solemnity far beyond his years, in a frock-coat that is always tightly buttoned up, in an old but over-carefully cleaned black hat, with his unmoved face, the slightly protruding chin, the lids bulging heavily above his eyes, the two fingers held sometimes against his mouth—he who sees him like this thinks: he is a boundless hypocrite. But just listen to him speak! Sensible; with caution; short-spoken; crossing off questions with malicious vitality; in astonishing, obvious, and joyful compliance with the universe, a compliance that inevitably straightens the neck and elevates the body. Many, who consider themselves very clever and who, for this reason, so they thought, felt repelled by his outward appearance, have been strongly attracted by his words. Then again there are also people who feel indifferent about his appearance but to whom his words seem hypocritical. I, as his father, do not wish to decide here, but I must admit that the latter judges are certainly more worthy of attention than the first.

My eleventh son is frail, probably the weakest of my sons, but deceptive in his weakness; for at times he can be strong and decisive, although even then the weakness is somehow underlying. It is not a shameful weakness, but rather something that only appears to be weakness on this earth. Is, for example, the willingness to fly not weakness? After all, it consists of fluctuation and uncertainty and fluttering. Something of this sort can be seen in my son. Such characteristics do not please a father, of course; they will obviously end up destroying the family. Sometimes he looks at me as though he wanted to tell me: "I will take you with me, Father." Then I think: "You would be the last one that I'd entrust myself to." And his eyes seemed to say again: "Well at least I'll be the last then."

These are my eleven sons.

A FRATRICIDE

It has been proven that the murder occurred in the following way:

Schmar, the murderer, positioned himself at nine in the evening on a moonlit night on the street corner that Wese, the victim, was certain to pass as he turned from the street where his office was located into the street in which he lived.

Cold night air chilled everyone to the bone. Schmar, however, had only put on a thin blue suit; and furthermore, his jacket was unbuttoned. He felt no coldness; he was also constantly in motion. He kept his murder weapon, half bayonet, half kitchen knife, firmly in his hand and fully exposed. He held the knife against the moonlight; the blade flashed, but not enough for Schmar. He struck it against the bricks of the pavement so that it made sparks, then regretted it perhaps, and to make up for the damage, he stroked it like a violin bow across his boot sole, as he, standing on one leg and leaning forward, simultaneously listened to the sound of the knife against his boot and any sounds from the fateful side street.

Why did Pallas, the man of independent means who was observing everything from his second-floor window nearby, tolerate all this? Try and comprehend human nature! With his turned-up collar, his dressing gown girded around his ample waist, he looked down shaking his head.

And five houses further, diagonally across from him, Frau Wese, with her fox fur over her nightdress, was looking out for her husband, who was lingering for a particularly long time today.

At last the doorbell before Wese's office rings out—too loud for a doorbell—above the town and up into the sky, and Wese, the diligent night-worker, still unseen in this street, walks out of the building, only announced by the ring of the bell; the pavement soon begins to announce his steady steps.

Pallas leans out far; he mustn't miss a thing. Frau Wese, reassured by the bell, closes her window with a clatter. But Schmar kneels down; because no other parts of him were bare at the moment, he presses only his face and hands against the stones; where everything else freezes, Schmar glows.

Just at the border separating the two streets, Wese stops, with only his walking stick to lean on for support. A whim. The night sky has allured him, the dark blue and the golden. Unaware, he gazes at it; unaware, he smoothes the hair under his raised hat; nothing moves together up there to reveal the immediate future to him; everything remains in its nonsensical, unexplorable place. In and of itself it is quite sensible that Wese walks further, but he walks into Schmar's knife.

"Wese!" shouts Schmar, standing on his toes, his arm stretched out, the knife descending sharply. "Wese! Julia is waiting in vain!" And to the right of the throat and the left of the throat and thirdly deep into his stomach, Schmar stabs. Water rats, slit open, make a sound similar to Wese's.

"Done," said Schmar, and throws the knife, the superfluous bloody burden, at the next house front. "The bliss of murder! Relief, invigoration from the flowing of someone else's blood! Wese, you old nightshade, friend, beer-bench comrade, are seeping away into the dark depths of the street. Why are you not simply a blister full of blood so that I can sit on you to make you disappear altogether? Everything is not fulfilled, all dreams are not blossoms that ripen, your heavy remains lie here, already dead to every kick. What is the point of the silent question you are asking?"

Pallas, choking on all the poisons confusedly coursing through his body, is standing in the double-leaved doorway as it flies open. "Schmar! Schmar! I saw everything, missed nothing." Pallas and Schmar eye each other. Pallas is satisfied; Schmar finds no end. Frau Wese, with a crowd of people on each side, rushes over, her face aged with horror. Her fur opens, she falls upon Wese, her body in its nightdress belongs to him, the fur enclosing the couple like the grass of a grave belongs to the crowd.

Schmar struggles to stifle the last bout of nausea, with his mouth pressed against the shoulder of the policeman, who light-footedly leads him away.

First Sorrow

A TRAPEZE ARTIST—THIS ART, PERFORMED HIGH IN THE DOMES OF the great variety theaters, is acknowledged as one of the most difficult of all that are humanly attainable—had arranged his life, initially only due to his striving toward perfection, later also due to a habit that had become tyrannical, so that as long as he worked for the same company, he would remain on the trapeze day and night. All his needs, which were incidentally quite modest, were fulfilled by attendants who took over from one another, watching from below and sending everything that was needed above up and down in specially constructed containers. Particular difficulties for the world around did not ensue from this way of life; it was only slightly distracting that he remained up there during the other program acts, which was impossible to conceal, and that, although he usually remained still at such times, glances from the audience would now and again wander over to him. But the management excused this because he was an extraordinary, irreplaceable artist. They also perceived, of course, that he was not living in this way out of willfulness, and that this was really the only way for him to remain in constant practice; only in this way could he preserve his art in all its perfection.

It was healthy up there as well, and, during the warmer seasons, when the side windows all around the arched roof were opened, and the sun forced its way along with the fresh air into the dimly lit room, it was even quite beautiful. True, his human interaction was limited; once in a while a fellow acrobat would climb up to him on the rope ladder, and they would both sit on the trapeze, leaning to the right and left on the tethers and chat; or builders repairing the roof would exchange a few words with him through an open window; or a fireman inspecting the emergency lighting in the uppermost gallery would call out something to him that was respectful, but hardly comprehensible. Otherwise everything around him was still; once in a while some employee, who had strayed into the empty theater in the afternoon for instance, would gaze pensively up into the heights almost beyond visibility, where the trapeze artist, without knowing that someone was watching him, practiced his acts or rested.

The trapeze artist could have gone on living peacefully in this way, had it not been for the unavoidable journeys from place to place, which were a great inconvenience to him. True, the impresario ensured that the trapeze artist was spared anything that unnecessarily prolonged his suffering; for travels in the cities, racing automobiles could be used, at night or in the earliest morning hours if possible, to chase through the empty streets at the highest speed, however too slowly for the trapeze artist's longing; in the railway train, they would reserve an entire compartment, in which the trapeze artist could, as a miserable substitute for his usual way of life, at least spend the journey up in the luggage net. In the next venue for their guest performance, the trapeze was already in place in the theater long before the trapeze artist's arrival, all the doors leading to the theater were opened wide, all aisles were kept free—but the best moments of the impresario's life were still those when the trapeze artist set his foot on the rope ladder and, in a heartbeat, was finally hanging up high in his trapeze.

Although the impresario had already managed many journeys successfully, each new one was still distressing, for apart from everything else, these journeys were certainly destructive to the trapeze artist's nerves.

Once, when they were on such a journey together, the trapeze artist was lying in the luggage net and dreaming. The impresario was leaning in the corner by the window opposite him reading a book when the trapeze artist addressed him quietly. The impresario was at his service at once. The trapeze artist said, biting his lip, that instead of the single trapeze he had used for his exercises up to now, he now must have two, two trapezes facing one another. The impresario approved immediately. But the trapeze artist, as if intending to demonstrate that the impresario's approval was just as inconsequential as his objection would have been, said that from now on he would never and under no circumstances ever perform on only one trapeze again. He seemed to shudder at the thought that this might happen one day after all. Hesitantly and observantly, the impresario declared his full approval once again, two trapezes were better than one, and besides, this new arrangement was favorable, it would give the production more variety. At that the trapeze artist suddenly burst into tears. Deeply startled, the impresario leapt to his feet and asked what had happened, and when he received no answer, he climbed onto the bench, stroked him, and pressed his face to his own so that it also overflowed with the trapeze artist's tears. But only after many questions and words of flattery did the trapeze artist say with a sob: "Only that one bar in my hands—how can I go on living!" Now it was easier for the impresario to comfort the trapeze artist; he promised to telegraph the next guest venue from the very next station regarding the second trapeze. He reproached himself for letting the trapeze artist work on only one trapeze for such a long time, and thanked him and praised him for finally bringing this mistake to his attention. In this way, the impresario managed to reassure the trapeze artist, and he was able to go back to his corner. But he himself was not reassured; he observed the trapeze artist secretly over his book with deep concern. Once such thoughts had begun to torment him, would they ever completely cease? Were they not bound to keep growing? Did they not threaten their livelihood? And indeed, the impresario thought he saw how, at this moment, in the seemingly peaceful sleep in which the weeping had ended, the first wrinkles began to engrave themselves on the trapeze artist's smooth, childlike brow.

A DREAM

JOSEF K. WAS DREAMING:

It was a beautiful day, and K. wanted to go for a stroll. Hardly had he taken two steps, however, when he had already arrived at the cemetery. The paths there were quite artificial and impractically winding, but he glided above such a path as though atop torrential waters, hovering unwaveringly. Already from a distance, his eye caught sight of a freshly dug grave mound that he wished to stop at. This grave mound seemed almost to lure him, and he thought he could hardly get there fast enough. But sometimes he barely saw the grave; it was obscured by flags, whose cloths twisted and flapped against one another with great force; the flag-bearers were not to be seen, but great jubilation seemed to prevail.

While his gaze was still directed into the distance, he suddenly saw the same grave mound next to him on the path, indeed almost behind him already. He jumped quickly into the grass. Because the path continued to race beneath his jumping feet, he stumbled and fell to his knees directly before the grave. Two men were standing behind it and holding a gravestone up in the air between them; no sooner had K. appeared, than they drove the stone into the earth and it stood there as though cemented in. Immediately a third man emerged from the bushes that K. recognized at once as an artist. He was dressed only in trousers and a poorly buttoned shirt; on his head he had a velvet cap; in his hand he held an ordinary pencil, with which he was already depicting figures in the air as he approached. With this pencil, he now positioned himself at the top of the stone; the stone was very tall, he didn't need to bend down at all, but he did need to bend forward, for the grave mound, on which he did not wish to tread, was separating him from the stone. So he stood there on his toes and supported himself with his left hand on the stone's surface. With particularly skillful handling, he managed to produce golden letters with his ordinary pencil; he wrote: "Here rests——," each letter appeared clean and beautiful, deeply engraved, and in flawless gold. When he had written the two words, he looked back at K.; K., who was very eagerly following the inscription's progress, was hardly concerned with the man, but looked only at the stone. The man actually did prepare to continue writing, but he couldn't; there was some hindrance; he lowered the pencil and turned around to K. again. Now K. also saw the artist and noticed that he was having great trouble, but couldn't name the cause. All his previous vivacity had disappeared. This also troubled K.; they exchanged helpless glances; an ugly misunderstanding was present that neither could resolve. At this untimely moment, a little bell also began to ring from the cemetery chapel, but the artist waved his raised hand, and it stopped. After a little while, it began again, this time very quietly, and, without specific orders, immediately stopped again; it was as though it only wished to test its sound. K. was inconsolable about the artist's predicament; he began to cry and sobbed for a long time, covering his face with his hands. The artist waited until K. had calmed down, and then decided, as he could find no other alternative, to keep writing anyway. The first little stroke that he made was a relief for K., although the artist had obviously only drawn it with the utmost reluctance; the script was no longer beautiful, either; above all, the gold seemed to be missing; pale and uncertain was the line; the letter was only very large. It was a J; it was almost finished when the artist stomped angrily with one foot into the grave mound, so that the earth flew into the air all around. Finally K. had understood him; there was no more time to beg his pardon; he dug with all his fingers in the earth, which offered hardly any resistance; everything seemed to have been prepared; a thin crust of earth had been constructed only for show; just behind it, a great hole with sloping walls opened up, into which K., turned onto his back by a gentle current, sank. While he was down below, however, with his head still raised upwards, already being absorbed by the impenetrable depths, his name was driven with mighty flourishes across the stone.

Delighted by this sight, he awoke.

ACKNOWLEDGMENTS

The translator would like to thank Marylou and Jürgen Pelzer for their advice and attention to detail; Utz Tayert for his insight and reflection; Luis, once again, for his patience; and Harda, for guidance.